# The Isle of Kheria

# The Isle

## A NOVEL BY

McPherson & Company

# of Kheria

ROBERT CABOT

Kingston, New York 2012

Published by McPherson & Company, Publishers,
Post Office Box 1126, Kingston, New York 12402.
Manufactured in the United States of America.
Designed by Bruce McPherson. Typeset in Centaur.
First edition.

1 3 5 7 9 10 8 6 4 2

2012   2013   2014   2015

Library of Congress Cataloging-in-Publication Data

Cabot, Robert.
   The isle of Khería : a novel / by Robert Cabot. — 1st ed.
      p.   cm.
   ISBN 978-0-929701-98-1 (hardcover : acid-free paper)
1. Male friendship—Fiction. 2. Grief—Fiction. 3. Self-realization—
   Fiction.   I. Title.
   PS3553.A28185   2012
   813'.54—dc23

                                          2011051524

*To Penny*
*thank you*

# The Isle of Kheria

*Part One*

*S*eas break against a rocky spit, tossing bits of rainbow to a setting sun. A man, naked in the rising wind, hurls himself into the sea. He strikes out, strong against the mounting waves. Far beyond, where the darkening sea and sky are one, an islet waits for him——black cliffs, twin peaks, hostile in a gathering storm.

Distant now, dim in the fading light, the swimmer is thrown high on a cresting wave. He raises a hand——defiant fist, a final curse torn free? An open hand, a gesture of farewell? And is gone.

On a ledge above the reach of spray, a figure in white looks out to that sea. A long dress presses against her. Sleeves of voile trimmed with lace at the wrists. With one hand she holds a broad straw hat to her head, its brim flattened against her cheek, hair escaping, flying in the cloudless meltémi gale. Her other hand reaches out to the empty sea, draws back to press for a moment against her breast. She picks up a basket, hurries off toward a whitewashed village, her dress streaming before her.

High on a headland a dark figure stands against the faint green twilight sky. He is dressed in a somber, conventional suit. One arm is raised to hold his black fedora against the rip of the wind. He too looks out to the empty sea. With a gesture of resignation, another job to be done——a lift of his shoulders, palm turned upward for a moment——he signs the Orthodox cross, three fingers joined. He turns to go——saddened, it seems, weary.

. . .

*An empty sea. Drifting, sinking into black waters——a last few bubbles rise to the silvery surface, to floating embers of a dying sky. Your hair flows in curls above you, your lips are parted, your eyes look upward, smiling, eyes of deepest blue that I once knew well. That scar on your cheek——a sliver of a German grenade, or was it friendly fire? You would never say. You whom I held in my arms, in my heart, whatever the perils of our twisting paths.*

*Your fist raised from the heedless waves, your curse.*

*Drifting, sinking, gone.*

# 1

I, Joel Brewster, here on this far side of my world. A mournful return to these islands of Greece. My son, my Andréas, came with me as far as Athens from our quiet life in Canada, our Twinflower Farm. We were taken to Aidan's grave by his daughter Persephóni, and her daughter, Mélantha. We stood there, the four of us, silently, then moved away together. We walked up Aidan's street, past his rough blue door, the one window shuttered, and on to a kapheneíon for coffee and baklavá.

Andréas insisted I come here without them to this Khería, this island, the village where Aidan, my friend of a saddest past, was drowned in a storming sea.

Drowned? His choice? His despair? For Greece, for his life, for me? I, had I failed him?

My private path, Andréas knew—I must find my way alone.

. . .

Twinflower Farm, our home. This cabin, we built it, she and I. My dearest Silda, she's there, that shelf above our cookstove, a simple stoneware cookie-jar urn. Warm, safe, always there. When I'm back from chores—the milking, the mucking out, the garlic-braiding, the oil change for our 1931 Ford tractor, the farm's books to update, a horse to shoe, potatoes to wheelbarrow to the root cellar, fruit trees to prune—she's waiting there for me. Chores that never end, blessedly never end.

From my bed here in our cabin's loft I look across the room—she's there in the last flicker of embers through a crack in the stove top. When dawn finds its way through the stained-glass window—we'd found it in a junk yard— it wakens her ever so lovingly.

You others, often you drop in—a friendly call. My son Andréas too, back from college, living behind the barn in a yurt. A report on farm affairs, a loaf of bread just out of the communal oven, a bowl of yogurt. Excuses, friends, I know, you're here to check on Joel. He seems so solitary, obsessed. He'd dropped all interests. No lectures, no more ventures into citizen diplomacy, no articles to write, no mixing with neighbors, the farm's apprentices, even us. Only his chores and his Silda there above the stove.

*Soto voce,* —"Will he never let her go, let her return to the earth?" *Then to me,* —"She is gone, Joel, at peace, death has taken her, it is time, six, seven years, time to let her go."

Death? Of course, of course, I'm no stranger to the word. So many. Parents, friends, colleagues, fellow sol- diers, foes—I know. But Silda? No. It's been years you say? No matter, I cannot let her go. No, she must not go, nor I. This work—flowers, fruit, vegetables, honey, eggs, milk—Casilda's joy, it's also mine.

Here, I have something to show you, here beside Casilda on the shelf. This stone heart with a fossil starfish on one side, warm red, smooth, her special gift to me so long ago. She found it, a girl on a Dorset beach.

And here, this watch fob. A bronze coin of ancient Greece, thick leather to frame it, copper rivets. Aidan, my oldest, my dearest friend, he found the coin near the top of Mount Olympus, home of the gods of his Greece. He made this, he gave it to me long ago. I keep it there too, beside Casilda. Aidan, however different we may be, whatever his despair, he is my other partner. I cannot let him go.

—"Yes yes, Joel, you showed us often before." And they mutter, I do hear well when I choose, —"A worry, his grip, he's losing it, right enough."

It is time to bring in the cows. I'll go now. No, I'll leave the meetings, those decisions, all that I'll leave to you, my friends. Thank you for the visit, friends. Be well.

Losing it. The easy way, why not? And the doctors always said, the family genes can show up any time.

. . .

Alder branches, roots, rocks, mud, sod—a beaver dam to pull apart. This grapnel anchor from our skiff, set it well into the center of their dam. A line to our ancient tractor. There, that did the job, a rush of water through the gap, a corner of our hayfield reclaimed. I'll just keep at it—every few days, I guess—till our beavers get the message, relocate well upstream.

A drink of water, a munch on a bit of peppery watercress from the brook, a rest in the shade of the tractor. A cry, a figure waving from the far side of the field, is that Andréas? He's coming toward me. Andréas, tall and skinny, loping across the stubble, his ponytail swinging.

A letter, special delivery, urgent. Dog-eared, grubby, twice stamped Return to Sender, its earliest postmark nine weeks ago. It's from Persephóni.

*My father. . . swimming off Khería, late afternoon, a meltémi. . . drowned. . . the funeral. . .*

Drowned. I dig my fingers into the earth. A beaver slaps his tail against the dwindling surface of his pond. A jolt searing deep in my skull—a silent scream. I turn my face in the moss, a wave washes the mud bank. The crumpled envelope, the postmark ATHÉNA, Greece—I must leave, I must go, I must know.

. . .

Come with me, Andréas, please do come.

Goodbye, my Silda, I'll be away for a time. Wait for me, my dear. And here, I'll take my fossiled heart, the ancient coin too.

. . .

Andréas, my only child, glowing with his twenty years, there in that kapheneíon after our visit to Aidan's grave. On his right, Persephóni, a handsome woman, striking, a braid of white hair to crown her head. On his left, Mélantha, a girl, a young woman of a luminous Grecian beauty.

He was right, he should stay with them, I must go on alone.

## 2

My lookout, here in the fragrance of thyme and rosemary. A limestone ledge, worn, hollowed by time, padded with mosses and lichens. I lean against a bank of mint and lavender and dry grasses. Below me, a jumble of white, this island village, Khería.

Smoke rises from a dozen chimneys into the still evening air. Khería's tiny harbor is a half circle enclosed by the arms of a breakwater. In the twilight, the blues and whites of fishing boats moored to the stone quay are fading to grays. The green and red lights of the breakwater entrance are brighter against the darkening Aegean. On the strand outside the harbor two caíquia are winched up for the night, three, four men unloading their nets into a donkey cart. The murmur of their voices, the whisper of pebbles washed with each retreating wave, the mutterings of gulls settling down for the night, the low whistle of the scops owl. The donkey cart rattles up a cobbled alley.

. . .

They gave me a local newspaper, rumpled, already yellowing, Aidan's photo on an inside page. A naked corpse discretely fig-leafed with a towel, stretched on a blanket on the stones of the quay. They'd searched that sea for days—fisherfolk, the military, by plane too—they found nothing. His friend, Gióia, she saw him vanish, swimming far out toward Khímaera, a barren rock. A fist raised against the cresting waves, a cry. A hand raised in farewell. Then nothing. In the end, a fisherman quite by accident caught him in his net. Rowing against the current, dragging him in.

Stories of his death came in flurries for a time—accident, murder, suicide? No answers. The police held Gióia for the inquest—a few days, then released. The funeral was properly Orthodox, I learned. A crowd, he had many friends, though a son, a daughter, a wife, they stayed away. One other daughter, Persephóni, and her Mélantha were there. There was no sign of Gióia at the funeral. I was absent, only hearing weeks too late.

This morning I sipped ouzo with the fisherman. He had found the body days after that evening when Gióia had hastened to the village to report the loss. He told of her tears, her distant look, her beauty.

He took me in his caíqui to show me where Gióia said Aidan had leapt into the sea. I walked out there later, imagining where they likely had picnicked—a shallow cave, a pool teeming with little crabs. I stood on the ledge of that final leap, looked out over the silver sea to his goal, Khímaera, a far-off islet rising from the sea, its two peaks piercing the sky—the horns of a goat, they say, a fearful place, a lion's roar, his breath flaming in the night, a serpent wrapping the cliffs.

A deadly monster, an illusory Chimera, was that your bitter goal, Aidan, was that your despairing choice? Your hand raised from the heedless waves, was it an angry fist, a final defiance? Of your Greece, your Gioia, me? Answers, is that why I have left my Twinflower, torn from the comfort of quiet grief, a quest for answers? For sanity?

In my left pocket, Silda's blood-red fossiled stone, in my right your ancient coin, Aidan. Both hard against my flesh.

. . .

From my warm ledge, here, watching the evening enshroud the day, I can still see that finger of rocky promontory stretching out into the floating stars, pointing toward a speck of an island, lost in the uncaring sea. I would return to that fatal evening, I would rise, I would hover in the paling sky over that finger of no return. I would hear that final cry.

I close my eyes, time slips quietly away.

. . .

A flash of green on the horizon, the sun's farewell. Sea whipped by the rising gale. Three figures. Aidan, his shaggy head, his defiant fist, his cry... But no, I cannot make it out. Sinking now into the dancing sea, into flashing bits of voile torn from a crimson sky. A Jason, despairing, his golden fleece is lost. You, Mister Death, yes, Thánatos, I know you standing there on the cliff—you in your black fedora, conforming to the local Orthodoxy—resigned to yet another melancholy task. And a woman in white—a beauteous Aphrodite, some here say. I watch her closely. Holding her hat with her left hand, her gown blown in the gale, her right hand gestures out to the empty sea, beseeching, then is held for a moment against her breast. She turns, picks up the picnic basket, hurries toward the village.

. . .

Aidan, Aidan. You of our shared brotherhood, shared loves, dreams. Whatever our bitter differences—your Hellenic resolve, my winding path, your anger and despair, my fossiled heart—were we not destined to return, always to return, to find each other?

. . .

Far piping of a floghéra—the goatherd has finished with the milking. The resinous scents of the maquis, the evening air flowing around us, settling to the sea. Sheep's bells of the last stragglers, the rush of a diving nighthawk. My ledge is warm from the sun. A down jacket, and the winter nights are mild. My bed at the inn can wait. I drift, I curl into dreams

. . .

Come, old friend, sit by me where we can look out over our lives. Yes, you'll need that shaggy sweater—its sour scent of goat's wool—the rock is warm, but the dew has come early. Your eyes, it's dark now, are they still that angry, stubborn blue?

# 3

The eyes, they are blue, but the anger is washed by the sea. Two, three days ago you came to the cemetery near my Athens home. I know, you stood by my grave ringed by the rough stones Persephóni and Mélantha had placed there. I saw them too, standing apart with your Andréas. Even in that sea of polished marble—cloying angels to perfume the nastiness, rotting roses, plastic flowers, sepia oval faces—they must have thought those stones were fitting, fitting for the man I sought to be, for the Greece that I had lost.

I shan't be there long—the unpaid rent, those hideous stones. They'll dump my bones in a common grave, a death pit, to be visited no more, my stones replaced, no doubt, by a shiny mausoleum, a monument to avarice.

Yes, you were there. You looked out over that snarling stink of a city through your tears, you whispered your goodbye. I saw, I heard.

You bear age well, Joel. Standing there by my grave, back straight, eyes still their own innocent blue. Graying, balding a bit, but...I saw you too, striding through the heather, sure of foot, down to the rocks of my lover's leap. Class, you have it still. Yes, I'm still impressed by bloodlines, mine being a tangle of deceits.

You shake your head. You'd protest?

### JOEL

No, not protest, Aidan. But bloodlines? I've a thing or two to say about bloodlines, mine as well as yours. Saved for later.

Lead off, old friend, do. I'm more than a bit worn out—that empty sea, the muddle of memories. You started, keep going. I know, you told me some of that bloodlines bit. Gibraltar your unlikely birthplace, no doubt the source of your rock-hard stubborness and your romantic inclinations. You would go on and on about The Rock, a bit much. Invincible, that blackened limestone, pillar of Hercules protecting ancients from the terrors of beyond, ruling its world, bastion of empires through the ages, Phoenicians, Greeks, Romans, Vandals, Visigoths, Muslims, Spanish, British. And Odysseus, Tariq, Pelayo, Isabella, Nelson, Monty, Ike. And American expats? Yet there you were—with the Admiral himself, and your mother Yvette.

### AIDAN

You never met him, no, of course not. Rosswell Allard, Admiral, United States Navy, retired. Yvette—that's what I called her—you did know her. She and I, we finally moved to England, and much later to New York, long before you and I first met under that college clubhouse elephant head. In my early years I idolized him, deified him. Tall, a lofty voice, commanding, he could do no wrong. He largely ignored me, the adoring child, I can see that now, but there was the occasional gesture—the tiny monkey carved from an elephant's tooth, the peek at his medals, the *first-rate-my-boy-bully-job-top-hole*—that kept me in thrall for a time. Then...

. . .

Six candles and I blew so hard and I'll get my wish to play with the baby ape tomorrow when we picnic, our special place high on The Rock. My leg aches so awfully and I can't sleep and 'Vette is gone to Ladies Books Group and Sir said not to bother him but it aches so and I mustn't touch the Sloan's Liniment and I'll just have to ask Sir to. His study door, it's open and he's there on the sofa, no clothes on, Nanny too, kissing and ...

Sir? Then he's shouting and grabbing me and my pajama rips and what is that thing? He slams the door.

Father did it, can't we sew it up? And he and Nanny and I don't know what and .... Don't cry, 'Vette, I love you so and .... He makes her cry 'most every day. —"How could you, Rosswell?" And he slaps her and her lip is bleeding and I pound and pound and pound at his leg.

. . .

Two-star Admiral Allard, Ret. *Retired*, ha! Strutting about the world, bagging big game—two-legged, too—National Geographic team close behind, whole rooms in our Gibraltar home just for his glassy-eyed trophies. The elephant head, remember? No, you wouldn't, you were nearly blotto—toasting the trophy he'd given our college club.

His Congressional-Medal-of-Honor manner was always there. Sir, may I please be excused, I... Sir? His exploits, something about convoy duty, 1917, torpedoed, sinking, but the U-boat is destroyed too. And the rescue—he was a great swimmer, I'll give him that, once swam the Straits to Africa. When a sailor was swept from their lifeboat he dove in after him, and later he fished a German codebook from the freezing sea. His luck—no codebook, no medal.

· · ·

We escaped to England, Yvette and I. I was perhaps eight or nine. After that I was largely free of him—one or two visits, attempts at reconciliation—icy cold, steamy anger, done and gone. We found a cottage by a village not far from Cheltenham. We settled in, American expats again for a time, then rather part of the scene.

It was there my childhood idyll began.

· · ·

Springtime. I skip down our grassy lane to school, satchel bouncing, my muddy green Wellies on a string round my neck in case I choose my wadey path along the stream for going home. The bell clangs at us, I drop my bag and boots, plop behind my desk, just in time. I shouldn't want Miss Roberts to be upset. I shall marry her, you see, when I grow up, pretty and sweet and kind.

Class outing today, she tells us, lunch satchels, hats, boots if you brought them. Seven of us, four girls, three boys, we dash to the beech wood above the cricket ground,

Lady Ellen Park. Here it's closed in, moldy leafy smells, squirrels scurrying—elves dance on a giant toadstool, a frog croaks to be rescued, a fairy flutters by. The girls hold hands and giggle and I wish so very much they'd stop. I'll stay back, here, better, now I can hear the rooks, they're chattering at the cuckoo who really doesn't care, just goes right on with his cuckooing, his wife laying look-alike eggs in a borrowed nest. They'd have pushed some of the owner's eggs out, clever but lazy, as teacher says, and they'll leave their eggs, their babies, to unsuspecting foster care—and go on mocking with their cuckoo-cuckooing. And what's the moral we're supposed to learn?

Through gnarly tree trunks, whispering, legs of giants, secret stalking, circling, just when you're not looking, stealthy, closing in. Jump away, they'll not succeed, escape their spell. Ah! There! Now! The sun comes through, defeats their wicked plan. We've made it to the edge of the wood. To a mossy wall, a stile, the kind with flat rocks sticking out each side, like steps both up and down—Public Footpath, this way—up, and down. And beyond there's a sunny field with sheep and Herefords and a million thistles. Look, come, over here, a comfy ledge, it's thick with lichen, sunny and soft. Can't we have our lunches now, Miss Roberts? We'll brush away the rabbit droppings.

. . .

Autumn. Chatterings, squeezings—while the school bell still rings—through the double door, escaped the chalk dust, the silly girls, the Aidan-to-the-blackboard-for-the-class. Shouts from the cricket ground behind the hedgerow, I kick a stone—scuffy boots—up our lane, past the pub, two farmhouses, a copse of oak and beech, rooks, they swirl about and scream at you from their rookeries, kick and kick, twenty-seven times to the stone slab bridge over the brook. Poohsticks with Yvette, sometimes, my stick mostly beats hers floating under the bridge. I nudge my stone across. On to the end of the lane where it widens enough to turn a farm wagon. Past our rusty Austin—Yvette's finally managed to buy it. A last kick into my special pothole, ready for tomorrow. Jolly good shot, old boy. Capital!

I take a twirl or two on the stile, drop off into our weedy garden—hollyhocks, things gone woody, Yvette would say, and wallflowers, and I don't know what. Our stone cottage waits for me under its slate roof—tiny, it's just for us. A well with a rickety pump, a privy in the back—but nobody to see me, I'll just pee here, behind the roses. I can't hear it splatter in the dust, though, for the noisy rush of the millstream over the dam, there, through the bank willows, and the gabbling of the geese that will hiss at me if I get too close, and the quacking ducks—I can see them, over our fence, in the millpond, tails up bobbing for bottom tidbits.

There's one room for cooking and eating and living, a curtained corner for washing, two cubbyhole bedrooms, a stove—coal or coke, sometimes bits of wood—to warm and feed us. And there's a grate, embers in the ashes. To lie elbow-propped before it, dreaming—on this saber-toothed tiger pelt, to the sizzle of roasting tiger meat. Or to toss in a pinch of salt for its sparkle and spit. Or to kneel before it to brush stars into Yvette's night-black hair.

. . .

Winter. Walking home from school. Snowy, lumpy shadows lurking just beyond my torch light, a ghosty dreadful wailing, it mimics the hoot of an owl. Our pond now, a friendly murmuring, ducks, I pick them out with my torch, they paddle a patch in turns, keeping off the ice. Our twirly stile, dead flowers in the snow. The door latch, the matches, paraffin lamps, a candle. Yvette, you will come back soon, oh do! House tending for London weekenders—how dare they find our village! How could you work for them! It feeds us, you say, and The Admiral's checks don't by half, you say, and all right but it's quite black outside and I'm not sure how long I can keep the goblins and demons and harpies out.

Here, I forgot, I'll open the stove damper, more coal, put on the kettle, scones to warm in the oven, butter there on the frigid windowsill, I'll warm it a bit on the ledge above the range. Tea cups, the pot and cozy, plates and knives and Pooh's pot of honey, more candles for her return. Poke up this morning's grate, a lump or two, one more.

Is that our creaky stile? A thump and rustle, stifled coughing, wheezing just behind the door. Unlocked! A violent banging, the latch lifts, the door is flung open. Cowering by the hob, I scream and scream and scream. A monstrous giant, one thumping wooden leg, a belt of pistols, snarling mouth and two black teeth, eyes that glare at me, saber raised, strike off my head.

You're here! I cling to you ever so tightly and I love you so much my dear dear Yvette. I touch your cheek.

. . .

Older, two years or so. I go to public school, a bursary boy, Cheltenham, boarding, weekends busing or bicycling home. It's such an elegant city, trees and tulips, boulevards, parades, spas—it suits me. George the Third made it so with his love of the baths—strange to think he was king to both Nelson and Washington. And my own mother's great-great-great-greatest signed We, the People of …. And now we're here, rebels returned to the fold, and quite unnoticed, by now just two of the crowd—whatever the traces of nasal American, of Gibraltarian llanito, they seem successfully hidden behind my stylish stammer. I'm hazed no more than others.

. . .

Bank holiday. With our Austin firing well enough, spark and choke reset, crank handle back in the boot, we pick our way, cautious of our rutted lane, and head out. To the west, to Wales. Castles to hold off the English, Monmouth, Powys, the Black Hills as twilight slowly climbs the hillsides. Our headlights find a faded sign offering us,

> BRACKENDELL
> BED AND BREAKFAST

We turn off the metaled road down into a valley on no more than a track. Sheep in the warm dust scramble out of our way. A nightjar, sleeping in the grass between the ruts, looks at us red-eyed in the lights, hops grumpily off to the side. Horses stomp and whinny in the dark. Carts, a sheep shed, stables, gates to open and close. We stop at a rambling, thatched farmhouse, only one window alight. The lower half of the Dutch door is ajar, it opens, a tiny woman, bent double, comes through it—no need to open the top—makes her way painfully toward us, peers at us, head tipped to her shoulder and turned up, greets us, rather warmly, I'd say, invites us to come in.

Inside it's toasty warm, well lit with two paraffin-mantle lamps hanging from the low-beamed, blackened ceiling. The floor with dips and tips, rugs mostly threads, a battered stove, a fireplace with a smoldering log, a heavy oak table, four chairs, a sagging sofa, cushions, an open book on the floor. Like ours, it's a room that serves for kitchen, dining, living, all in one.

Miraculously she manages—politely refusing offers of help—a scrumptious omelet with herbs and onions and garlic, her goat cheese, fresh brown bread, salad from her garden, home-brewed ale, and her pudding of custard and fruit.

She struggles over to sit with us as we finish. She rests her head, left side down, flat on the table—nearly bald, deep leathery wrinkles, eyes rolling to find us till they seem turned all to white—off-putting at first. She jokes about it, though, apologizes.

I look intently into the one eye I can see, look at nothing else—she is lovely once again. Her voice is soft and singing, young and beautiful, a country voice with a Celtic lilt, well-spoken.

### GENNA

I was born here, this hidden valley, farmed for thousands of years. Its own world, complete, yet so small, so unlikely in our austere hills, defenseless yet largely unnoticed through the unending ages of war. There's a stream, from a spring on the hillside. It meanders, a few acres on either side, good earth, a woodlot of oak and beech, steep grassy slopes all round. The village—church, pub, school, a shop with the post office in the back, a blacksmith, that is all—it's a good hour's walk away.

Genna, yes, that's what they called me, Guinevere, in Welsh that's white and smooth and soft—can you see me like that? School, I loved our school and read and read and read. I met my husband at a village fête, a dance in the church—mouth organ, fiddle, and song. He'd left the coal mines, after four years buried half a mile deep, came back to the farming he knew. We were married, and here's where we settled. My father was crippled by then, my mother already dead, no others, so we took on the farm. Hard work, it was, good work. Two Shires, Sun and Moon, for the ploughing and mowing and tedding, for the threshing, the hauling. We had a saddle horse, sometimes two—ponies we call them—and the cows, the pigs, sheep, chickens, ducks among the reeds in our little marshy place, usually a goat or two or three. And our two golden-haired, blue-eyed daughters—fairies right out of a book. Ach! We did love them so.

One spring Sunday after church and farm tasks—we'd honor the Lord's Day best we could—I prepared a picnic basket for Efrem and the girls. Milk—fresh, still warm— hot scones and clotted cream, my elderberry jam. Boots, pullovers, anoraks just in case. They're off to explore the caves and craggy places a mile above our spring.

No, they never came back.

Those were solstice days, those June days, when the evenings stretch on and on. The nightingale had begun his sad evensong. The cows were in, I'd milked them, put the jug away in the springhouse. I clanged and clanged our supper gong, a rusty pipe hung from the eaves for when Dad—or later my husband Efrem—was out in the fields. Nothing. I lit our storm lantern and set out in the dusk. High I climbed, higher, calling, in terror. Not far from the top, a track turned off, faint, overgrown, forgotten for years. I'd been there once, though, once as a girl, and I knew just where it led, and I knew just what I would find, and I knew.... My heart stopped and my breath stopped and I ran and ran in the dark. First came the scent of new-turned turf, of rock dust, of bracken and grasses crushed. My lantern found the rubble.

Someone, but long long ago, had dug into our hill, mining, or hoping, for …. Coal, I suppose, lead, or diamonds, gold, or the Holy Grail, oh God! I don't know, I don't know. Torn hands, my fingers and knees all raw, cold fear. Towards dawn—a mourning dove in the scrub oak, our rooster far below—I found it, her little hand, her imploring hand. Mummy, oh Mummy come soon.

Something snapped, like a knife in my back, my heart too, my soul, all my life. I worked on, my back a searing pain, slower, hopeless, half mad. Here, my own little girls, their bodies unhurt. Efrem's torn, mangled flesh. He'd covered his daughters, holding them tight, as the rock crushed down on them.

My back, it wasn't at first this bad, I still farmed a little, the animals, the vegetables, the routine tasks. I had managed to get the mare saddled that day, had gone to the village for help. They came, they took out my loved ones, they cleaned them and dressed them and stretched them out—here, just here, on this table—and I fed my guests and thanked them for their kind words. But something was troubling them, even I in my state was aware of it. Weeks later I learned by mistake, I overheard whisperings at church—I was kneeling, hidden in my pew—of another body they'd found when they'd dug farther. A young woman, a friend from a neighboring farm who'd been seen with Efrem at a church dance that spring, me home with the children and chores.

It was then my back slowly gave up, in a year I was bent almost like this. I closed down the farm, kept only two ponies, their tack, put up that sign at the village turnoff, painted it myself. Thirty years or more ago.

And I've come to be content.

### AIDAN

She brings us an enormous breakfast—poached eggs, a mountain of bacon, grilled tomatoes, toast, butter, her elderberry jam. She has to rest often, detouring to her pillowed sofa nest, curled there almost purring, watching us it seems with something like delight. She says she still has horses.

—"Two Welsh ponies, gentle, responsive, though they'll be frisky—unridden for more than a bit. Visitors are scarcer now, you see—the Depression, the talk of another war. Would you not like a ride?"

Why, yes, that would be lovely.

Frisky, quite so. At first, they had seemed to be practicing an entirely new step, a sideways diagonal skip, they'd shy at the least excuse, snort, toss their heads about. But we've managed this far and they're calmer, the trail now is much steeper, demanding their full attention. I'm not much for riding—for The Admiral another large negative—but this, it is ever so different, a quest for the Grail, and dragons to deal with en route.

Quite unprepared, we come to a pile of rubble in our track, half covered with bracken and thistles. On an outcropping above, three weathered wooden crosses are fastened with brackets. No one had dared put a fourth.

We climb on, steep, I hang to a handful of mane. Our boots are wet from the dew on the heather, blossoms jeweled in the sun. Sheep start up from their slumber, dash off terrified, as if they'd never seen a horse or a person before. A pipit has found a spot in the trail where the sun has dried the dew, time for a morning dust bath, fluttering, shaking like a terrier back from a swim—a tiny yellow cloud. A calf stumbles on her knees, heaves up to chase a sleepy tiger moth—a brand-new incarnation from a woolly-bear past.

Here, we got here, Maidshead, high upon her shoulder. Far below us greens to blues to grays unfold. Hedgerowed fields, winding lanes, the flash of sun on a window, dark woods, the clap of a hunter's gun. Farther, all fades to the distance, mingles with the sky. Faintest church-bell tolling, slow, ripples in the stillest air—cadenced steps of casket bearers, the flag, the rifle salutes?

We dismount, tether our horses, loosen girths, unstrap our bags, spread a blanket on the grass—careful, the sheep dung there, rabbit pellets sprinkled round, here, it's better here.

Finished with our picnic, we stretch, lie face up to the sun. A skylark begins his singing—bubbles of sound. He slices high to the sun, hovers, wings clap-clapping love calls to his mate. His calls are answered, she rises from the gorse, circles, spirals up, ever higher till they join, wings embracing. They tumble unheeding in joyous song. Close overhead they spread their wings, a feathery whoosh, and fly off their separate ways.

We walk our ponies down another path, a circling track we'd found. Stretch our legs, spare theirs—it's very steep, ledges, steps, some sliding scree. And here we rejoin the morning track. The rubble grave is round this turn.

Yvette, I'd like to stop.

She holds my pony, I scramble up the pile. Ivy covers most of it, honoring the dead. I break off a stem, a yard or two. I pick two lengths of minehead timbers, weathered, shriveled through the years, I'd seen them when we'd passed. She'd used them, I guess, for her dreadful digging through the night. I bind them carefully. Propped in place, wedged in mossy rocks, I clamber down. Yvette has brought up the ponies. She's looking up, tear-filled eyes.

—"I'd thought the same, my darling, a fourth cross, it's right, whatever the story beneath."

. . .

You have a questioning look about you, Joel. Why did my story skip to Wales?

I had no plan. It just happened. But reflect on this. You knew me first at college—the clubby snob, prancing about, bagpipes, kilt, and the famous knobby knees. Then you knew me as a shell-shocked dogface. And you saw me often in Greece, my adopted—and adopting— home. In London too, quite memorably for me. I may well have seemed to be a different person—unswerving, devoted to certain aspects of Greece, intolerant with a vengeance, cruel. Yes, it's true, don't object. But I was once that schoolboy, too.

# 4

*JOEL*

Spittlebugs. They spit—bubbly spit—on timothy stems and the goldenrod and the wild tiger lilies. First thing summer mornings. Sometimes we call them froghoppers, they look like tiny frogs with wings, and they can hop as far as I can, farther. A little bit disgusting when the spit brushes off on you—like now.

Through the gate. Remember to close it—cows in Mother's flowers, flowers everywhere around our cottage, really Uncle Will's, he gave it to us—to forget the gate would be the end of me. Off through the pastureland, fire-breathing bull to watch for, thistles and nettles and thorny holly leaves—trials and demons and dragons, third son, the prodigal, off now to seek his fortune. I've made it, neither slain nor slaying, quick through this gate, slam it shut. That buzzing sound, dragon scales scraping against the barbed wire—bees busy in the raspberry blossoms, rows and rows and rows.

Then the strawberries, a bird got a bite out of that one. The yellow tomatoes, the red ones, lettuces, cabbage, parsley, onions, garlic—for the help, Mother says, not for us, garlic's not genteel. The chard, carrots, sweet corn with the tassels just beginning, and what's-that-stuff?

The gardeners' house, the barns and sheds and paddocks, hidden among the cedars. Uncle Will's gardeners,

Portuguese, Antonio, his wife Louisa, Fernando, and Hazel the milk cow. Louisa's there to greet me with the newspapers, our mail, a glass of milk she's scooping from the pail Antonio's just brought up—milking's very late, Hazel got out during the night.

Luísa's English is funny. —"You aunt, she send you come her morning quick."

She's my great-aunt really, but no need to go into that with Luisa, they don't understand me any better than I do them, and anyway I call her Aunt too, just like Father and Mother. Aunt Abby, Uncle Will.

She's zany, fun, wild red hair, all angles and bones and huge freckles. She taught me cribbage, more or less. He is very wise with white hair and white pajamas and he can't turn his head, and we have to go right to the foot of the bed so he can see us. He's an invalid in a body cast, right up to his chin. That's his tower room, there, top floor, fourth or fifth, with the balcony high over the sea. Huge stone castle of a house, I'm sure it's been there forever. Elevator, lots of servants with white gloves and little hats, the men servants wear tails.

Yes, he's very wise, Uncle Will, Father calls him his mentor, but I wish he'd learn kindness from Uncle Will— but he never will. I think they are very rich, but when I asked them, Father sent me straight home, without dessert, alone and in the moonlight by then—we were all there for the summer-welcome supper—and straight to bed. But Uncle Will did give me a secret wink as I got up to go.

So....

Past the currants—will they ever get ripe?—and up the rise, onto the croquet lawn with her roses all around and the stone statue of Peter Pan, it looks like, except that he's playing pipes. The seagulls are circling Uncle Will's turret, squabbling with a crow who would steal their catch.

What does Aunt Abby want? I can't think that I've done anything that naughty. Through more gardens, across the driveway, up the long stone steps, onto the wooden porch that circles the castle—a moat, of course. And she's standing there in the portcullis, an elderly princess already rescued.

—"Joel, child, good morning, thank you so much for coming to see your old aunty, though I did rather order it, I know. I rang up Mother to tell her you will be with me for a time, and that she must not worry. Come, we shall have hot chocolate—oh no, I quite forgot, your nasty allergy, we'll make it Horlicks instead—and sweet little cakes that Ellen just made. This way, on the porch in back, it's sunny there and we can listen to last night's nor'easter rollers breaking on our rocks."

We sit in her black-painted wicker chairs before the black-painted wicker table with a starchy white tablecloth and everything all set. She rings a little china bell—I think it's china, dainty, by its brass handle shaped like a leaf—and Lucille arrives with her loaded tray.

. . .

—"No no, you certainly may have another, I am *in loco parentis* now, my dear, my rules here, not theirs. No, no cribbage today, Lucille, but I thank you all the same. And tell Ellen her cakes are delicious.

"Now, I must tell you something, it's more than time you knew. Rumors would soon get to you, perhaps they already have—but no, you needn't tell me whether....

"Your father has another brother, two years older, Charles, who has been living here with us ever since your grandparents died. When he was only a few years old, your grandmother came to realize that his mind was drifting away. The doctors in those days quickly called it a congenital mental condition. They wanted to put him into hospital care, but your grandmother chose to have him at home. She devoted the few remaining years of her life to him. When he was perhaps eight or ten, he got a terrible disease. He was left paralyzed, speechless, his body twisted. He's been completely bedridden ever since.

"There's nothing, nothing that can be done. It's better that he be here with us than in some hospital. He loves us, we can tell by his eyes, how they light up when we visit, Lucille and I. No, not your Uncle Will, it would be difficult to get there, wheel him in his bed, I suppose, carry him, and he would really rather not. And your father simply cannot deal with it, leaves it all to us—that is why I am telling you. Understand, it was awful for your father. An older brother, a half secret in the house, no one mentioning it in any way. It hurt him, that you must know, scared him—would it happen to him some day?—made him ashamed."

Can she see me wriggle, avoid her eyes?

—"I know you see your father as strong, sure, knowing everything, always in control. That is the way the world sees him too: Donnelly Brewster, president of his huge company. But to tell you of his brother? That he could not do. And remember, we can love your father all the more for this vulnerable side he has. He knows I'm telling you, he asked me to, knowing that rumors would get to you anyhow and likely of something far worse.

"There is certainly no need to visit Charles, no. Now, you must go."

. . .

Standing here in the rose garden... I need to pee. Watching a bee in a blossom, half thinking of that childish book that father had left lying in an obvious place, something like *The Birds, the Bees, and You.* Humph! Grownups are so innocent.

That other turret, that must be where Charles is. Where we're not allowed to go, even Thanksgivings—all the family, cousins and all, maybe forty of us, playing Going to Jerusalem, a long line snaking through the house, someone banging on a piano—can't hardly hear it up here. Or Sardines in the Box—finding secret places. That locked door at the top of the stairs.

*Congenital, the male line,* she said, I know what that means. George, my cousin, first cousin—I heard mother talking about him on the telephone, how worried my uncle was, she said it too, *congenital, the male line,* and how George—I never knew of him till then, no not at all—how he lived in what mother called a home. My father, somehow, maybe …. Me? Mother yelled at him, I heard her, crazy she called him, heartless, always judging, strict strict strict. I see him now, here, looming over me, strict strict strict. What Aunt Abby called my father's vulnerability, what did she mean? Is all this why I'm scared, so scared? Why I just can never seem to love him, is he scared too?

· · ·

A whippoorwill starts his silly song. Poor Will.

Poor Charles. I'll find him, I'll be his friend. It's cloudy-rainy, now's the time, today, I think I can. I've finished *Lorna Doone*. My plan, it's simple. I need another book. And as always when the weather's bad, my long read after lunch—if there's no sailboat racing to endure—instead of swinging in my hammock between the cedar trees, it will be indoors. And often that means in the castle library, Uncle Will's big old leather wing chair—before he got tuberculosis of the spine—any book I want, thousands and thousands there. At that hour no one stirs, the castle seems to sleep. And I know just where the house keys are—on a big ring by the pantry door.

The plan proceeds, I've got it right, let's go. His turret room is up these stairs, from the library spiraling up. Four flights, there's his door, this must be the key. Open it softly, mouselike, ever so slow. My heart is skipping and jumping, I cannot breathe. No, I must not go on, he'll see me and scream and I'll be banished forever and ever. Too late, the door is swinging quietly in, there's no going back.

A hospital kind of bed, cranked up so he's half sitting, still beneath the covers, dark hair, awfully pale, his eyes are open, bright blue like mine, they turn to me, his eyes—are they pleading?—a baby's look, smiling, wondering, asking, so alone. I cross the room to his bedside, his eyes, they seem to be talking, begging me to stay. A baby, he's older than father, a baby with kind eyes.

Somehow I'm singing, singing him a nursery song. He hears, I'm sure, his eyes say thanks. Another song, a special song, Mother would sing it to me by my bed. I sing on and on until.... It's late and I must go, I'll be back, though, baby Charles, I'll be back to sing to you. Goodbye.

And I went back often, I sang all the songs I knew. And each time it was that special song—why can I not remember it?—that put stars in his eyes, that brought tears to mine.

. . .

The afternoon sun slides in low through the motes, riffles in the amber of Mother's long skirt. —"Joel dear, why are you so often sad?" Her heels click as she moves away—pretty Mother, my Jorie—her head with its pinned-up bun on the back shaking worriedly. A frown floats in the shadow she's left behind.

Why does she think I'm sad? Am I?

That song from summers ago, that special song, a dying echo, to be sung no more, for baby Charles is dead? My song is forgotten, is that my sadness? Or that I feel so

… different, misplaced, not understood? But I was simply standing here, nothing special, nothing I'd think she could see. Here by the window, listening to the drips of melting snow in the downspout, watching the occasional car go by, a Buick, a Model-A, a Pierce Arrow, an electric car like Grandma Brewster's, watching passersby hurry through the streetlamp's cone of light. I fiddle with the tassels on the blood-red brocade curtains, just waiting for Tom Mix time.

My crystal radio hides in my room behind Jules Verne and Thackeray, with the earphones and the bottle of Carbona to clean the crystal. Scratches, fading, shifting stations. *The Lone Ranger*—Hi ho Silver, away! Hooves drum, racing through the sagebrush—silver spurs, if I send in a box top …. Ralston? Fifteen minutes later I search again with the cat's whisker on the crystal—Who can it be?/ It's *Little Orphan Annie.*/Bright eyes, cheeks of rosy gold,/ … Arf! says Sandy—they'll send a supersonic dog whistle for ten cents and an Ovaltine label. Later, when Mother's come—hide the earphones—lights are out and Mother's finished singing about Leary the Lamplighter—not my Charlie song, my forgotten song that I must have learned from her, she sings it no more—then I skip over Major Bowles's *Wheel of Fortune* and find *The Shadow*—Who knows what evil lurks in the hearts of men! Then *Grand Central Station*—Crossroads of a nation! And, when the radio adventures are finished, it's Benny Goodman in the *Starlight Ballroom* with his licorice-stick clarinet.

# 5

A star skims the purple sky, dies beyond Khímaera. Stiff, cold, joints cracking, have I slept here long? Is there a lingering scent of goat's wool? My heart is warm from memories, I flinch with pain.

Two beginnings, Aidan, me. Two boys, innocents, generous hearts. Two scornful Olympian fathers, are we both the children of an insufferable Zeus? My burden, too, my fear of mad genes. And Aidan, your burden?

I pick my way through the star-shadows, the maquis, the scent of heather, moist in the gathering dew. To my inn, my bed. Aidan's bed once, they told me...and Gióia's? His arms are around me now.

## AIDAN

College days, before the war. It was my knobby knees that did it, they'd say, and my rather ostentatious little eccentricities. Kilts and bagpipes, the artful stammer, that kind of thing—peacock plumage, Simon would call the lot. Simon, you'll remember, my roommate, fellow peacock. He'd sometimes join us, you and me, Joel, racing Poohsticks under the campus footbridge. We'd drop our sticks together on one side of the bridge, race to the other side to see whose would first emerge. It took skill, choosing the best spot to drop your stick. The current was slow, there were snags and eddies to catch you.

Poohsticks became our substitute for flipping a coin—skill and cunning, not just dumb luck. Who'd pay for the midnight homework-break of cinny-roll and milk at Hayes-Bickford? Who'd get to choose the jukebox tune? Who'd have first choice on a double date with the gorgeous Baker twins.

There were glimmers too of another me, a secret me, a me with no prize yet in Poohstick games. My secret to keep from you till our whiskied night in Athens—my revelation, our hilarious disaster, my devastating loss.

A different you, a different me. A different meaning to our game.

## JOEL

The peacock you, my college *ch-chum*—mind a bit of teasing?—how did I see you? Ever sure, no doubts. Your poems in the literary mag, your screeds. Your high spirits. Your British conversational knack. I admired you, I loved you. Hugely popular—parading the campus paths, your bagpipes blasting Cock 'o the North, your knobby knees. A nod to a clapping co-ed, an eyebrow raised to a football jock. Might I have seen a tilt of the kilt for him as well as for her?

Aidan Allard, son of the famous admiral. God, you were handsome, those knees above the tartan stockings, those very blue eyes, the wavy dark hair, a trace of a scar on your cheek—what is its story? Maybe you were a bit on the short side, but never mind. And there was that hint of a charming upper-crusty English stammer.

Steadfastly romantic, yet quite unaware, it seemed, of the turbulence in your wake. You had a snobbish veneer in those days before the war, perhaps we all did. Snubbing the green-panteds, the two-tone saddle-shoeds, buying into those exclusive club rituals.

That time we sailed up the East River on a classmate's family yacht, you balancing on the bowsprit, bleating your bagpipes, the rest of us toasting Manhattan with mint juleps. You mumble, was it, *Precious shits!*?

Then the you I saw four years later dabbling in a puddle of Austrian beer, trembling from the horrors of war, rifle propped against the wall. And the you of your Aegean idyll in the arms of your Dimitra. The you my companion of Pindos mountain adventures. The dancing you, the laughing you. The you who wanted what I could not give you. The you of fratricidal Greece, released from torture chambers, lying in the arms of a dying youth. And the you who gave your pregnant daughter to the safekeeping of my *Arianna* and me. The dissident you—your novels, your poetry, your scathing pen. The despairing you who swam out against a gathering storm, who gave himself to an impossible Greece, who came to rest in that circle of stones, whose bones would soon be tossed in a pit.

A long way we've come, you and I, Aidan. Old embarrassments fade into bemusement. How did what once was elitism, snobbery, become in your adopted Greece a relentless militant communism, asceticism with a stubborn romantic streak—and despair?

### AIDAN

No no, Joel, you've got it wrong, not militant, not bitter. Angry would be better, angry—their corruptions, violence, greed, injustice, God help the innocent. Not they with their trumped-up Orthodox God—a key to the horror. Yes, I did convert, it's true—the godparents, the new white shirt, the new name, Aléxandros, Aléko, Aidan doesn't work in Greek. I turned to an idea, a pageant, a practice, though, not their tyrannies and lies.

But let me move back, December 7, 1941.

. . .

This classmate, Joel Brewster, why would he invite me for Sunday lunch? Do I belong up here on Hoity-Toity Hill? Well, where else, with my mushy British talk and the stammer to set it off? Anthropology 101, sitting together right at the back, a hundred or more nodding heads, boring, we doodle, a competition, cartooning the prof. After his lecture, we chat up a bird or two, it makes the course worthwhile, yessir, after all. Well, actually I do the chatting up, this Joel, he is rather stiff, withheld. Nice chappie, though, in his way, for a Yank a bit of all right. Well, yes, I'm a Yank too, it seems, transplanted. Smashing looks, he has, when he takes off his spectacles. If he'd only toss out a few crumbs, the birds would come a-flocking.

So he invited me, for whatever reason. I'll try it out, why

not? I took the underground—the subway—walked up The Hill—they definitely pronounce The with a capital T—on its bricked pavements—sidewalks—real gas lamps strung along. The streets are named for trees. That's better than for bloody battles the way they do at home. Or rather, what was home, now I guess it's here, or actually a three-hour train ride away where Yvette's selling her soul—fabrics, snotty stuff, the kind if you're anybody you've got to have.

Here, the numbers dwindle, I must be getting close. White front doors, brass knockers, discreet curtains. —"No, my dear, we simply do not call them drapes."

A formal lunch with servants bringing a mediocre soup, a roast, Mr. Brewster carving. The first slices are for Joel's mother—dainty and, I must say, rather gorgeous, for her age. —"The outside piece, well done, yes, thank you, Donny dear." That's what she calls him, diffidently, the meekest wifely way—echoes to me of Gibraltar from that gratefully distant past. A gravy boat is passed around, following each delivered plate, and roast potatoes, carrots. The pudding is what they call floating islands—appalling, blobs of beaten whites of egg bobbing on a sea of yellow glue. Demitasses in the living room, chocolates. Donny Boy lights a cigar, turns on the news.

Pearl Harbor, Honolulu, Japanese bombers, American fleet, major damage, White House, war to be declared, Germany, Italy too, the Axis Powers. Stand by for more. And patriotic music.

We're quiet, a few good Christian expletives with *excuse-mes*, mostly quiet, we avoid each other's eyes. The terror and awe and exhilaration, for me it seems almost a repeat. Luftwaffe, the RAF, the ack-ack batteries in Cheltenham's tulip beds, air-raid shelters, the Home Guard, gas masks, Loose Lips Sink Ships, all that. It's come here too, at last, my Emerald Isle, now here. Again that patriotic stiffening, can that be me?

Back to college, the subway carriage rattles round me, the stinks of piss and tobacco. The averted eyes, each alone in silence. Words, images, strung together helter-skelter. My bagpipes, peacock's plumage still, or to incite war fervor like Winnie or FDR? America Firsters, Lindbergh, Hitler, Jesse Owens—America at Last. The patriotic music, get Americans off their duffs. Anthro, Dante, Herodotus—or draft or volunteering, or save my sacred arse? Here, this lurching filthy tube carriage. An eye lights up at coming glory, shoulders back, a straightened spine, a fist to smack the other palm, soundless cursing, firing up. America firing up.

FDR again, —"The seventh of December, nineteen forty-one, a date which will live in infamy."

Today? Well, I sit here on the vastness of the library steps, empty out my book bag—regulation green with black draw-string strap—scratch a match on New England's granite, light my Sterno burner, tin cup balanced on it, water from a whiskey bottle, tea in a strainer spoon close at hand. My tea ceremony under way. Two girls come up the steps, they sit nearby, try me on some casual questions, behave as if I know them, but I don't. I'll be careful to ignore them, mostly, play it right, just my usual tea on time. Peacock plumage working, Simon would say. Men go by, eyebrows lift, derisive snorts—that's new. December the eighth, all right, I see, and that, no doubt, is the end of tea times.

Will my bagpipes still draw the giggling girls, part of the plumage? Slow steps, the stately steps they'd taught me at Cheltenham, down a campus walk next midday. It has a martial air to it, though, *Cock o' the North*. New country, is this a new me, firing up? I'll sign up, yes, college ROTC, and Simon too, be rotsies now, Army officers in the end, the gentlemanly thing to be—and save our arses, at least for a time, go on with college, and the war will surely end soon.

Close-order drill to the football field, artillery training today, uniforms, the clapping girls, it's not such a bad war at that. The traffic stops while we march smartly across the bridge.

—"Our boys, they'll take care of the Japs." And waiting for us, to teach us how, is a graying Great War veteran and a lineup of seventy-fives.

—"That's all we've got, men, seventy-fives—millimeters, diameter of the barrel—French artillery, 1873 vintage, horse-drawn."

. . .

The library steps, I sit here again, we've been rotsies for almost a year. Many have gone now, enlisted, or missed some deferral and were drafted, or were grabbed by the navy as ninety-day wonders. Some by now are dead.

Joel, yes, he enlisted a year ago, right off, the first of our class, and as an Army private. It surprised us, his parents were distressed. They tried to get me to intercede, but no no, I certainly would not. Good show, Joel, rebel Joel, escape.

In fact my roommate Simon and I, we are about ready to sign up too. The ski-troops recruiter is giving his pitch, a bunch of us skiers, well, we'd skied once or twice. Bored with ROTC, antsy, and guilty, ready to give up commissions, to hell with being officers, let's get on with the war, it can't last much longer. And we'll have grandchildren some day to account to. And the girls have their eyes on the real ones on furlough, we're second best by a lot. And ski troops? It does sound rather glamorous, special. Right-ho!

. . .

They've put me on guard duty. Halt! Who goes there? Yell it three times, if there's no answer, shoot. Two in the morning, two hours to go, thirty degrees below zero. I'm relieving a soldier, they told me, whose eyeballs had frozen stiff. They gave me a World War I Enfield rifle and ammo, how to shoot it I haven't a clue—French seventy-fives artillery, yes, not Enfields. And this fort, so they call it—a railhead where they dump us poor blokes, then just miles of barracks and Quonsets, warehouses, that sort of thing. Where are the crenels and merlons, or at least the spiked wooden stockade? No defenses, just me—and the place no doubt swarming with Huns and Japs. Nothing, just me. The best way, the only way I can figure, is to keep my eyes shut tight. I'll surely hear the officer on duty when he comes out checking on me, and one Halt! should do it, I reckon, with a Who-goes-there? for good measure. No dereliction of duty, no court-martial, no lockup for the duration, no waiting for some future amnesty to give me back my civil rights.

Days later, still not quite frozen, they march us—we straggle—through snowdrifts, duffel bags piled in a truck, to the railhead, to the train waiting for us, waiting impatiently, fuming and hissing, MPs strutting about, a first looie—silver bar insignia, not brass, got it right?—sleepy, hung over, it's still only oh-five-fifteen, black, lights at the dimmest, a listless half-arsed blackout—I could show them a thing or two there. A first sergeant, old-time cadre, vet of that fucking—see, I'm getting the hang of it—Great-War-to-End-All-War, three stripes up, three down, diamond in the middle—got that one too—doing all the work. Lists and orders, barking out last names and we reply with first names and middle initial. Aidan, I've no middle initial ... Sir.

—"Just *NMI*, soldier, and *Sir* is for the brass. Smartly there, duffel from the alphabetical pile."

. . .

Seven days we've been in this miserable train. No idea, no one warned us. Our seven-day tomb. They told us nothing, where, when, how, or why, nothing. So Simon and I, we made it all up. A sort of variation on our Poohsticks race, besting each other's elaborations. Pullman cars, green-curtained proper beds, the porters, dining car with white-gloved waiters, an overnight, at most maybe two, to Idaho, Sun Valley—a luxury ski resort—Simon would know, the Challenger Inn, two to a room, full service, gorgeous blond Austrian girls—no no, they're the enemy, make them Swiss—to teach us how to ski. And other things.

Not quite.

Sealed in, we are, no outside connections, no talking with anyone else, the enemy's everywhere, listening, in case you didn't know. A turn-of-the-century coach, recalled from railway heaven to torment us. Seven days in a row it serves us—in a manner of speaking. Seats of filthy plush worn down to the springs, home for untold generations of fleas, bedbugs, lice. Benches come in sections, face-to-face, four assigned to each seat meant for three. So one of us is usually standing or has managed to climb onto the narrow metal grill of a handbag rack overhead. The cast-iron supports and fittings, their elaborate floral designs, are sticky and mostly black with the grime of uncountable hardworking hands. The one toilet is soon plugged, overflowing, the trap that should open to drop shit on the tracks just doesn't work. The solutions are varied. The window for a piss, the gap between cars for a shit, frigid sooty air up your arse, or a snowdrift on the frequent watering stops—our engine suffers from hardening bladder, prostatitis, both—and the occasional U.S. Army latrine. Meal stops at Army field kitchens, usually in bleak stretches of uninhabited prairie in the wee hours, where they slop goo in your mess kit. Except for the infrequent turn on the rack, sleeping is just sitting up. Chin propped on your fist, elbow on knee, until the ache in your teeth wakes you, probably thirty minutes at best. No other solutions are tolerated—head on a shoulder, feet on the opposite bench? No way.

Seven days, washing just once—at an Army field setup in Kansas. Geography pretty much escapes us, though, we usually haven't a clue. They manage to avoid the big cities, even Chicago, interminably shuttling us round. Shunting yards and empty spaces become our natural habitat.

We approach the Rockies, lined up there, a blue and white wall far beyond the sagebrush. Snow, ski troops— that's the U.S. Army for you. We slow to a crawl as we begin to climb. To Pando, Camp Hale, ten thousand feet, ten thousand tents and five hundred barracks, the snow a sooty gray. The dry clean air of the summer resorts, the TB asylums? Two thirds of us, of our fourteen thousand men, call in seriously sick—the Pando Hack. They say several have died of pneumonia—or is it TB and they'd not want to call it that? How clever they were to put our camp in this high snow-filled valley, closed in with major mountains all round, and the railroad passing right through. Coal-burning steam engines pouring soot into our pristine valley, and the coal gas from the hundreds of stoves in our barracks, that's what's doing us in. The inscrutable ways of our valiant Army.

But it might be worse. The Ivy League, the Swiss, the Austrians—they managed to sneak the Austrians in too, not like the interned Japs—in a sort of fraternal ski club. Officers and men are actually friends, regulations largely ignored.

This dream of a sporty dilettante crowd, the National Ski Patrol. They managed to sell it straight to FDR, his top brass bought into it too. And who wants to be shot clear out of the sky, or sunk straight into the sea? No, this was our brilliant answer, ski our way through the war, all of us friends.

If it weren't for the hacking lungs and the food, it is not a half bad war. Arduous climbs, sealskins on our skis, sixty-pound packs, mules, even Saint Bernard dogs, and the blizzards at fifty below. But then there's the smuggled wine, the song, camaraderie. We learn to make igloos at the end of each day's trek, warm, cozy, much better than tents. Our equipment is good, developed on Mount Rainier. And they'd figured out toboggans with motors, snowshoes with a new design, steel edges for our flat white skiis. And rock climbing, I'm good at it, they even have me teaching it now.

Would The Admiral be proud of me, is that why I'm here instead of back with those French seventy-fives on the rotsie range? Does he still linger, am I still in his thrall? Does he even now play a role in my choices?

And dearest mother? She makes no judgments, never bothers with opinions, my Yvette, she simply, quite simply, adores me, that was everything, beginning to end. At least that is all I can see.

. . .

Choices are over and done with, just look sharp and do what you're told. And that's not hard in the ski troops, in this boy-scout-outing war. Until ....

—"Pack up, men, we're ordered out. Write your letters, get them to the mailroom for the censors by noon, be ready to ship out tonight." A train again, but much better this time, and we're treated with some respect.

Fort Ord, California, for amphibious training. Ski troops? What did they have in mind, Fujiyama? The seasick drills, the head down, the leap into the waves, M1 held over our heads. The lore of the LCIs, the Landing Craft, Infantry. We'd seen it all in the newsreels, the *March of Time*, and there's no way they can prepare us for a head blown off, for pants soaking with piss, for death. Day passes to town are denied us, reading Steinbeck would have to do.

Some shipped out from Frisco, a detachment of us they put back on this train, a converted boxcar through the night, no idea where we are headed, we don't see a thing. Our train pulls right up to a dockside, it's Seattle. We board an LST—Landing Ship, Tanks, bloody arse-backwards acronyms. It's already packed with equipment, with vehicles, guns, LCIs strapped on deck. Are we really to be part of an invasion, my God, did we bargain for that? We hardly have time to pick out a pipe berth, go up on deck, when a whistle sounds, the bow ramp slams shut, hawsers are thrown free of their bollards, and blacked-out Seattle slips silently into the night

We stick to the inside passages north—are Jap subs lurking about? Thousands of wooded islands, abandoned Indian villages—a fallen totem pole rotting in the weeds. Tide rips, fog banks, I never see a buoy—had they moved them, pulled them up to deceive the invading Japs? We steam on through moonless nights, long misty days. Fjords, glaciered peaks, bear, deer, elk, leaping salmon, whales, otters, dolphins, eagles lording over it all. Distant snowfields in the spring sun, icebergs broken off from glacier faces float by, indifferent to the white-capped waves. And always the throb of the engines, the bow cutting through black waters, our wake ever lengthening.

North, northwest, west, even southwest for the last day. Winding through islands, heading for what? Familiar names—Alaska, two cents an acre seventy-five years ago, Sitka, Seward, Kodiak, Aleutians. Strange names—Umnak, Atka, Adak, Amchitka. Dreams of walrus tusks and sealskins, harpoons, whales, salmon, Aleuts paddling one-man bidarkas, big umiaks, signs still of the Russian traders, their genocidal rule—then ours. Trashy settlements ghostly through the fog, impossible cliffs, mountains reaching into pale sunlight. Slipping shadows, ships gathering, all about us, silence, distant shouts. Our stern anchors clatter, the ramp cranks down, we're set abruptly, unceremoniously, on shore.

It's a tacky military base, we settle down to wait. There's talk of a landing, instructors drawing diagrams, drills, haphazard dry runs, M1s handed out, ammo, target practice, awful food. And rain, never-ending rain now, just for us. Helmets, Army rain gear, ponchos, and a GI towel around the neck, they work moderately well—except our feet, our feet are never dry.

Attu, the tip of this island chain, we've taken it, they tell us, we hear rumors of a long and bloody fight. And a shipload of wounded soldiers is triaged to our field hospital. They wander round camp, bandaged, canes, some hang out with us. Most are silent, a few want to talk, to find some relief, exorcism, and to warn and prepare us for what may lie ahead. They speak of the grind of battle, of Jap soldiers wild drunk with saké, bayonet-charging the smoking machine guns. Other horrors we'd rather not hear.

The Attu campaign had bypassed Kiska, Kiska they'd left for us, thirty-five thousand of us, Canadians too. Simon and I are assigned to the same landing boat, and we're told which cove, which beach will be ours.

This is it. Simon, old friend, we're buddies as they say, foxhole buddies, it's official, and friends, roommates right through college, all of that. But Simon, have we ever really talked? Like what the fuck are we doing here? Like what is this, who are we, and why? Plato, Shakespeare, Nietzsche,

Jesus, Margaret Mead, our mothers, the lot, what help are they now? The fact is it's you and the fellows next to you, the pfc, the corporal, the sergeant, the looie that count.

If they get you, and I survive, what would you like me to do? Ask me the same and I'd not have a clue—well, no, maybe, maybe I'd like you to, let's see …. Get home, find Joel, play Poohsticks under that campus footbridge, a third stick dropped in for me. There, and likewise for you? Let's shake, here, and a hug too, old friend.

Frank, over here, we need your help. Here, a photo, we'll stand by our LCI, it's this button. Cigarettes dangling, helmets rakish, M1s casual—warriors, tough, a cameo for the Army tabloid, their *Stars and Stripes*. Maybe I'll make hero status after all, compete with The Admiral's lingering wraith—if he's dead. But… killing, killing another? Draw a bead, his head there above that rock, he's peering the other direction, breath held, squeeze it off, his helmet bouncing on the shingle, his face gone. Cold, deliberate, that's what they taught us. Can I? Oh God!

Shit! A shot, what was that? Willard? Shot himself in the hand? That's one way to deal with the future, but you must do it right, and be ready for Leavenworth, too. Sadsack Willard, he's botched it again, a scratch on a knuckle, that's all.

. . .

Over the purr of our motor there's not a word, not a shot. The gut-rumble naval shelling from our destroyers has suddenly stopped. There's not much to see, just an

LCI on each side, land is vague through the fog, kelp waving as we go by. They passed out mugs of steaming tea laced with GI rum, real rum. A beach, so they say, rocky, but really a beach, Jesus, they better be right! Was that our propellor hitting a rock, will we make it at all, will we end up just sitting ducks, Jap target practice when they've done in the rest?

Fuck me, we've really hit something now. Why are they lowering the ramp, lowering into the open sea? Just waves, and fog, and they order us out? Waist-deep, frigid, trip on a rock, M1 over my head, wet to my neck, oh shit! I'm so bloody pants-pissing scared.

That rattling sound, ladyfingers—Guy Fawkes? Fourth of July? or someone tossing pebbles, sorting through stones for some skippers? Oh shit—this idiot mind of mine—it's shooting, they've pinned us here, feet still in the sea.

Simon, quick, over here, get down, here, behind this rock. There, they're moving in, those shapes, you see, over there in the fog? I forgot, flick the safety, clip's already in, squeeze one, quick now, two, three, four, five. Oh shit! I broke my shoulder, forgot to hold the stock in tight, broken I'm sure. But I got one, maybe more, got 'em before they got us. Willard, get down man, what the fuck are you doing, you're ... Christ, they got him, that's his helmet, it bounced on our rock, shit, his head's inside.

I vomit.

Bloody hell, they're closing in, fast, a grenade might

do it, oh shit! I've taped all mine—those things, they scared the crap out of me during training. Simon, they're coming in, look out! Damn, I've lost them, lost in the fucking fog. That head, for God's sake throw it away. Gordie, Jesus, what are you doing, what the hell, you can't go out there now.

He's up, readying to make a dash, flat slap of muffled fire, a single sigh beside me, his helmet flies off, his eye is gone, he rolls toward me, the back of his head is mush.

Oh shit, Simon watch it! They're coming again, there, over there, see, where the fog has lifted. But, aren't those Americans?

Christ, we've been killing each other! I throw my rifle into the sea. And... Oh God! Fuck you!—my shout tearing my throat—fuck you, Admiral Allard, take your medals and shove them, way up, way up your insufferable arse.

Salt and sand and seaweed to soak up the piss and the blood. This violent shaking, both hands to get the food they've brought me up to my mouth. Triaged to a fucking chaplain, aspirins and a Bible. —"Pull yourself together, corporal, we've a war to win."

Body bags lined up, a chaplain mumbling ashes and dust, a rifle squad fires off their volleys, it's done. How many are mine, how many? Dark forms in the fog, falling, calling out. Mine. I'm there still, I lie with them on the edge of that uncaring sea, a dying wave to roll over me—and my world.

Before I leave the beach I find two pieces of driftwood.

Trembling, fumbling, our sergeant yelling at me, I tie them together with a bit of seaweed—a bit of vine on a Welsh hillside. A cross propped in the blood-spattered rocks.

Twelve of us are dead in the friendly fire, seventeen more from Jap booby traps and our faulty shells. Seventy-one lost, all hands, when a destroyer hit a mine. And the Japs had long since evacuated, probably just after they lost Attu. Our glorious glamorous mountain troops, no medals, no heroes, just dead. No skis, no snowshoes, no mountains to scale, just dead.

And a war to win.

. . .

Back to the waiting and waiting for no one knows what. No one, in fact it's completely unknowable, like what happens to us next. They're shipping the whole bleeding division, us heroes and the guys left at Camp Hale, to the snowy peaks, the icy cliffs of Texas, yes, Camp Swift, Texas, USA, summer of '44, one hundred and nine degrees in the few scraps of shade.

But Simon and I, when we'd unloaded in Frisco, the shakes largely displaced by rage and despair, we pull off a most classy hoax.

Compassionate leave, Sir, my mother, she's quite desperately ill, Houston, where she'd moved for her job. And, a day later so they'd not see the connection, Simon comes up with, —"Sir, my brother, flying-fortress gunner, killed, ack-ack hit his turret, Klagenfurt, shipped him back, the funeral's in Dallas." They give us rail passes for anywhere, report to Camp Swift in a week. And they never checked on our stories, at least not so far as we knew. Or maybe they saw through the subterfuge, but, maybe, —"We owe them, what the hell, let the kids go."

A first-class compartment to Chicago, the Union Pacific's art deco streamliner—Benito would love this, right on time to his kitschy modern Rome. We'd bought a few extra medals in Frisco, shined up our combat boots, and are treated like conquering heroes. They wine us, —"Cigars boys, cognacs, what'll it be?" Chicago I lost in a smoky blur, but we do make it back to our camp, considerably the worse for the wear.

Texas, Camp Swift, month after month, waiting, and for what? Was it maybe they're simply protecting us, protecting us from ourselves? They distribute Japanese language texts, maps of Burma, to ski troops! For God's sake, what's next?

Finally they have relented—November, Jesus!—they give us a new CO, General Hay. He manages to get us, all fourteen thousand, three regiments, onto troop transports, shipped out—east, the Atlantic, sending us to do in Jerry. A fast convoy, they call it, with token naval escort—the U-boat menace seems to be considered quite over.

Gibraltar. The Admiral, Yvette, baby Barbary apes sitting on my shoulders, picnics in the hills of Spain. Those hills against a winter sky, at peace, bloody fascist Spain, yet quite at peace. Germans, Japs, they lost this war two years ago—Midway, Guadalcanal, El Alamein, Stalingrad, half of Italy—yet they keep on with the slaughter, pulling back into their heartlands, which are getting bombed to shit. At least the Eyeties knew it was time to throw in the towel, Italy is for the taking if we can pry the Germans out. Mussolini escaped to the north, his Bicycle Boys kaput, remember them? Rommel with his thousands of tanks, Badóglio's boys on wobbly bicycles scurrying to escape our Tommies. They knew they'd lost, hopeless.

But Rommel, Generalfeldmarschall, he must know too. In fact, years later we were to learn the truth about him. One of the few humane and honorable leaders in the Wehrmacht, near the end of the war he died of injuries, they said, his staff car strafed. He was buried with highest honors as a great German hero. At the war crimes trials in Nürnberg, General Keitel, top dog of all the German armed forces throughout the war, a.k.a. Hitler's lackey— guilty and hanged—testified that Rommel had played a role in a plot to rid Germany of Hitler and end the hopeless war. They caught him and gave him the choice of either disgrace, execution, and the annihilation of his family by a public trial, or of suicide and a trumped up hero's parade. He chose cyanide.

We pass Algiers in the distance, then Sicily, Capri, Vesuvius. Naples, Lady Hamilton waving welcome from the mole, we get a glimpse of a dirty city, its forts, its immortalized funicular, the obligatory wisp of smoke from its volcano, the docks, the teeming, scheming city, urchins grabbing, stealing what they can. They say a Liberty Ship, one of Henry Kaiser's troop transports, had unloaded there, been left untended overnight, and had completely disappeared by morning, dismantled piece by piece into the black markets.

We're loaded into LSTs, on past Ischia, Ponza, Anzio, Giglio, Monte Cristo, Elba, on to Livorno where they herd us, straggling, ashore. No skis, no all-white winter gear, no snow cats, only our crossed-skis shoulder patches and our rock-climbing gear. Are we just ordinary foot-slogging infantrymen, cannon fodder, after all that razzmatazz?

We've set up camp along the beach, sunny, not really winter cold. We've tied our tents to the umbrella pines, spread our laundry on the mastic shrubs to dry, stretched out in the sand and grass, sheltered among the dunes. Wine appears quite magically, much-used fiaschi wrapped with raffia, some with remnants still of the Chianti cock label—the Dago red. A guitar or two, songs begin, our mountain songs—but out of place. We dwindle into silence, a bit depressed and scared, until someone starts up with *Santa Lucia*. The gathering local paesani join in, then teach us their rousing partisan version of the rice-growers *Bella Ciao*. A fast marching beat. —'E se io muoio da partigiano/O bella ciao, bella ciao, bella ciao, ciao, ciao..."

. . .

January nineteen forty-five. Past Florence, at the southern edge of the Apennines, we joined the Fifth Army. Heroes of North Africa, Sicily, Salerno, Monte Cassino, Anzio, three famous infantry divisions, the Forty-Fifth, the Thirty-Sixth, and the Third. Their casualties through these years were twice their total complement. I met a corporal who'd refused any higher rank—unlucky, unsafe—the sole survivor of his company, went through it all. And we, the Tenth Mountain Division, we have Kiska—now this.

Jerry's General Kesselring, north of us somewhere, had set up his Gothic Line. He'd left Florence smoldering, bridges all blown except Ponte Vecchio where he'd destroyed the buildings at each end, piled up their rubble as barriers. He pulled back into the mountains. Eighty-eights on every mountainside, they say, no way to get through. So they send us to the slaughter, pull the others back to rest.

Bitter snow, black cliffs, shattered groves of oak and olives, eighty-eights whistling overhead. Desperate trenching, piling rocks, —"Bad idea, soldier, a near hit and you're killed by your own rocks." Cowering in ferocious cold, days and nights of terror.

Word comes down the line. —"Corporal Allard, report to regimental HQ, on the double, now!" We assemble in a classroom of the village school, the requisitioned headquarters, sit on the children's desks, check each other out. It's obvious, they've pulled in the best of the rock-climbers. Great, now what, preen ourselves or head for sick call? The brass files in, led by no less than General Hay himself.

—"At ease, men, at ease, that's rear echelon chickenshit, not up here."

He proceeds to lay out all the thinking—to us, dog-faces, unshaven, scared GIs. Monte Belvedere—Mount Belvuhdeer they called it—they figured was the key.

—"Belvuhdeer commands the route, men, the only way through to the north. They have no aircraft, none left, but they can watch all our movements from up there, fire down on us at will, keep an eye on every village on the route. And they've stopped us there for weeks. Belvuhdeer must be taken. We've got to get major forces in close without them knowing, be ready to move forward when we've softened them up, distracted them. That's where you men, the very best, come in. The way to get at them is to take Riva Ridge, here on the map. I'm taking you up closer now so you can get a careful look."

Keep down, spread out... There, Riva Ridge. It's defended too, mortars at least, emplacements, but if we could take it, it would give us a high route, a clear and more protected route for us, more vulnerable for them, to soften them up on Belvuhdeer, then move in from below in force.

—"Pass these binoculars around, men, check it out. We're looking to a sneak attack, nighttime, you men to secure ways up the face, a battalion or more to follow, surprise attack, started well before dawn."

We figure out. —"Four, maybe five, ways up, Sir, could be done, yes, even at night, steep, but easy rock work, we'll fix ropes where needed for the others. Ice in spots, mostly melted out with this sirocco. Can be done, Sir.

Can you give us any light?... No, of course not, Sir, but could our searchlights aim at the cloud cover, seem to be searching about? The reflected light could help us. And, Sir, the others that follow, they'll have to be single file, dangerous, defenseless, at all costs they must be totally silent, Sir... Thank you, Sir, we'll do our best, count on it, General, Sir, our very best."

Well, no skis, I guess, not in this war, but at least there's this rope work. But what's there if we make it? Shit!

They sneak us—we ten rock-climbers and several companies—by night, no lights, no noise, just on foot, up the valley, to a village near the foot of the ridge. The villagers—what's left of them, Jerry had tried to evacuate them all—the villagers hide us in their houses, their barns, ply us with polenta, sausages, wine. We're out of sight through the day, no shelling from Belvedere. So far so good. Now, twenty-thirty, time to start our climb. Alone this time, no Simon, he's been made company clerk, typing requisitions, morning reports, service records, adding in some medals for us, for our road to glory.

We're loaded with slung M1s, ammo, grenades, ropes, carabiners, pitons, hammers—they'll bring up the BARs, mortars, more ammo next phase. Hammering pitons in the dark, fixing ropes, it's clumsy work, but not too bad.

We're there, the top, and no sign of Jerry, not yet. We signal, up the others come. They're good, they're here, and not a sound. The fog is thick, we dig in, shallow foxholes, they may counterattack. Get ready, the hand signal, advance. Belly crawl, M1 on our arms ahead, pull with our elbows, push with our toes, heads down and sideways to look ahead. Regulation crawling, it works. Midnight, they must be sleeping. Their emplacements are dim in the reflected light, roofed over, sandbags, only the narrowest of openings. Our lieutenant makes the signal, hand grenades explode like rapid fire.

They're ripping us with machine-gun fire. Someone just ahead is thrown back on me. A shriek, a sigh, a patch of his flesh slaps my hand, sticks, I shake it off in horror. Our desperate fight has begun. Slide in behind that rock, splinters pinging on my helmet. My grenades—pull the pin, stiff-arm overhand. The first one falls short, throws mud and snow in my face. The second makes it—their emplacement explodes, a machine gun with a severed hand sizzles in the snow just beyond my rock.

Screams, medics, wounded lowered down the cliffs. Death's gurgles to the rhythm of machine guns. Someone calls in artillery, explosions just ahead, ripping off my helmet, pounding in my gut. On and on.

Exhausted, utter terror, black tears—my blackened face—splattering on my wrists. Oh fuck, oh Jesus, no! I've done my best, I'm finished, the others can do the fucking rest.

They did, they mopped up, Riva made secure. They ran the ridge at dawn, into the fire of Belvedere's rear defenses. Some found protection in the dark, many found death. The way was open now, defenses were softened for our main forces to come on in. Not long and Belvedere was ours.

They find me, half frozen, shaking, spasms, stretched in the bloody grass, I'd been there through the day, they tell me. They evacuate me with the wounded and dead, tied to a stretcher, lowered down the face of the ridge on my own rope. They thaw me out, a bowl of soup, fresh bread brought up from the rear.

—"Nothing wrong with you, Corporal, they're coming soon to interview you for a citation."

A medal, I suppose. Fuck the medal, fuck this fucking war... Sir.

An effective word, fuck, it often has served me well, and this time it gets me a three-day pass to Florence.
—"Division's regrouping, we can spare you."

Simon juggles papers, gets himself a pass too.

We hitchhike back to Florence in an Army four-by-four. The road is jammed with tanks, armored personnel carriers, truckloads of soldiers, convoys of ammo, supplies moving in, empties and the wounded and the dead moving out. Our driver, a Third Infantry Division pfc, chatters on and on.

—"It has its good sides, this driving. Mostly independent, detours for trades with the locals, never at loss for excuses, always room for a girl or two and to hell with the MPs, and damn few of them anyhow up here at the front. There are the mines, but you infantry, or the tanks, or the engineers with their Bangalore torpedoes and sweepers usually get there first. And the snipers and shells. But we're mostly pretty far back."

He takes us straight into the center, sailing through checkpoints, MPs waving us on, drops us in front of Palazzo Vecchio. Florence seems half deserted, stripped of all possible ornaments, not a statue to be seen. No banners, no kiosks, no sidewalk cafés, umbrellas, awnings, potted plants, carrozze, the things you'd rather hoped for. Well, winter and war, what might you really expect? What we get is masculine Florence, with its phallic town-hall tower, its relentless stone, hollow echoes. The Duomo with its Baptistery and Giotto's colorful bell tower seem oddly out of place. But we'd look about later.

Our very first order of business was something we'd planned for weeks. —"But, Aidan old buddy, old hero, are you really up to it after all that back there?" I am, and we do it. We climb through the rubble, up onto the Ponte Vecchio, our dreamed-about, agreed-upon bridge—the only bridge Jerry had left intact. We pass by the shops on each side, iron-barred, padlocked closed, gold no doubt squirreled away, not a soul, up to the central balcony-like opening. We lean over the upstream balustrade, drop our Poohsticks in the Arno, race to the other side, cheering on our contenders as they emerge. A tie. —"If only Joel were here, maybe a three-way tie? Or is he... No, I shan't... He's somewhere over here, two years ahead of us, under fire too, he wrote once. No, no..."

Next must be food, though it's only midafternoon,

the very best. But the only place we find is this cellar restaurant at the end of our bridge, not quite the place of one's dreams. Thick-fogged with our breaths and GI cigarette smoke. Bitter wine, spaghetti with a light sprinkle of Parmigiano, a few drops of rancid oil. Girls, black hair, flashing teeth, unbearably sexed, they rub against us—tomorrow, ragazze, too desperately tired.

Late afternoon, the sun dying in the sepia Arno, flashing blood-red, we find a pensione on the Lungarno. The lift is a fretted cage, a contraption with ropes you pull hand over hand to ascend. Our room is enormous. A dusty chandelier sways in the draft beneath a swarm of cherubim, shreds of faded damask on the walls. There's a dead toilet up the corridor, but they show us the ceramic chamber pots, the basins, a pitcher in Forlí's yellow dragon patterns, chipped, blackened cracks repaired with lead staples. Two candles, a thin box of wax matches. Letto matrimoniale, non c'é altro—that's all they have. Unlikely couple, Simon and I. The bedspread is a canvas cow blanket with rust-red block prints of milkmaids. The dank sheets are finally warmed for us with the suora, the pregnant nun, the belly-shaped wooden rack dangling its earthenware pot of embers.

No rattling gunfire, no slamming of their eighty-eights, no foxholes in the frozen rocks, no frozen bodies. Sleep.

Breakfast on our bit of a balcony—the sun is weak, wintry, but it's bone-chill inside—steaming bread rolls, olive oil for butter, bitter chicory coffee, hot blue milk.

We'd brought sugar from our K-rations, but the signora puts a pot of precious honey on our tray. Honey—not GI gelatinous marmalade slopped on our mess kits—sugary honey, in our coffee, on the rolls, on our fingers as we clean out the pot. She tells us it was honey from her brother's farm, honey of the field poppies and wild onion and rosemary and the tiny white olive blossoms—she is rapturous in her broken English.

Through the railing we watch an organ grinder sitting on the rubble at the end of a dynamited bridge. He's cranking out a Bersaglieri march from the last war. His monkey, Turkish cap clutched to his belly, sleeps in his master's lap. Old men muck in the Arno's slime, installing props for a jerry-rigged bridge span. Sewage stinks mix with the reek of cordite and death in my combat fatigues.

We wander a Florence stripped of treasures, hidden from the war. The galleries and museums boarded up. Churches shiver in their silence, boots treading the tombs. The Battistero is shuttered, but the Duomo is crowded. The bell tower sways over a red-roofed blackened city. Beatrice slips away in her hooded cloak, Dante smitten, quite transfixed.

The next morning, early, a bus rattles us up the Chiantigiana into the hills, drops us off at a roadside shrine. After hours of walking, the sun slicing the cold, at midday we crouch outside a cemetery wall—lichened stones, clinging capers, ivy, a gap of rubble where a shell had torn a cypress from its roots, hurled it through the wall to lie

dying among the dead. We spread out our déjeuner sur
l'herbe, partake daintily—a bottle of black wine, a loaf
of bread, an onion, cheese for a traded pack of cigarettes.
We quote Wordsworth to each other, it seems to keep us
warm. Snotty literary-mag types at college, buck-arse GIs
conjuring an Arcadia from the ruins.

When we've run out of Wordsworth, we wander on,
cold, quiet to the slow far tolling of a funeral bell. The
winter haze is heavy with the smoke of carbonari burning olive wood in sod ovens for the charcoal—prunings
to give strength for next season's fruit, trimmings to clear
away the shatterings of war. A pair of white oxen strain to
the yoke of a wooden plough, a black figure struggles on
the handles. No reins, few commands. —"Brrrrrra!" he
calls, leaves them standing, steaming, pissing on a patch
of snow. He's bent and shriveled, too old for war, his
back twisted under a rag of a coat, a tattered gray scarf
wrapped around his head, his hands in the remnants of
mittens, bony cheeks blue with the cold, eyes black and
smiling behind the bushes of old-age eyebrows.

He comes stiff-legged to us, invites us to follow him.
Beyond a tangle of blackberries we come up to his casa
colonica. Stone, the stucco mostly gone, a shell hole in
the red-tiled roof patched with an ancient canvas cow
blanket, smoke lifting in the still air, an arched loggia
sheltering a cage of mewing pigeons and mourning doves,
a yellow-eyed dog on a chain, chin on paws, watching us
cautiously, chickens twitching on the ladder ramp to their

rusty tin-roof coop, a vaulted outdoor oven for figs and bread off to the side, a well, its hand pump wrapped in burlap against the winter.

He leads us in, it's dark, one pane left in the single boarded window, musty, smoky. His wife, her body doubled over almost down to her knees from a lifetime of hoeing, twists her head to peer up at us, holding out her root of a hand, greeting us with her smiling gums.

We sit, four of us, by the open fire under its massive stone hood supported on smoke-blackened oaken beams. The stone benches are softened with sheepskins. She rises to bring vin santo in thimble glasses—honey amber, honey sweet—a plate of herbed olives, slabs of bread she toasts on a grill over the embers, rubbed with garlic, sprinkled with olive oil and salt.

They thank us, their liberators. We empty our pockets of cigarettes and gritty melt-proof GI chocolate bars. Addio, compagni, e buona fortuna.

. . .

Back to their senseless war. The eighty-eights, they're rumbling again, is Jerry brain-dead, even stupider than we are? Yes, I know, the usual litany, his Beethoven and Schiller, his Nietzsche and Einstein, his Goethe and Hegel and Bach—let's leave Wagner out. He must know he's lost, yet he goes on destroying, and killing, and dying—so do we.

But, well, maybe some have finally got it. Our road back is lined with battered soldiers, no helmets, no guns—Jerry. They're mostly unescorted, just our MPs at spaced-out checkpoints, counting, phoning back numbers, sending them on alone. There are even weary waves from them as they trudge by. Losers, just kids like us, the living few.

. . .

We slog on, snow to mud to springtime, February to April, slogging slowly on. The whole division, and the others, the Brazilian First on our right, the British Eighth Army on down to the Adriatic, the U.S. First Armored, the Thirty-Sixth, leapfrogging, pulled out, others come up, the Buffalo Division, no way to keep track of it all. Stubborn, disciplined resistance, Jerry's never on the run. Our aircraft fill the skies, the Germans have none, not one. Their supply lines are battered, ours untouched, a flood of ammo, tanks, men. Village by battered village, we move on. Simon's back there somewhere on a truck or a jeep. Me, I cling to the top of a Sherman tank. On to the next village, the next river, then fan out, watch for the snipers, keep my arse down, hope they'll pull out or surrender. Resistance, a machine gun may be in that bell tower. Down, fast, it's coming in! Damn! Their mortars, they've found us again.

I pick up pieces of a Pando ski instructor who'd just propped himself up on his elbow to piss. I try to put him back together. Tears, vomit, shaking so I can hardly pull off his dog tags, wave the medics back. Just his dog tags in my pocket, that's all that's left.

Another day, more horror? From what I've seen of our platoon leader's map, we're closing in on the Po river. A chicken colonel, no less, has come up in his jeep, striking a cliché Patton-like pose, calling for volunteers.

—"A circling dash to a bridgehead, get there ahead of Jerry, secure it. We do it, men, and the war's nearly won. Volunteers?" Not a one, so they volunteer us. My name's on the first sergeant's list, Corporal Allard. They've volunteered me.

Well, we've made it, outflanked Jerry this time, got ahead of him, we're sitting here holding our end of the bridge over the Po, munching our K-rations, the colonel too—that will get him his medal if this bridgehead operation won't do. And Jerry, he's left his wounded behind, he's crossing downriver, some swimming, some rafting on driftwood, logs, poles, discarded tires, empty petrol cans, even a wooden ammo box. Poor bastards, they're lucky, though—we raced up here light and don't have the firepower to waste much on them. We lob a few mortar shells across the river to keep Jerry away from their end of the bridge. A kid lying in the ditch beside me reaches for his MI, takes the prone position, sights on a raft of Germans, looks over at me, puts the rifle down, rubs at his tears with the back of his wrist.

They're over, they disappear on the other side. We start across the bridge, over the river Po. Simon, Joel, they're not here, I scratch in the paint of a girder,

*FIUME POOH*

And on to the Adige river, crossing with amphibious Ducks, barges, and later a pontoon bridge. Resistance ever less. Our momentum picks up, we requisition everything on wheels—German lorries, touring cars, wagons, motorcycles, sidecars, Fiats, bicycles. *We're* the Bicycle Boys now. On to Lake Garda, Malcesine. We work our way up its eastern shore, but it's slow going, they blocked several tunnels as they retreated. Others of us advance on the west shore. Several of our brass drown when their amphibious Duck capsizes while shuttling across the lake.

We make it to the north end of the lake.

We celebrate May Day with a partisan detachment, communists to a man. Flags, whatever was at hand, stars-and-stripes, hammer-and-sickle, the red-white-and-green, no ribbons round a maypole, this was their Labor Day. And we liberate a German warehouse, blast through its concrete door, Kesselring's private stash, the finest French champagne. So it's *Bella Ciao* again, to the delight of our partisan friends, to the swish of admiring skirts. Girls waving branches of red plum blossoms, singing with us, perching on our knees. I'm too battered, and beat, and drunk for more than a kiss and a squeeze. Church bells begin their frantic, joyful chorus, calling out over the lake. Bats escape from the belfries, to dance with the myriad swallows, a twilight impromptu ballet.

There's a radio out on the terrace tuned in the BBC. Cease-fires on the Italian fronts, surrender to be signed tomorrow. Formalities in the days ahead, surrenders up the line, Lüneburg, Rheims, Berlin. I fall in a bed of lilies, joyfully, wonderfully, finally blotto.

And in that bed of lilies is born a plan. The gardener of my perfumed dreams, Aldo, tells me later, —"They're not just ordinary lilies, compagno, they're belladonna lilies from Africa, the flowers like a bella donna, no? I grow them for the bulbs, the signori hereabouts pay good prices for them, or will again now they've got Benito strung up by his heels, and Adolf by his single ball, they say."

Yes, well, emerging from that bed of lovely ladies, I have a plan. They'd had two brutal years of war, the U.S. Fifth Army, Algeria, then Sicily and Italy's toe. They almost made it, toe to tip, to the top, the border in the Alps. My plan, I'll just keep going, on to the top, to the Brenner Pass, finish that last bit for the men who didn't make it, for the tens of thousands who'd be lined up forever waiting under their white crosses and Magen Davids and whatever suits them best.

I'd been summers to the Italian and Austrian Tyrol, with Yvette, learned enough German, I should have no trouble. Finally free of war. Will I need Simon, his creative forgeries, passes, missions, his intricate, hoax-filled mind? But I've left him far behind. No matter, they'll never miss me, I'm already detached from my company, thanks to the colonel for that, no, they'll never miss me, and who'd care if they did? I'll find my way back to my company, just take a day, maybe two. Good old Simon'll be there, he'll take care of me then if need be.

I tell my compagno, Aldo, no one else, just him. He lights up like a sparkler, says he'll come along too. But no no, he can't, his grandson is expected back the next day, back from Milan with the partisans, back from stringing Benito up. —"Si si, compagno mio, by the heels, Piazza Loreto, his mistress, Carletta, too. The buses, compagno, they run north to the Brenner at least once a day. No, there's no petrol problem. They're converted to coal gas." I dust off bits of the lily bed's compost, pick up my rifle, helmet, mess kit, ammo, and pack, and just go.

The roof of the bus is an open-air market. Glassy-eyed chickens tied by their feet in a bunch, a sow with piglets in a willow-wand cage, sacks of potatoes, cabbages, on-ions, and carrots, cages of songbirds, two bikes, a dog, a machine gun, three huge demijohns, wine or oil, in their rotting wickerwork baskets. And smack in the middle, on leaky sacks of flour, sits a wizened old fellow—Tyrolean hat, filthy loden cloth cloak, S-shaped pipe, the kind with a silver cap—picking out partisan songs on a squeeze box, mumbling the words through his pipe-clenching teeth, a brown dribble of spit on his bristly chin, eyes shut, quite carried away. He switches to a Great War song, passengers, hanging out of the windows, joining in.

*O, Gorizia, tu sei maledetta...*

Inside it's packed, but they tug me, shove me, squeeze me into a seat, put my gear on a rack. The din of their greetings, the kisses and cheek-pinching, the wine poured down my throat, the stink of tobacco, horse shit, urine—too much in my hung-over exhausted state.

We rattle along, a dust cloud behind, dodging the potholes, pitching, bouncing, violent lurches. The window is streaked with pig piss, yellow drops make their way down through the dust of my reflection. With one hand I cling to a handle on the seatback in front of me—my Sherman tank handhold. With the other I prop my head, elbow on the window ledge—Willard's head rolling on the shingle, torn flesh. Nothing stills the shaking, the screams, my sobs.

A hand is on my cheek, a wedding ring, a young woman all in black. She dries my tears with a torn bit of lace-edged handkerchief, reaches across me to pull open the window.

To a gorgeous spring day. Vineyards carpeting much of the land, their twisted vines almost hidden in fresh green. Poplars standing guard by the side of our road. The shrines for the worshippers, the crosses where partisans died. Farmhouses, villages, painted churches with onion steeples. Donkeys loaded with firewood or panniers of sickled grass to fatten the calves, oxen carts hauling flour from a mill. And everywhere—walking, bicycling, piled on carts, clinging wherever they can, buses, one or two trucks, sidecar motor bikes—men heading home from war, men who'd been forced to go on killing or face the firing squads. Most have managed to find at least some bits of civvy clothes—patched woolen pants, a moth-eaten cloak, a battered hat, but never a rifle, a helmet, a bandolier—shedding war. Some wear red bandanas on their arms, partisans embracing brothers, reluctant enemies before. Many are wounded, limping, on crutches, in filthy bandages—the ragtag ends of Benito's empire finito, kaput, done.

We pull up in Bolzano—it's horribly damaged by American bombs. I still recognize the Mareccio Castle's five towers, the Dominican monastery, and the cathedral is largely intact. But the stench of cordite and death linger, we are silent, the accordion player climbs down. We hurriedly unload, reload, take off again to the north.

The Alps gather slowly round us, the Ötztal and Zillertal chains. High snowfields, glaciers, sharp peaks, and down here a chill in the air still, hay fields just turning green. The railway follows beside us, then tunnels while we climb, laboring up the hairpins. The stream—is this where the Adige is born?—drops through shaded patches of ice and snow. A young girl is fishing from a bomb-damaged bridge, waves, then blows a kiss when my uniform—well, my filthy fatigues—catches her eye.

As we climb, our bus gradually empties, village by village, into these mountain homes. Trees thinning, rocky meadows, sheep terrified at the sight of our bus, the pass opens up before us. The Brenner, the Austrian border, where Charlie Chaplin, his blob of a black mustache, and Jack Oakie, the bulging chin, the silly fascist salute, where they met, where the Axis was born. I'm the last one left on the bus, just the driver and me. He backs the bus onto the shoulder—must be his usual way to turn round, head back. He stops, gets out, so do I. Nearby is a fountain, spring water splashing into a stone trough. I drink from my hands, put my head under the spout. My reflection is shaking violently, I grip the stone with whatever strength I have left. The sun wavers behind my skull, someone is sobbing, I sink to the grass.

Have I slept? Sorry. The driver helps me up, hands me a bit of bread and a sausage end. We look round, poke open a door or two, no one, no customs, no police. The red-and-white barrier pole is up, the Grenze sign on it smashed, replaced by a carefully painted

*Tirol Über Alles*

We look at each other, the same moment, a questioning eyebrow, a gesture north. We climb back on board, head off.

Austria, Innsbrück, far down in the valley, which Yvette and I often had made a base for our hikes in the Karwendlthal, for our Faltbooting on the Inn and the Enns to the Danube, our bicycle trips up the valleys. And the concerts, an opera, Schuhplattler in a beer hall courtyard, Lederhosen, Dirndlkleider, and all.

The streets of Innsbrück are crowded, people milling about, women, children, men in discarded bits of uniform, insignia torn off, many missing legs and arms and eyes, GIs in rear-echelon olive drab, jeeploads of snazzy MPs. The scene is largely subdued. Perhaps the Austrians worry that their status is in doubt, anxious to be German no more.

I find the Goldener Adler, our favorite, Yvette and me,

but, —"We've filled the very last room, Sir, every hotel is full."

Why the fuck am I here, and AWOL at that? And the bus won't go back till the next afternoon. A park bench, a whorehouse? My night with the lilies and wine. Riva, the Ridge-Runners, Belvedere, the slogging slaughter north. The distance to go, to get back. Bone weary, filthy, in battle fatigues, MPs prowling about. Better just turn myself in? Helmet, rifle, pack, why am I here? This crowd of rear-echelon types, Eisenhower jackets, ribbons, thinking to add to their story, their glory. I collapse at a last lonely table in the hotel lounge bar.

Herr Kellner, bitte, ein Bier.

And later, Noch einmal, bitte.

Well, old Joel, you know the rest. Me at that round slab of marble, drawing pictures with slopped-over beer. I saw you first in that puddle, an upside-down house-of-mirrors reflection. Spectacles, your brown hair GI-trimmed, properly combed, ribbons and medals on your jacket, trousers tucked into well-shined combat—so-called—boots. I knew right away it was you, God knows how. I didn't look up, I wasn't ready to believe it, didn't want to believe it, for God's sake no!

And then you said it, that selfsame hometown college-kid voice. —"Aidan! it's fucking well you!"

# 6

A shattering moment, an impossible moment, our private pincer moment, that Goldener Adler moment in the bar. One frontline dogface, the rest of us rear-echelon. An MI, battle gear, alone, a marble table, across the room. You are shaking, spasms, you'd slopped some beer, dabbling in it, lips muttering silently, pale and pinched as death. You look up slowly, stare, groan, fall forward sobbing in your beer.

An MP lieutenant comes over, all decked out, white helmet, everything polished, the works. He helps me get you and your gear up to my room, to lay you on my bed. Without a word, no document check, no salutes, he shakes my hand in both of his, turns, tiptoes out.

You lie there, calmly by then, tears pouring down your cheeks. I draw a steaming bath, undress you, help you stumble in. I soap and scrub and rinse and dry you, and still you've not uttered a word. I half carry you to that double bed, pull up the feather bolster, turn off the flickering lights. I undress, lie down beside you. I hold you in my arms all through the night.

You awake late in the morning, but there is still time for a lunch before your rendezvous with your bus driver and for one thing more you quietly ask me to do. I come with you to the bridge over the Inn for our private fraternal rite, our Poohsticks. Two bits of splintered wood from a shattered shutter. We drop on the count of three, they land together. We dash to the other side. They float from the shadows, still close. We turn to each other, we smile, we hug. You tremble in my arms.

Released then, face to face, your hands reach out to me, fingers lightly to my cheeks. They hold me, my eyes to yours—tormented, lost beseeching. I can but turn away.

We walk silently through the streets of Innsbrück. Flags, banners, garlands of flowers—smiling crowds to-day, gay colors. Children dancing around a fountain to a beribboned accordion's tune.

We find the bus, your driver friend is asleep on a pile of army blankets in the aisle. You pass your kit up through a window, turn to me. —"Thank you Joel…your care… this beaten, broken me."

My hands to your shoulders, your haggard face is blurred through my tears.

· · ·

Forty years ago that was, Aidan. Long journeys for us, many changes of course. Long journeys intertwining. Lost promises. Wars and loves and disasters. So many violent deaths, so much unjust and devastating hurt. Torn bodies, ravaged hearts in useless conflict. Despair.

How did I get there, to Innsbrück, how could that be? You were completely drained, it was not the time to exchange stories, never really has been—till now.

· · ·

My Grand Tour war, my cushy tourist war, that's what it was, my cushy Grand Tour war.

That last summer, with the war hotting up, Roosevelt ascendant, the draft starting up, Lend-Lease warships to England, fascist Charles Lindbergh routed out, I got me a job. A machine shop pressed for help to make its contracts with the Navy. Bench lathes, turret lathes, drill presses, routers, the works.

I work my butt off, prove who I am or am not. But they all seem to know, the silver spoon's still stuck in my mouth. I'm good, very good, work hard on my job, my image. I drive up in an old heap of a car, work overtime, take on the toughest of jobs, eat from the snacks truck with the guys, make my name into Joe. But still there it is, that hateful spoon. The Brewsters with all their assumptions, The Hill where we live, the unearned privileges, father forever cultivating his Important People, harvesting them like a crop.

. . .

Then Pearl Harbor. I volunteer, and soon—Brewster, Joel, report to your Army Recruiting Station.

—"Undershorts, everything off, men." A finger jammed in my crotch. —"Cough, cough again. No hernia. Short arm inspection... like a toothpaste tube. Good, not venerealed, not yet. You're in. Glad to have you on board, son. Patriotic. Report to the sergeant." A private soldier among millions, not on an officer track, not me. With the secrecy of wartime—I'll be thoroughly out of reach.

So, I've made it, just turned eighteen. I'm in, anonymous at last.

. . .

Medical probings—of the congenital thing, no record, no trace, certainly no fessing up. Only my deep, my hidden terror. Lectures, armloads of uniforms and gear, conflicting orders, foul food slopped on mess kits, barracks, never-ending rows of basins and toilets cheek by cheek.

Thousands of us, milling about here in what was an old dirigible hangar, hundreds of desks, each manned by a junior officer. They have our records and fat catalogs to match up supply and demand. —"German and college math, I see. You're reclassified, soldier, field intelligence work. Dismissed. And smarten up that salute."

A miserable train ride, then Camp Crowder, Missouri. Basic training. —"Prone position, men. Heels down. Remember, squeeze it off. Ready on the left, ready on the right, ready on the firing line. Commence fire!" Fucking M1 busts my shoulder. And my ears.

—"Rifles on crooked arms, men. Push with your toes. Elbows and toes, men. Get that ass down! That's real barbed wire and real ordnance. Love that mud, soldier. You hoping for an extra hole in your ass?"

Parading in the pouring rain, presenting the colors. What the fuck! Where's *my* umbrella, General... Sir? Better the forced marches, heavy packs, at least we get to see the scenery—if we don't die, that is.

Climbed into this huge pot, scraping at the burned-on

goo, and my twenty nonstop hours of KP duty have just begun. Scrub the ceiling next, no doubt. And when do they tell us how to use a condom? How to kiss ass?

—"Sergeant, that bunk there, check it." He'll drop a coin on my blanket. Shit, it doesn't bounce. —"Mummy didn't teach you how to make a bed, soldier? Put him on clean-up detail, sergeant."

Cigarette-butt searching in the dead grass, beady-eyed corporal, —"Asses and elbows, that's all I want to see. Any goldbricking goof-offs get KP from midnight on." Field intelligence work? must be.

It's mostly just a blur.

Another train ride, three days of frigid hell. To pine woods, meadows, snow, red mud, more marching, more asses and elbows, more polishing, pressing, dusting, tight-tucking, KP duty in turn, extra for your goldbricking GI sins.

Gratefully, just a blur.

The serious study—Morse code, Japanese, radio language and traffic analysis, ciphers and codes, radio direction finding triangulation. We are good, mostly old fogies, thirties or more. PhDs, all of them draftees—and chickenshit, ass-licking, college-kid volunteer me.

. . .

Here, on board HMS *Queen Elizabeth,* not to the Pacific, that wouldn't do for the inscrutable Army that had us learning Japanese, no, to Europe somewhere. Eight, ten thousand of us—we sleep in three shifts, three to a pipe berth, tiered four high, six hours sleep, twelve hours on deck or wedged in some sheltered and blacked-out space— creeping in convoy at the speed of the slowest converted tramp. U.S. Navy circling on the horizon, flashes, blasts now and then, rumors of U-boats and sinkings. Empty lifeboats drifted by yesterday. Big turnout for chapel on deck this morning.

To London. We, we survived the Birmingham Replacement Depot, the repple-depple, the Army's storehouse of live bodies to replace the dead. Now London. The Luftwaffe is blitzing the city again, well, little-blitzing. It's exciting. They've cranked up the ack-ack battery in Portman Square next door to our requisitioned quarters in Montague Square. We'd rush out to Hyde Park to see the show, duck under Marble Arch for protection. Two of their Heinkels or Junkers make it into London—searchlights and gunfire. They got one, circling down in flames.

Reveille call, oh-five-hundred, me the acting first sergeant. I drag a few from their sacks, we straggle out to the street, sort of line up. Pitch dark. I snap out, AttenSHUN!

An officer's voice from the gloom, —"Morning report, Sergeant." All present and accounted for, Sir. I salute to the night. And most are sleeping on till the last minute.

We slouch our way from our bombed-out row-house quarters to Baker Street, British Y-Service officer teaching us what could be learned about radio eavesdropping on Jerry.

It's tea break, elevenses, and I'm planning my evening, my dive into the Underground—crowded stations, squalor, every platform jammed with pipe berths layered up to the ceiling—to vaudeville at the Windmill, to a play, a concert. Bitter cold, these blackouts in the fog, a few taxis—no private cars—headlights masked down to slits, groping, feeling my way.

—"Your seat number, Sir? Tea and biscuits at the intermission? I'll bring it to your seat. Thank you, Sir, thank you." Solemnly standing for *God Save the King*. The audience is jittery—when Air Raid Alert lights up on the proscenium, many will walk quietly out, down into the bomb shelters of the Underground.

Sunday, wandering. Just back of Saint Paul's it's cratered down to Mithraic origins. The pubs, their by-appointment-of, King-certified ales, their bitters and bangers and pickled eggs, rationed. The fish-'n-chips barrows, greasy newspaper cone. —"Yes, vinegar please. Why sure, Ma'am, we're glad to be here, glad to help out."

Sadsack corporal, me, lunching at Claridge's with Air Marshal Bomber Command himself—a most tenuous tie through a U.S. Air Attaché uncle of my college roommate. A gesture to the Yankee ranks. Wartime regalia, kowtowing white-gloved service, sherry, whale steaks, cabbage, tapioca goo. Nothing whatsoever to talk about.

That was Bomber Harris, I'd remember that. The only top British brass not made a peer in 1946. At the end of the war the Labor press took him on. Wanton, useless saturation-bombing, Dresden worse than Nagasaki. Just stiffened up Jerry's resolve.

. . .

They've not told us where we're going. Sailed from Liverpool, a P & O steamer, British privates, Aussie privates, and us. We're mostly corporals and sergeants—noncoms—privileged, put in real cabins and on the traditionally preferred port side—posh for Port Out Starboard Home, so we're told, the north side, the shady side for the upper-crust colonials on the England-Orient-England passage. Plausible? We're assigned to man the fifty-caliber machine guns on the wings of the bridge—noncoms, so they assumed we must be well trained. Nothing like PhDs for protection. Swinging around on the seats, kind of fun, cranking the barrels, sighting on clouds. And yesterday at a Junkers, Jerry's weather plane—at Baker Street we'd worked on intercepts of their daily radioed reports. We actually let loose, tracers, the clatter, though they were way way out of range and the bridge officer suggested we quit. —"Just swinging around, checking out the ammo, Sir."

Landfall. Tangier off our starboard bow, Trafalgar to the north. Hercules straddles the Straits, Gibraltar to Monte Hacho. The Iberian hills catch the sun, blues to greens. Fields, forests, groves of olives, vineyards, crystal streams, I reach out, held by the ship's rail, longing. To lie in the sun, a goatskin of wine, bread, manchego, a fig, a friend. Peace there in blood-drenched Spain.

The P & O, the bitter war, we sail inexorably on.

The Axis, they're beaten, they've lost, for God's sake it's time to give up. The Battle of Britain, Doolittle's raid on Tokyo, Midway, El Alamein, Morocco, Oran, Algiers, Stalingrad, Attu, Guadalcanal, and the U-boats mostly sunk I'd guess. the Luftwaffe moribund. Strengst durch Freude, Lebensraum, Drang nach Osten, and the Ever Rising Sun. Lost, what the fuck, can't they see? Hegemonical, the world? Maniacal!

Sailing inexorably on.

Algiers, a golden city. Teeming with troops, tanks, trucks, the harbor jammed with warships, transports, supply ships, landing craft—hospitals overflowing, they say. Brits, Americans, Aussies, Canucks, they've taken over this Frenchified Arab town. Allied HQ—Eisenhower, Montgomery, Alexander, are you up there scheming? Did you learn some lessons at Kasserine Pass, old Ike? They really did beat up on you. But Monty, his Desert Rats and a thousand tanks, they'd crushed Rommel at El Alamein a few days before. By now they'd just about pushed Rommel's Afrika Korps into the sea. Scheming, up there at HQ, getting ready for something. Churchill had already told the world in his stirring though pompous prose. —"We shall strike at the soft underbelly of the Axis before the leaves of autumn fall."

. . .

We're on a day pass, two hours by truck to Algiers from our billet in the mountains. I'm heading for HQ, halfway up the hill. Ike's up there near the top, his palace wrapped in barbed wire. The guards check my dog tags, let me inside. A captain, the parachute patch, a sloppy peremptory salute returning my very GI one.

—"So you want to sign up for the paratroops? That's great, my boy, uh, Corporal, we need men like you, men with pluck. You'll hear from us soon and good luck." He's a friendly sort for one of the brass, why? Is there something I just don't get?

And what had led me to such insanity?

They had put us in trucks as soon as we landed, no Aussies, no Brits, no other GIs, just PhDs and me. Two hours deep into the Atlas mountains, a run-down colonial spa, Hammam Melouan—hot springs, baths, filthy cubicles. They put us quickly to work shoveling gravel, day after day. A month of that and the paratroopers looked like a great solution—to blisters, to useless boredom. Adventure, join this war. Will they transfer me soon? We shall see.

In the meantime, a three-day pass, four of us, to do with what we will. A rickety bus, just Arabs and us, two hours west to a village on the coast, Tipasa, Phoenician they say. An empty church, Roman ruins, four thermal baths on the cliff's edge. It was once a rest-and-recreation camp for Roman legions back from the outposts of empire. Like us.

We have a French pension to ourselves, a lone inn on a bluff above the sea. Our elderly hosts are effusive, so grateful to be freed at last from Pétain and the Boche. For breakfast they bring us chicory café au lait—their own cow's milk—croissants, their butter still milky from the churn, maquis honey. Real china, silverware, curtains, sheets on our beds with cats to keep our feet warm.

We roam the beaches and cliffs, the ruins. Sherds, a Roman coin in a ploughed-up field, an amphitheater, we quote Shakespeare from the stage to each other, lunch on wine, cheese, black bread we'd bought in the village. We dash naked into the waves, toss stranded starfish back to the sea. We play Bach on the church's pump organ, see a jittery movie at the village cinema with Garbo in scratchy French.

We bus back to Algiers, we sneak into the Casbah, OFF LIMITS. I buy a battered gasoline burner for six cigarettes, have a mattress cover stuffed with grass, quilted. Back to the gravel—my skills in great demand. Then at this morning's formation, still dark, I'm ordered to fall out, report on the double, the CO himself, no less, brass of the brass, what could I have done? The Casbah, outstayed my pass?

—"Corporal, you're way out of line. No paratroops for you. Your transfer's rescinded, I had to cable Washington, no less. We've spent thousands to train you, not to hang you from a piece of silk for their target practice. KP, three days. Dismissed."

KP and more gravel, while Sicily, Winnie's underbelly, is freed. They manage a very bloody landing at Salerno, roll on to Naples and the slaughter at Cassino. But our orders finally came—this morning, they called us out, six of us, ship out tomorrow. We pile our gear on the makeshift parade ground, my mattress, my cook stove—sure Corporal, no problem—and a scattering of similar loot.

. . .

Corsica, Bastia, we've joined a radio-intercept company. Our war has begun. The company had bivouacked where a German SS Panzer Division had been only three days before. We learn from our radio intercepts, from breaking their ciphers, from tracking their radio signals, that they'd crossed over to Italy to help deal with the Allied landing at Anzio, near Rome. And they had mined their camp as they left. One of our radio operators loses a leg when his truck is blown to bits.

A few days later we climb into our company trucks, jeeps, vans. We are self-mobile, self-sufficient, a traveling circus—dogs and cats, a cage for three songbirds that dangles from a truck stanchion, mattresses, footlockers, stoves, and on and on—convoying over the top and down to L'Île Rousse on the northwest shoulder of Corsica. Preparing for an invasion of France? They claim—a cover story?—that we'll get better reception there of the radio communications of the German artillery units surrounding the Anzio beachhead. We keep the beachhead HQ informed on where Jerry will move his guns to each night.

L'Île Rousse. A tidy little town with its bars, its deserted deluxe hotel, its harbor for the fishing boats, and its gorgeous coral beaches. We have it pretty much all to ourselves. We've settled in an olive grove five minutes up from the sea, a village of tents and trucks and vans. No more washing clothes, shaving, bathing in our helmets, hot water scooped from the chow-line mess-kit-washing vats, helmets propped in the dirt by our cots. They set up showers yesterday in the field, near the latrine. That latrine, a deluxe twelve-holer over a trench, the shit burned daily with high-test aviation gasoline. It makes an amazing stench.

Our antenna towers are up, our hillbilly radio operators tune in around the clock on the Germany military frequencies, scribble reams of ciphered messages, over to us enlisted men in our converted moving van. The Intelligence Platoon—cipher breakers in the front, two of us traffic analysts in the middle, two order-of-battle men in the rear sticking pins in their maps. Our officers—three lieutenants and a captain—putting together our findings and radioing them to Fifth Army HQ on the Anzio beachhead near Rome, radioing on our super-secret Sigaba enciphering machine. Sigaba—we enlisted men couldn't touch it except, in the likelihood of imminent capture by Jerry, to pull the timer lever that would explode the dynamite on which Lady Sigaba was sitting.

Swimming, wandering the maquis, bar-hopping in the town, forays into the mountains in a borrowed jeep—*Little Schmuck* painted on her side—to trade cigarettes for fresh bread, wine, laundry, a French lesson. An evening climb to the stone village on the hillside above our olive grove for black bread and cheese and bitter new wine with the family of the girl I'd found to do my laundry—my adolescent lust repressed. A meager dinner in the empty dining room of the Hôtel Napoléon Bonaparte, a brocaded bedroom, a hot bath. I lie in my canopied bed. I weigh my good fortune, I wonder where friends, where Aidan may be. I dream.

Oh-two-hundred, black cold, we jeep up into the mountain barrens of Cap Corse. A boar hunt arranged by a tent mate. He'd befriended a wild Corsican mountain man, a man who only a few years ago had guided a boar-hunting party off a Rockefeller yacht. We hike for hours. By dawn we crowd into a goatherd's cave, hot bread, goat milk and cheese, eau-de-vie-de-vin. Berets, GI wool caps, assorted firearms—an Italian Beretta pistol, German Lugers, a black-market Garand, Lee-Enfields of the Boer War, our carbines, a World War One BAR, even a bazooka. For hours we stumble through the maquis in a ragged line, dogs racing about. Shouts, a rush in the bracken, shots, volleys—a feral pig ducks between the goatherd's legs, disappears. We straggle back to our jeep.

A few weeks later, three looies and I, their intrepid, acrophobic guide, manage an ascent of Monte Padre. Fog and ice and fear and my unerring luck—we make it. And slide down a tongue of snow, down into flowering maquis, then scrub oak, pine, vineyards, figs and olives, the sparkle of distant streams, the call of a goat's bell.

My spring and summer idyll, war gods close at hand.

A faintest thrumming, a swelling, a throbbing, filling the air, inescapable, drumming deep to your core. Each day now in the early morning. Over the mountains to the southeast they come, specks catching the sun, wave after wave, seven hundred, a thousand, our B-17s, our friends, cousins, brothers, the Flying Fortresses, Italy-based, Foggia. Thousands of tons of death. How many will be missing on their return?

Last week, those bodies on the beach. A crippled bomber came roaring toward us, faltered, too low, bounced on a rocky reef, twisting, skipping the wave tops, skidding almost to the beach. A parachute pack stenciled U.S. Army Air Force washed up on the sand. Plexiglas turret, its gun bent in a U, water rising in it, blood-red water, white face, eyes staring out, pleading, dead. Another, washed up, his head gently rolling in the wavelets dying on the beach. His last denial, his incredulous No.

A lovely spring afternoon, off duty, three of us are sitting on the grass in the local school yard. Our mademoiselle French teacher—young, most desirable, most unavailable—with her blackboard nailed to a tree, we with a bottle of bitter wormwood absinthe to loosen our tongues, she in exasperation mixing Corsú curses with her French. A rumble of trucks, a small U.S. Army convoy goes by. Till now we'd been the only soldiers around. They stop in a field near the base of the harbor mole, we can see them begin to unload and set up. We go over, watch them, try to figure it out—they weren't talking. Electronic equipment, antennae, some sort of radar is our best guess. And an hour or two later another convoy pulls up, a squad of Rangers, armed but horsing about. They join us for drinks, smokes, and news. Italian–Americans, they'd been parachuted in behind the German lines north of Cassino to make contact with partisan groups—sent here for a rest and as guards for this new installation, whatever it was.

Working the night shift a week later we hear popping down in the town, fireworks maybe, a marriage celebration, no big deal. A banging on our door, the officer of the guard.

—"They're all dead, every last one. A German torpedo boat had landed, slit the throats of the two men standing guard, shot the rest in their sleep, taking the electronic stuff with them. Keep your carbines with you, ammo clips, always. Captain's orders."

Most nights, when we're not on shift, we doze off in our tent to *Lili Marlene*, then *Sing, Nachtigal, Sing.* —"Ici Radio Monte Carlo." Mother had sent me in a shoe box the Sears-'n-Roebuck radio I'd had by my bed. We can get the BBC, drowning out the German radio with the Morse code V, the dit-dit-dit-dah of Beethoven's Fifth, Winnie's V for Victory, BBC news if the Germans haven't managed to jam them out. And often those opening notes of *The Bells of Saint Clemens*—oranges and lemons—some sort of code message, we figure, maybe aimed at the French Resistance, the Maquis. Tonight we get Lord Haw-Haw, Jerry's pet turncoat, in his Oxford English, telling us we are losing the war. They interrupt with the air-raid report. —"Achtung! Achtung! Die Luftlagemeldung. Über dem ganzen deutschen Reichsgebiet gibt es kein feindliches Flugzeug." No enemy aircraft over Germany? That would be most unusual, the RAF by night, the USAAF by day, they're bombing the shit out of them, nonstop, that's what it looks like from here.

· · ·

A three-day pass.

—"Corporal, show me your orders."

Yes, Sir, here you are, Sir. Three days, Bastia.

—"Carry on, enjoy yourself, observe the Off Limits."

I have a school friend, a grease monkey at the Mitchell B-25 bomber base south of town. I find him, and the next morning I'm in the belly of their DC-3 on the first leg of their daily fresh-vegetable run—Bastia, Naples, Algiers, Bastia. They'd freeze the squadron's ice cream in the cargo bay on the flight back.

I get off at Naples, hitch on another DC-3 to Rome's airfield on the via Salaria. Rome had been liberated a few days before. I join a jeep-load into town. Watch out for the MPs, stay clear of the hotels requisitioned for the GIs. In a bar on the via Sistina, in my few words of French, I get invited to stay with a family in their cold-water walkup flat.

Delirious, joyful Rome. The fasces and swastikas and blackshirts we'd seen in the newsreels—gone. Glowing, beautiful Rome. Gelati, those delicious gelati, from a barrow by the Spanish Steps. The piazza Venezia, a herd of sheep under the balcony where Benito once held forth.

The Villa Borghese, a band tuning up, a street artist is cartooning the GIs. Me? Sure, why not?

Another hitched ride, back to Corsica, a Mitchell this time, crouched in the empty bomb bay. Frigid air blasts through the cracks, thin air, they'd warned me, breathless, heart working double time. They let me peer out now and then, Giglio, Monte Cristo, Elba, Corsica's snowy peaks. I make it to Bastia in time for our company truck. No one the wiser.

Normandy, June 6, 1944, Brits, Canucks, GIs, bloody beachheads secured. We have orders to follow it closely on our big order-of-battle maps. But Rommel is there again, and the colored pinheads on our maps seem stuck there week after week. For us nothing changes. Maybe we're helping, some possibly useful news about German plans—who, where, where to, when—in Italy and France and the Fatherland, the Eastern Front is out of the range of our radios.

Our orders come. Strike tents, fill in the latrines, bring in the radio direction finders from their hilltops, antennae down, mess closed. C-rations now, horrid stuff, dog-biscuits, cans of so-called scrambled eggs, Spam, the sandy no-melt chocolate bar—which I can't even lick, damnable allergy—cigarettes. Pile our traveling-circus gear in the vans. —"Stow it out of sight, men, best not to have it advertised, not just now, chickenshit brass to deal with where we're going."

Our company CO, he's been with this crowd of hillbilly

Tennessee National Guardsmen from the beginning—moonshiners, country-store clerks, mechanics, truck drivers, high-school kids made into jittery radio operators, communicating among themselves by tapping Morse code on each other's arms. Morocco, the Kasserine Pass debacle, Sicily, now here. Our CO's learned the ropes, nonchalant by nature, though we recently arrived noncoms of the Intelligence Platoon see little of him, are always treated a bit apart, newcomers, intellectual types. So... He's learned not to take orders too literally, it seems.

He leads our convoy to Ajaccio, the embarkation port, by the longer scenic route, up over the top of the island. Our colorful convoy, twenty, thirty vehicles. We stop at cheering villages. We learn of the liberation of Paris. More wine and kisses, tossing cigarettes and chocolate. Then winding our way on, the alpine route, it is spectacular.

But we've missed the boat.

The next day they find us a spare LST—spare, how can that be? We leave in the night, to Saint Tropez. The harbor is jammed with the invasion fleet. We hit the beach in late afternoon, August 16, D-Day plus one, drop the bow ramp on the shingle, drive ourselves off. No Jerry.

—"No time or place or safety to set up shop, men. Stay packed up, close by, we'll move out in the morning. Chase Jerry—at a safe distance."

Some of us stray into a nearby vineyard, gorge on half-ripe grapes. We watch in the twilight, out over Saint Tropez Bay, dozens, hundreds of ships anchored or moving about, five battleships we can see, dozens of cruisers, destroyers, transports, LSTs, LCTs, LCIs, supply ships, hospital ships, many with barrage balloons on long steel-cable tethers to discourage dive-bombing Stukas. One bomber hits a cable, explodes, setting a hydrogen balloon on fire. A spectacular show. Later a summer storm hits us, lightning strikes several balloons, enormous flares light up the bay. And we shelter in a stone tool shed, spend the rest of the night under its leaky tin roof, stomachs writhing with grapes.

Flowers, wine, eggs, extravagant kisses, whatever they had. We hang out over the slatted sides of our four-by-four trucks, toss cigarettes and candy bars. A touch, a kiss, a cheek moist with tears. Our joyous advance, racing up the valley of the Rhone, the Route Napoléon, trying to catch Jerry in his high-speed orderly retreat. Every town, every village, country roadsides, cheering, welcoming crowds, women, children, the elderly, the few men spared.

Lons-le-Saunier, Bésançon, Vesoul, each is a stop for a day or two to set up our antennae and listen in on the German retreat, pause while the American Seventh Army and the French First slow their advance to clear out stubborn pockets, to allow rear echelons, supplies, reserves to catch up. And now Épinal, Alsace-Lorraine on the edge of the Vosges Mountains, Jerry digging in, winter closing in.

We've set up in a beech forest. The booming of our artillery is not far off, with occasional sharper return

fire from Jerry's eighty-eights. It takes a day or so to sort
things out, intercept what we can, figure out where their SS
Panzer and their SA Divisionen are, their plans, casualties,
strengths. And we're back to our six-on-twelve-off routine.

Free time, time to wander in the autumn, kick
up the beech leaves. —"Watch it! Willy, the Motor Pool
mechanic, he stepped on a mine yesterday, field hospital,
dying, they say." We find a path through the woods up to
a hilltop, to a lone brick structure, maybe a factory once.
Over the door is painted  STALAG

Cautiously we explore the cells—Russian, English,
French, German, American, a defiant Star of David, sad
scribblings on the walls, pages from diaries, scraps of
clothing here and there, prisoners shipped off to the factories of war, of death.

Here, lying in a ward for the wounded, earache driving
a spike into my brain. And trench foot, Great War vintage.
The mud of autumn, the cold, the soggy boots. They
never got around to issuing us winter boots and the wool
tuques. I was done in by the freezing wind driving around
in topless *Little Schmuck.* We were scrounging chunks of
coal in the villages for the stove in our tent—cigarettes
and my horded chocolate bars in trade.

Groans—some mine. Screams, death. An infantry sergeant from the Forty-Fifth on the cot next to mine, half
mad from the pain of his wounds, reliving two years of
his hell. Two years of combat—the Kasserine Pass, the
Sicily invasion, Salerno, bloody Cassino, the Gothic Line,

the Rhone, now here—the only survivor of his company's original complement. Half delirious, he's in the foxholes, M1 burning his hands, helmet machine-gun-smashed twice, deaf from the eighty-eights' blasts. Keep going, squad, keep down! Belly crawls toward longed-for death.

The chaplain—a captain—and his sidekick sergeant. What are they here for, another death? Not this time—a shoebox full of medals, purple hearts all around. Making their way down the line, like handing out candy, not quite the cure these poor bastards need.

—"Name, rank, serial number, soldier."

Me! Fuck that. This fucking war, just fuck off, give me my aspirins...Sir...please.

My neighbor turns toward me, thumbs up, grins, shakes his head—and groans.

. . .

There's a break in the weather, our twelve hours are here, the artillery thunder has stopped. We borrowed *Little Schmuck* from our friendly lieutenant, headed off for a jaunt. East and south into Alsace, more German than French, it had switched many times through the centuries. The ghosts of a thousand warriors, they say, still wander here in the Vosges. High into the hills, still green through the snow, pine woods, meadows, steepled villages, smoke from stone farmhouses inviting us in for a bowl of warm milk or their eau-de-vie-de-poire, their schnapps. This is the French First Army's sector—random tanks scattered about, washing draped on the turrets, a hammock slung between gun barrels, black African poilus with their laughing girls dancing to a mandolin's tune. They ply us with eau-de-vie and dried figs.

. . .

God! Here it comes again, the GI radio network, they play it once an hour, this *Great Speckled Bird.* Roy Acuff. He wiped out Sinatra in the Army vote. Our old friend *Lili Marlene* is dead. My trusty radio—smuggled a wire, buried in the muck, two hundred yards from our van. Here, four of us squeezed in an attic, warmed by the family and cows below us, and the mound of steaming, composting manure piled against the front wall—we could step out our window onto it.

Cigarettes are still the best currency—one carton a week, you can't afford to smoke. Wine, coal, the fresh-baked bread, sometimes an egg or two, a haircut, maybe even a hot-water shave on a trip to the nearest town. And I'm told it takes only six fags to buy sex from the girls.

On to Sarrebourg in the heavy snow. Jerry has just moved out. This house, six of us, it's still warm from the coal-burning furnace, half-eaten breakfast on the table, German magazines lying about. I'll stash away some of these swastika armbands, medals, photos, mail them home when I can.

Bastogne, deep in snow, zero weather, Jerry almost made it, almost got to Allied rear HQ. The Battle of the Bulge. We had sent back an urgent report warning of a massing of German armies, seemed headed for the Ardennes.

Ignored, didn't get to the right command, who knows?

But Jerry's regrouping again, we picked it up, reported in this morning. They're headed south—toward us. Did HQ hear us this time? Perhaps—a U.S. infantry division moves forward past us.

Jesus, that's rifle fire! Coming closer. Outflanked, broke through? Jerry's headed at us. Midnight, and they're closing in. Pack, pull out! Retreat into a subzero blizzarding night.

. . .

On the move again. In early March the U.S. First Army had grabbed a bridge over the Rhine at Remagen, upstream from Bonn. Hadn't the Germans got it mined in time? Or was it, as some were saying, that the German field commanders wanted to let the Western Allies through to occupy as much of Germany as possible before the Soviets got over the Oder?

A pfc from the radio intercept van banged on our door this morning, waving his pad of message forms. He'd copied down a message, in plaintext, German—he couldn't read it.

*The battle will be conducted without consideration for our own population, all industrial plants, all main electricity works, waterworks, gas works. . .all food and clothing. . .destroyed. . .create a desert in the Allies' path. Your Führer, A. Hitler*

Not a comforting message even for a battle-hardened Prussian.

The breakthroughs have begun, the Rhine is crossed in several more places, bridges repaired, gaps Bailey-bridged where the engineers could. We've moved up fast. Into

Germany proper, through the Saar, factories smoldering, to Worms. The worst of horrors—not a building left standing, bulldozers clearing tracks through the rubble, uncovering countless corpses, the stench beyond belief. Disgusting banter from one of us about a Diet of Worms. This gorgeous city I'd visited eight years before, city of Martin Luther, of Liebfraumilch wine, the Niebelungen-lied, flattened yet again—the Huns, the Thirty Years War, the French, and now the American and the British bombs.

A woman carrying a child in a bundle on her back is searching the ruins as we roll by. She stares at us, venomous, moves on. The shame of victory, I can't sort it out.

Two of our men were stabbed yesterday, left for dead in a ditch near where we'd camped overnight. One managed to tell us that they'd been invited by village women to bed.

NO FRATERNIZING

It was posted everywhere. We heard others have died when given buzz-bomb juice, the fuel for Jerry's V-1 buzz bombs, disguised as schnapps in ersatz orange juice. Demonize each other, appropriate a god, drive us to kill and be killed, this is what you get—in victory or defeat.

Augsburg, we've set up there, listen in on the German's last hope. Festung Europa they call it, their final fortress, rumored to be in the mountains by Berchtesgaden, where Hitler had gobbled up Austria, gave Chamberlain umbrella status, built himself a mountaintop retreat. We comb the likely radio frequencies—nothing, nothing to it. In fact, the messages we do pick up now are in plaintext, even

English at times. Generals lining up to surrender, hoping, I suppose, for special conditions.

Some of us have been sent to Innsbrück, over the Alps, to connect with a sister radio intelligence company. Bells are ringing, every church, every school, every firehouse, ringing still, nonstop. May seventh, the Germans surrender at Rheims. May eighth, again in Berlin.

The Austrians are cautious, but they've poured out on the streets. I found a hotel, the Goldener Adler, their last room. My celebration begins with a bath. Relatively resplendent in my Eisenhower jacket, clean shirt, tie, polished combat boots, I go down to the bar, crowded with half-drunk GIs. Across the lounge, a dogface, alone at a little marble table—muddy in combat gear, helmet, M1 rifle, dabbling in slopped beer from a pewter stein, trembling, lips moving silently.

A bath, a feather bed, my arms around you, our Poohsticks ritual on the Inn. You to climb into your bus, tears, a wave. Goodbye, old friend. Till stateside.

. . .

I jeep to Karlsruhe, to the waiting, endless waiting to go home. Paris on a three-day pass, trucked there, a bunch of us, twelve hours on miserable war-beaten roads. A hotel on Place de la République. A dutiful sightseeing tour, the feelthy peectures at every stop. A four-star restaurant— was it Chez Lapin?—but only passable food, and then the *Folies Bergére.* Streetwalkers are everywhere, dirt cheap. Twice they almost had me, but...

A two-day trip to Munich, *Little Schmuck* still going strong. We drive through a countryside of lovely rolling farmland, but very few cattle, some fields going to seed. Crowded villages, refugees from flattened cities, hostile and fawning, hungry, hands out for whatever we might have, sullen. We keep our carbines well in view. On the back roads, detouring the bomb-cratered highways, we see only the occasional battered motorcycle, one tractor, mostly oxen, it seems, drafted back to do the ploughing.

A lone chapel, Wies. We stop in the shade of a nearby wood for our picnic. The little rococo church is open, undamaged, a wildly corrupted baroque—and for me baroque is already an architectural corruption. Fun, though, bleeding hearts, skeletons—trick or treat—many windows, sunlight, brilliant colors. And it is good to see something in that world still intact. We detour to pass near Neuschwanstein, mad Ludwig's crazy castle, a Disney set for *Snow White*'s Wicked Queen.

Then Munich? Everything flattened, we can't even get close. We turn back.

Back to Karlsruhe. To the Armed Forces Network announcing, —"Hiroshima...atomic bomb...historic breakthrough...atomic fission...one element made into another...major step for humanity." The alchemist's dream, lead into gold, the Midas touch? That's what the announcer seems to be saying.

Humanity? How many killed? Victory, shame?

· · ·

Ravaged Germany to bounteous Switzerland. Compassionate leave, they called it, a week's leave for those men who have blood relatives in Switzerland. That's me, yessir. Poor auntie, she'd no doubt need compassion.

The trains were running smoothly, bridges, tracks intact. The cities ruined, stinking of death. Classy train sailed right on through, Strasbourg, Colmar, Mühlhausen, and the border crossing, greenish uniform, cocky cap.

In English, —"Just your Army pass, Sir, that will do."

Sir! I like that. And then the wonder of a normal, undisturbed civilian world, a thriving picture-postcard-chocolate-and-cuckoo-clock-and-watches-and-cheese country. Fat, clean, complacent, they're intensely curious, in their stolid way, at maybe their first sight of a combatant—so-called, I quickly add. They'd issued us Eisenhower jackets, caps with the Signal Corps piping—our helmets, were they turned in for good, would they pack us off for the Pacific?—some colorful ribbons, hash marks, medals, the unit citation patch we'd been awarded, my combat boots would have to do. Do I look enough the part? In Basel I take a train to Ascona, Lago Maggiore, the south, to the address I had for her. No Aunt Alice, but a delightful sunny day with a swim in the lake and a feast of fish and rosé wine. I finally find someone who knows her and gives me her Bern address. I phone, find her, zip there in another of their marvelous electric trains. Hugs and kisses, and she takes me to the Hotel Royal Palace, puts me in the royal suite—I mean it, me a still somewhat-muddy sergeant—that looks out spectacularly over the gorge of the Aare.

Wined, dined, pampered outrageously, a special banquet put on by the American minister just for me—the OSS chief with his cast of spies, a couple of military attachés, U.S. generals who'd passed a lovely war, and best of all the American minister's gorgeous daughter who accedes to a date for the next day. Toasts, welcomed ego-building questions, my stories taking on some extra height, demitasses, cigars, cognacs, the works.

My date starts with the obligatory sightseeing. The pathetic bears in their pit, the Zeitglockenturm, with its mechanical puppets doing their number before every hour. The arcades, the fountains. We go back to her elegant house for dinner en famille. Except it isn't. Our worthy minister is summoned to the phone, comes back to tell us surrender messages from Tokyo are coming in, relayed through neutral Switzerland to Washington. Much excitement, staff coming and going, my date perforce most decorous. Ah well, and if it had come to a pinch? Our hero would no doubt not have carried the day.

Aunt Alice puts on a cocktail party to honor her warrior hero. But this time it seems I am not the center of attention. Across the room is a cluster of guests around a great white-haired bear of a man, introduced by Aunt Alice as the renowned Carl Gustav Jung. Now who the hell is he?

. . .

A United Fruit passenger-and-cargo steamer made over for troops, reasonably comfortable for once. Out past my blue hills of Spain, past Gibraltar, under Hercules' crotch, west, Europe left far behind. Two days later I'm perched on the prow, my favorite spot, whatever the boat that I'm on. The early sun is warm on my back, a herd of dolphins leads the way. I doze for a moment, wake with a start, the sun is full on my face. Off the port side I see our wake has become a U, we've certainly turned back. What the fuck's happening? The skipper forgot his wife in Gib, or the war's started up once again, or a U-boat's still out here on the loose, or they've gone back to pick up that chickenshit major, the one we'd dumped off the stern?

—"All hands! We have turned back to Gibraltar. A propellor shaft bearing is overheating." An hour of seething disbelief, then the sun's on my back again. —"All hands! We've found a spare bearing. Repairs are under way. We trust there's been no inconvenience."

No no, most certainly not.

Land ho! It's Staten Island, not Manhattan, but what the hell. We pull up dockside, decidedly listing to starboard with a thousand men crowding the rails. A band blares music-hall ditties and patriotic stuff, majorettes wave American flags, a few civilians, a lone man in a fedora, and a hot-dog wagon or two. The gangplanks reach up, hands to secure them. The good old US of A.

—"Sergeant Brewster, Joel, NMI, report to the bridge, on the double." Shit, now what have I done? The crew shows me the way, a saloon astern of the wheelhouse. He's there, the fedora, it's…my father, my nightmare, in the flesh. I get it, he's a director of the company that owns this fucking boat.

I thought I'd escaped, but I haven't. No no, quite obviously, by no means, no, not yet.

# 7

A distant chug chug—a fishing boat coming in, a night's catch with the acetylene lamps. An old moon, late, weary, has slid down into my window. For a moment I am strutting, bemedaled, the conquering hero, the exhilaration of war. Then chagrin. My head shakes in the pillow, my disbelief. Those war stories, why had we never shared them? His kill-or-be-killed, my detached involvement. Our different paths.

I turn away, rearrange the pillow, slide into sleep. I hold him again in my arms.

### AIDAN

Torn bodies, torn minds.

You remember Henry Neff, college class below us, how he ended? Perhaps you never heard. Just twenty, he was a platoon lieutenant in the Battle of the Bulge. They were in slow retreat in the Ardennes. He'd called in for artillery on a Tiger tank, snafued the map coordinates, half his men were blown to bits by friendly fire. A few months back in college, he wandered off to the Alaskan oil fields, blew his brains out.

Or take Simon. When he hit the big time he turned his back on me. Small-town son, he'd climbed the ladder, became a distinguished publisher, and he rejected all my manuscripts from Greece, Not appropriate in this political climate. Some such rubbish. Simon, Simon. Later he started his own company, went bankrupt, and in the court proceedings it was revealed that he had awarded himself those extra medals. By then there was to be no penalty, but he couldn't take the social disgrace, shot himself in the ear with the Luger we'd liberated from the frozen corpse of an Oberleutnant.

We survivors, friends, rarely traded stories or did the veteran thing—the Veterans of Foreign Wars or the American Legion. Or the patriotic thing—the reserves, the National Guard, re-enlist. In 1945 to call us veterans meant no more than to call us young American men. War was an everyman's experience, like school and parents, either it was not worth much mention or there were private horrors we were desperate to forget.

## JOEL

Yes, Aidan, you came back to us a different man. That precious shit, that peacock-plumed was no longer there. Your response to old friends—witnesses, perhaps, but not frontline players in the horrors—often it was silence, a blankness, your eyes sliding quite away. Books, studies, silence. Bursts of anger at banalities, conventions, hypocrisies. Ever more stringent judgments of the just and the right. A different man.

For me, studies were routine, silence was embarrassing, anger was out. And girls were in—with comical and cruel self-imposed limits.

. . .

A double date to a fancy deb dance. With a Poohsticks win, I took the gorgeous June. You, our redhead Roselle. First, to a restaurant dinner—tuxes, long dresses, corsages, the works.

### JUNE

Joel, dear God! But, no no, you do age well, you two. And me? I'm forever twenty-one. No need to dye the tresses, Botox the wrinkles, pump up the withered lips and boobs, battle the cellulitis. Sexy, am I not?

. . .

This deb dance, I'm glad it's over, Joel. It's nice to be here just with you, *Good Night, Ladies* to end all that. The dance cards, the clumsy sophomores treading on my toes, the attempts at conversation over Ruby Newman's big-band swing, the constant cutting in. It's flattering, sure, but it can get rather rough, crushed corsage, champagne stains on my gorgeous gown, leering down my cleavage, my hair sweaty and out of place, sticky hands holding me, moving downward uninvited—yes, I know, we do invite it, sort of, but... And the others, the men left out, too shy or scared—yes, I knew you were one—they hang around the punch bowl, trying to seem disdainful, above it all, but we see the frequent glances at us girls. And the poor wallflowers, the plainer ones, overdressed or underdressed. My gown, it brushes past them, oh yes, I'm showing off, I know, but really I'm also moved by their distress. The dancing, I love it, the twirling ever twirling to a waltz, laughing, my head thrown back, tongue tip peeking out. Or a slow fox-trot with that gorgeous man, tall, curly hair, he hard against my belly, me, my breasts, my nipples—does it show? Dizzy, idolized, and lusted after, no, not bad, not bad at all.

But then…I do like just being here, with you. And gosh! your lovely Studebaker two-door, factory-fresh, your mustering-out cash, your reward for getting rid of Hitler and the Japs. Here, I move a little closer, my head lightly on your shoulder, my hand that falls by chance upon your knee. Yes, that's my house, number nine. There, there's a place to park. The streetlight is burned out—convenient—I can just see your profile when I turn my head a little, still resting, though, just gently pressing on your cool tuxedoed shoulder. Your blue-blood aristocratic profile, could that lie beside me in my bed? Me, the crypto-Jewish princess, or not so crypto, I know they call me JP. Still, crypto enough to get me in their snotty country club. I'm a first-class catch, as Mom would say, Yes, go for it, my girl.

But all that's really stupid, what I want is just to be here, here with you in the dark. I reach up to touch your distant cheek, come closer Joel, I kiss you, just a gentle brush. And then, well, heavy necking, they call it. It's really oh so sweet.

But me, I wanted more.

. . .

So, a skiing weekend, and this time I'm Simon's date. Joel, you're with Roselle.

The baked potatoes in the ashes, burned steaks—the place still stinks. The fire's down to embers, the lights are out. Eight of us in sleeping bags, air mattresses, we're scattered around the floor. No, scattered is not the word, we're paired. Two couples are in the shadows, they seem to be asleep. Joel and Roselle are nearby, I can see them in the embers' glow. A moonbeam sneaking through a skylight shimmers in her hair. Simon and I, we've zipped our bags together, slipped off all of our clothes. We giggle, quiet, we whisper, we caress. We are the humpbacked monster.

—"Slow down, Simon, lump head, no, shhh!" We hold our breaths, ease off a bit.

I hear Roselle whisper, —"Joel, do you wish you were doing that?"

A pause, then Joel, —"No, I guess not, not really."

You'd know the rest, no interruptus est, the last is quite the best.

### AIDAN

Joel, did you really buy into that piety rubbish, the chastity-purity line, the what-would-Mother-think? The multitudes willing and wanting, Africa, Italy, Corsica, France, Germany, Austria, you the victor. And here, they're here by the score. My God what a fate! To keep yourself as your mummy would want till a certificate makes it all legal. It stretches belief.

. . .

Graduation. Cranking up the pomp for their elaborate rites of passage, though war had done more than enough of that for most of us. Strange, I'd not thought before—honorary degrees to Eliot with his *Waste Land* to tell us the truth, to Marshall the Just, with his Plan to tidy things up, Apollo and Ares, take your pick.

My mother, my Yvette, she sat with your parents during the proceedings. She'd climbed up a few rungs by then, what with her acquired British accent and her decorated son—she did her best to parade him around.

As a graduation present, she took me to Nantucket for a week, rented a cabin on a beach. A tandem bicycle came with the rent. We explored the island, picnicked, swam, went to a posh restaurant in the town, to the whale museum—the *Essex* and her cannibalizing survivors—sailed a dinghy on the leeward side. We loved our little cabin, isolated in the scrubby pines, the dunes, the beating of the surf.

One foggy night, sitting before our fire...

. . .

Here, Yvette, let me brush it for a time, as I used to. A few silver threads now, shall I pluck them? The fire needs a stirring up, here, a bit of a poke. A Bach partita, is that your mood? Luxury, thick hair, the electric snaps as I caress it.

### *YVETTE*

Oh don't stop brushing, Aidan, so soothing, your gentle touch. Don't worry about the perm, I have to get it done again soon anyhow. Good. Yes, dear love, I did hear you, though that Bach you put on is a bit, well, heavy. How about something... Gershwin perhaps?

You asked last night where your name came from. Yes, it is time you knew. Here's how I remember, those flapper days, Gibraltar.

. . .

Rosswell, our heroic Admiral Allard, he's off for three or four weeks, bashing about the bush, darkest Africa, with his photographers and guns and entourage. Dare I feel relief? How did he come to be my husband, why are we here? Adventure has its romance, the small-town girl swept from her file-clerk spot at the National Geographic, the distinguished older man. There was no saying no. And Gibraltar, he says, because it was where they'd landed him from his heroics, hospitalized him. He owes it to them, he says. And also, I'd guess, because it was sort of British, he being rather Anglophile, and it's civilized and near his Africa. Tax advantages too.

After White House glory, promotions, retirement, he'd shipped us here. With the other apes, he'd say, no complaints I'm sure, and perhaps you'll better yourself, they say the library's not bad.

I do love it here on my rooftop—early morning, the west wind fresh off the Atlantic, blowing in from Cádiz,

Trafalgar, Tarífa, Algecíras. In the half light those shapes to the south—Tangier on a clear day, the Rif Mountains, Mount Hacho and Gibraltar, the Pillars of Hercules guarding us from the wicked Atlanteans. Our Rock hides the dawn. A pink cloud collects on the peak, up there with the wild olives and pines and Barbary apes. And their searchlights and radio masts and horrible guns.

Guns, Rosswell, his brutish world. Me, here, raped and abandoned, I'm just another trophy—his occasional visits and marital demands, the kindness that is gone or never was, scornful of my petty pursuits.

I must visit Barclays, get my ration of household cash he said he'd have wired to me. Street sweepers are sluicing the gutters by our house, the Maltese shopkeepers clatter open their shutters, a ferry blasts some sort of warning, the gulls search the sky, complaining. It will soon be time for Barclays to open. Will he be there? Amory, he said, Amory Ailesworth, at your service, Ma'am. Quite proper, quite comical, these British. He's down here, he said, from the Edinburgh branch to check some accounts for a month or two. He was neat, civil, helpful, even gracious, I'd say. Trim mustache, darkish complexion, lonely asking eyes. He was attentive and reserved at the Governor's Royal Navy reception—some visiting dignitary, their empire a bit threadbare, but still hanging on. Damn their empire!

What were my signals, what were his, was there no well-enough for either of us to let-alone? I want him to be there, his office door open, and I'd said I would be calling for the cash today, this morning.

I'm discreet with the makeup, playing down the American for these British. These silly hats we have to wear—tea cozies. And this bodice to perk things up a bit, my skirts to flap about my shins, and no gloves today, it's far too hot. Now my parasol. Just right, not bad, well turned out for twenty-five. Here, a Gib candytuft blossom, just opening as my summer passes by, tucked behind my hat ribbon. Sashay, they'd have said back home, sashay, girl. Yup, Rosswell my boy, this girl's on the make, and it's more than about time.

So, the next day, Amory and I have made it to the Spanish hills. We've left our rattly hire-car Morris at the bottom of the field, successfully bypassed a bull. Our picnic is spread out just so, rug, basket, corkscrew, glasses, tea cups, a thermos, napkins—well that's what we call them, darn it all—cutlery picked up at the house, wine, tea in the thermos, white with a touch of sugar, pork pie, cucumber sandwiches, cheeses and biscuits, messy persimmons, Eccles Cakes bought on Main Street. We sit demurely—my bodice adjusted, skirt tucked in, his trouser creases carefully dealt with at the knees and crotch, our hats quite discreetly set aside. Here on my tartan lap rug in a cork oak's shade.

Cicadas wind their shrill strings around us, insisting, then in unison they're silent. It's time to uncork, swallow the harsh Riója, just time, for they start their piercing chorus again, inviting, pressing, urging. Arousing. Yes, the nipple tingle, a warm unease, and I see through my eyelashes, as I set down my half-empty trembling glass, his comforting adjustments, other signs. The cicadas stop again, teasing. Time for your lips, Amory, I'll test the tickle of your mustache. We empty our glasses, the picnic is shoved aside.

Finished, and I suppose, objectively, that was a straight-forward encounter, unexceptional as Brits do say. But here—I pull things back in place, he struggles behind the tree—for me, it was, by contrast, quite marvelous. My Scottish trophy, sweet and kind, and there are weeks still before Rosswell returns. It's true I was thinking of him as we embraced on my tartan—never mind. Were he to hear of us, he'd... I dare not think.

The very next day we find a special trysting place, high to the edge of Gibraltar's own private collection of clouds. It's only a few steps from the highest viewpoint—tuppence telescope, lipstick graffiti. No one comes here this time of day, and we're hidden by a cloud.

Weeks later, and we come often, we lie here in the heather. There are tiny white flowers in the black of your hair. The afternoon sun lifts the flying mist, finds us lying mostly naked on our tartan. You sleep now, my Mory, your head turned from me. Here's a cardigan to cover you, rest now, spent. Your passport, it must have fallen from your pocket. Amory Ailesworth, you were younger then, no mustache, divine—and even more so now, oh yes. Clipped in back, a folded document, you'd not mind, I want to know you every bit. Geburt...it's too blurred, birth certificate? Augsburg, 1-2-1891, Amos Inselwert, Jud...

Jewish? My God! Why didn't I know? Ashamed, scared, all that behind? My God, my God, I know none, not really. They're different, it's said, yes. How different, what must I say, what must I do?

Mory, my love, I must wake you.

You're Jewish, are you? Forgive me, it fell from your pocket. No, of course not, why should I mind? Should I? And a baby, Amory, a baby is coming, yours and mine. But of course we'll keep him, you want that too, yes? It will be a boy, quite certainly, yes, of course, mustache and all, and when he's born we'll have a bagpipe parade to honor your Edinburgh too. And I've already found a Scottish name, I think it's Scottish, Aidan... Yes, Gaelic, of course, that's what I meant. Aidan, baby Aidan. Will that be all right, now that he's Jewish and all?

And Rosswell will never know. I'll put up with one more of his bedtime horrors as soon as he arrives. Then I'll say the baby's premature, all that. And he's here any day now, the cable said. And you'll be leaving soon, my love—how can I bear it?

I'll absolutely insist on the name. Aidan, you do like it? And after a time, discreetly, Aidan and I, we'll just pack up and go, leave Rosswell for good, a new life with you in your Britain. He'll be off with his guns and his cameras, and I'll just go. Are you happy, my love?

### AIDAN

You heard her, Joel, her rambling guiltless confessions, or is that an oxymoron? My hot-stuff, salivating, cuckolding, dissembling, small-town flapper of a mother. And it took you, Yvette, seven horrible years before we left. Just you, me, the Rock, and The Admiral when he'd deign to be there, scathing, brutal.

A caning for just a bit of unchewable gristle. And never a word from you in my defense. Seven years. You needn't tell me why, Yvette. Let me guess. Your Mory wrote to you, told you not to come, told you that he was already married, that he'll always love you, but... I see I'm right.

Jewish, what was I to make of that, or maybe are there other secrets lurking hereabouts?

At least, Joel—are you shocked by all this, did I never tell you?—she didn't put me on the chopping block, poor scrap of a newborn. I came upon a circumcision when I was wandering the streets of Tangier—my stinking freighter had stopped there on the way to Greece. The father invited me in to celebrate. It was an elaborate ceremony, the blood caught in a ritual bowl, parading the baby about, then cakes and syrupy mint tea and hookahs, and they tossed the baby's pleasure to a begging cur.

Me, the bogus Gentile, fraudulent, sneaking round the college quota, rowdy among the college-club antics, Amos's shofar traded for bag and pipes. That precious me before the war.

I kiss you, Yvette, I curse you. I slam the poker on

the hearth, storm out onto the beach. Perfidious woman, spineless, just sweep all out of sight, your stupid silent suffering, your hapless discarded years under U.S. Navy command, then your snotty fabrics. Mustachioed treacherous banker hypocrite, *that's* my father now? I'll track him down, I'll hound him, expose him, I'll drive him from his staid and dusty world.

I'll beg him for his love.

No. We'll meet and have Scottish ale in his King's Head at the foot of Castle Rock. He'll be polite, I'm sure, embarrassed, worn, and worried. There's no point, no anger, no love. Just, I am your son, Aidan. And go.

Here, my slippers fill with sand, the still sea whispers. A step farther through the dark, the sand is moist. A dying wave slides over my feet, stars' reflections mix with the phosphorescence. A barn owl hoots in the pines behind me, a rabbit shrieks of death. Their cries echo in my skull. I am spun, hurled into the floating stars, falling, shocking cold. A wave nudges me, extinguished, blackness. All is nothing.

Is that you, Yvette, have I been here long? Cold, so very cold, so tired, is that blood on the sand? Here, I can hold the torch if you could just give me a hand, a shoulder. Which way, where are we, is it late?

Yes, just here, I'll rest for a bit. My head, confusions. A fit, you say? Spasms, rigid, bit through my tongue? No no, I don't have fits, I fainted, hit my chin on the hard sand. The heat from the fireplace, the shock of your story, the cold. Just fainted.

. . .

But no, not sorry, not now, not ever. I'm not asking for forgiveness for my anger, or for my epilepsy, nor do I forgive you, Yvette. Sitting on all that for so many years, protecting me. Absurd, astonishingly stupid, and of course I hurt you, you've earned it. Yes, do, for God's sake, go!

# 8

*JOEL*

No compromise, Aidan, not even with your mother?

So that's your snarl of deceits. And there are more to come, I should guess. My lines? They have no tangles you said, the Brewsters are nothing if not proper. Proper, yes, but propriety wounded us, stunted us. Hilariously, poignantly, needlessly—take your pick, listen.

· · ·

Roselle, dear Roselle, come, join us, here in my dreams. Your warmest, green-eyed smile, your lovely form, your hair ablaze. That flicker of a smile, how I did love it! That wry twist of your mouth, drawing it ever so little to one side—your sardonic response, or a gentle barb about to be voiced, or your silence to my inanity. You'll not know of that last sad time I saw you. They called to say you were dying, that you'd asked for me weeks before but they'd just found me. I came, too late, you were comatose, curled tight, shrunken, shriveled, half of what you were before. They said your bones were mostly melted away.

I had loved you, my dear, loved you in my strangled way.

*ROSELLE*

Joel, dear Joel, you were a good companion, fundamentally good—not the best of words, but nothing better comes to mind—well, maybe nice, fine, somewhere in there. But troubled, yes, I knew, you told me of your uncle, your cousin, your fear.

I called out to you, more than once, to come with me, to be my friend. We did so much together through those last college years after the war. I asked you often, even begged you, to join me, to study in the city library, to share a meal nearby, or a strawberry float at the Rexall soda fountain. Your salon teas with Window Shoppe cakes, friends, talk, your jazz collection. Skiing, many weekends, and sailing—that week of cruising up the coast to deliver that fellow's yacht. Europe on the postwar student-veteran cheap—London, concerts, opera, Paris.

Yes, good times, they were, dear Joel, with no regrets, neither you nor I. But it had to end. There in Paris. I told you that it was time to go our separate ways. I could not go on, despite and, yes, because of your despair. You were such an ardent suitor, both ardent and withholding. It was much too much, I told you. I simply knew no way to handle it.

How many times we had lain together, a blanket in a field of flowers, a beach to the music of the sea, a bearskin in the glow of embers. Touching, embracing, reaching, but never, never...

Paris, that final time. My father had staked me to it, the ritzy Hotel Continentale. I'd told you the day before that we must part. But one last time? I asked you to my room, it was very late, to share a farewell cognac. Through that flowery lobby, ridiculously ornate—room

307, I still remember. And once again we lay together.

Did you know, Joel, what my name means? Rose, of course, and perhaps I already had red hair when they named me, but for the early Christians it meant the Rosa Mistica, the Virgin Mary, and, however hard it is to believe, I was that still.

I was ready then, I longed for you, I reached out to you. So sweet you were, so shy. Your sad whisper, —"Dear Roselle, no no, I, we…we must not." And you slipped away—a whimper, a sob.

The following midday—I was still asleep—there was a knock on my bedroom door. You were to leave the next midmorning, take the train to Pau for your cours de vacances. The garçon had brought a box—a flower, a note from you. It was a white lily with spots like drops of blood. And your note was so forlorn—remorse and farewell.

The next morning—Vite! Vite!, je vous en prie!—I sent you a perfumed note. I know its every word still.

*Quoique il soit longtemps fâné,*
*je n'oublie pas le beau lys,*
*touché de sang.*

You smile again, yes, I did love so to show off what I thought was my impeccable French.

## JOEL

Roselle, when I left your hotel that early morning, I wandered through the empty streets. The rue Royale, past the Louvre, to the Île de la Cité. I stepped into Sainte-Chapelle, lit a candle. A lone black-hooded figure knelt before the altar, crossing herself, murmuring in the enormous silence, lost in the misty vaulted void.

I was in torment, confused. My remorse, the hurt that I had done. My loss, my wretched loss. My promises—my self, my mother. I wandered on, sobbing, and at times a seething anger, fist bashing at my forehead, kicking out at Edith Piaf on a pissoir's cast-iron shield. Sad and amusing now, I suppose, the Puritan in Paris, so many thousands before, far fewer since, but then? Roselle, my love, it was for me an excruciating time.

Somehow I found myself back at my hotel. From a shop nearby I sent you that lily. I stumbled through the day. The next morning I packed, paid, shouldered my bag, and took the Métro to the Gare Montparnasse. At the station gate the hotel porter miraculously found me, handed me your note, winked, and refused my handful of coins. I waited till we were under way, my fellow passengers settled, and then opened the envelope. The sadness, the touch of perfume, the poignancy of your words, the irony, the hurt, the rebuke of that withered lily spotted with blood. I could not stop my tears, tears of anger, remorse, and yes, a most humiliating embarrassment. That I had been oblivious of the significance of that lily when I had sent it to you added to my torment. I longed to leap from the train, rush back to you, beg forgiveness.

. . .

But must you, Roselle, must you leave just now? I reach for you, your smoothest cheek, your Titian hair.

. . .

Yes, yes, quite right Aidan. Shake your head in disbelief. So do I. But we were talking of bloodlines, of tangles, of propriety. Listen.

You knew my parents, you were with us several times after that Pearl Harbor Sunday lunch. Donnelly Brewster, Marjorie. I called her Jorie, remember? Don or Donnelly, only Mother could call him Donny. She'd tease him for the split in his chin—he'd nick it often with his straight razor. We'd watch for it at breakfast—secret looks. Black hair, dark brown solemn eyes, she must have thought him handsome, his lieutenant's uniform, wings on his chest, pilot in the Great War. His full-length portrait hung defiantly on our stairway until his death. So did hers, for that matter, demure, diffident, beautiful in her sweeping blue velvet gown, her modest eyes.

He was a driven man, some would say crazed, you must have seen that. Successful in all he went after. A fierce grasp of facts, an extraordinary memory—would that I had but a small piece of it—and he'd never be gainsaid. Cruel with the put-down for anyone who failed his standards or disagreed. Belittling, humiliating, taunting. He'd hurt Mother cruelly with his probably fabricated tales of other women friends. Or maybe he was low on libido. I once heard him say how grateful he was that Mother had no urge for sex. What to make of that?

For him there were no dreams, no songs, no music. No hugs for his children. I tried a hug once before a parting. He lifted his elbows against me, held me off with, —"Only homosexual men embrace." Poor man. Poor man and no doubt scared—the family gene. Was he forever racing, terrified of being caught? I suppose my escapes were different, inconsistent, forever turning away. But I know the haunting fear that likely was with him too.

. . .

Sweet Mother, though, our Jorie, pretty, you'll remember, a kind face when she wasn't in the grip of migraine. Donnelly her demon, he'd put her head in a vise, tighten down till it split open like a pomegranate. Her name-day saint, she told us once as a bedtime story, was Margaret of Antioch, who refused to bed with the bishop—Mother put it more discreetly, I'm sure—was put on trial, thrown into a pit with Satan disguised as a dragon. The dragon swallowed her whole, but her sanctity upset him so that he vomited her out unharmed. Dragon Donny.

Dear Jorie, she too did escape, at least for a time, through music. Music for her was a joy, a spiritual release. For Donny it was mere entertainment, frivolity. Not long after I returned from the war, she and I had gone to an afternoon concert, a Mahler symphony, I forget which one. We had finished dinner at a nearby restaurant and were sipping a very sweet Madeira, her favorite, chatting, when she quite suddenly paused, looked up at me intently, touched my cheek with a finger tip, and...

## JORIE

Joel, my dear son, I promised myself I would tell you, tell you my sweetest story when you had come back to us. It is time now.

You know how much I love these Friday afternoon concerts. Your father could never take the time, poor dear... well, Wagner, sometimes, that was more than enough for him. I guess I'd become something of a fixture there, yes, long before you were born, dear. The luncheon lectures, the special invitations to the teas to meet the soloists. By the time I was engaged, Kostóvic—you know, the conductor for years—he knew me, and we would exchange a few words every week. Always *Mr.* Kostóvic and *Miss* Coddingworth, until I became *Mrs.* Brewster, of course. And he would introduce me to the visiting performers, to select members of the orchestra.

One Friday they had played a long and rather tiresome mass with the Choral Society. At the tea I was introduced to the first violinist, Boris Something-vich—I could not pronounce it. A mane of golden hair, a charming accent. We talked of this and that—the program. He was so attentive to my meager comments. He spoke of his childhood in Russia, of the rigors a violinist must face. His greatest relaxation from it was piano playing. I told him of our Steinway grand that Donnelly had inherited, of its sad neglect.

—"Ah, the Steinway, quite my favorite. I should be delighted to try it, to play for you, my dear Mrs."

. . .

Boris… Forgive me, I simply cannot manage your name. I'm so glad you could come. This way, yes, your cape. I'll just ring, Isabella will bring us tea. Here, we call this the music room. My mother-in-law was a very good pianist. It was her Steinway. Me? No, just light-opera sing-a-longs. Mr. Brewster, Donnelly? What a funny sight that would be!

Why am I so nervous? And I'm still carrying his cape and beret around with me. Silly-billy. So gentle, sad, playing a bit of a nocturne, Chopin. Look, they have that same delicate narrow face, playing beautifully, giving himself to the music. I shall ask him to come again, to bring his violin, why not? Symphony business, the fund-raising ball? Of course.

Marjorie Coddingworth Brewster, what has gotten into you? Now now, it's quite all right. He's such a good and gentle person and we are friends, yes, friends.

Goodbye, Boris, I so enjoyed your playing. Next week? We must help plan the ball. Will you bring your violin?

He kisses my hand. —"My dear lady, charmed, I'd be delighted."

Such a long wait, and…

The doorbell, it is Boris, I must run to let him in, it's Bella's day off, my hair has strayed a bit, I feel it on my forehead, am I blushing? Do come in, forgive me, it's the heat, I left my fan upstairs. How very nice, red roses, thank you, how very nice!

The beret, no cape, it's warm today. He takes my hand to his lips, I laugh, take both his hands, stand on tiptoe to kiss his cheek.

Up from the entrance hall, up these spiraling stairs. Yes, four flights, look up, here, from the bottom, its banister, so delicate—Bullfinch, he did the Capitol dome after the fire of 1812. Dwindling oval spirals—my chambered nautilus—will they go on up to vanish some day do you think?

Tea this time, sherry, sweet or dry? Just pull up on that cord, there, by that sliding panel, the dumbwaiter, thank you, up it comes from our basement kitchen. I've made these little cakes, will you? Here by the window, you must admire my bit of garden. Thank you, you're too kind. No no, I don't mind, why should I? Your beautiful hands, I kiss your fingertips. I need a friend, oh but I do.

. . .

You are pale, dear Joel, you turn away. But yes, he kissed me, he kissed me on the lips. I kissed him, we clung to each other, I trembled in his gentle arms. We saw each other often then. We were, yes Joel dear, I will say it, we were lovers, lovers until he left to join the Vienna Symphony a year later. No one, no one ever knew—Boris, me, and now you. So sweet a memory—to last for the rest of my life, to be my private answer to the callousness of Brewster propriety.

*Part Two*

# 9

Slowly waking, I turn from a flicker of sunshine slipping through a crack in the shutter, turn to a pillow of dreams.

Aidan, bleeding, lost in the sands by the edge of the sea. Had I known, had he told me, could I have held out my hand? Yvette rejected—cruel cover for shame, for the horror of that seizure? An escape to distant unknowns. My Roselles—can you forgive me, my chaste, my sad restraints, my denial of the dance? Jorie—sweet secrets— did she show me a way to that dance?

. . .

I go down to the harbor, I sit on a iron bollard at the far end of the quay. Gulls fight over fish heads, screaming in the wake of a caíqui returning with the night's catch. The village is busy now, unconcerned.

I move over to the kapheneíon, order breakfast, sit outside at a table under a thatch of cane leaves. A small boy appears with a plate of black figs, a roll with a sticky jar of honey, a coffee. Uninvited, he sits himself down at my table. From the pouch of his smock he pulls a pocket knife and a whittling stick. Something falls to the ground, a bit of foil. Putting his knife and stick on the table, he picks it up, smoothes it on his bare and grubby knee. He holds it out for me to see. Torn, still crumpled, but Planters P... is still legible in the flaking blue.

—"That Aléko, he gave it to me. Here, he sat right here, this table. I brought him coffee, he played the floghéra for me. He gave this to me, he did." He spits to the side, touches a forefinger to his teeth, crosses himself, presses his palm to his breast. —"I ate them all. That Aléko, he went off and drowned."

. . .

A bit of foil on a grubby knee, a splash of spit on a dusty stone

So he knew, that leap from cruel rocks, from that furthest tip of land, that leap would be his last? An arm reaching up from the angry sea, a final curse on Greece, on me?

. . .

I wander through the village, out toward the sea, past the finger of rock that points to Khímaera, up onto the headland. Not far off, for a moment do I see, standing on the edge of the limestone cliff, a figure dressed all in black? Looking back to the rocky finger, to its farthest tip, is it a woman, her dress that fluttering of brilliant white?

A shallow cave, a floor of sand thrown there by the winter seas. Soft, cool beyond the reach of the blazing morning sun, I settle there—a bottle of water, an orange, a wedge of goat cheese I'd bought in the village. Aidan, must you and I part in rage, remorse, despair? Our stories have long years yet to go. Our search cannot be done.

*AIDAN*

Nice spot you've picked, old friend. Bit of a snooze? Did I hear you grumping about...I have no idea what? Never mind, I'll just get on with my story.

I'd won a fellowship to Greece, PhD the announced goal—though not mine. It turned out that the degree they gave me that June was a master's as well as a bachelor's. Unheard of, and so was the subject, anthropology and classics combined. Quite by accident I'd taken several courses beyond the BA, written a jolly good paper that passed as a master's thesis. A special reward for the be-medaled hero that I was? So be it, no complaints.

With some research and the word of a British classmate who'd sailed by it in the war, I'd picked out an island deep in the Aegean, Artémisos, three hundred souls, as they say, one village, rarely visited. Participation-Observation, those were the anthros' buzzwords, the classicists tagged along. This island should do me rather well.

Before leaving, I bundle up my mustering-out uniform, replete with medals, pile it on those library steps, pour petrol on it, strike a match and toss it in. The campus police gather, but not a word.

On to Greece, to Artémisos, to my trumped-up anthro-classics project, my escape to a new life.

· · ·

So this is the meltémi, this etesian northerly fierce out of Turkey that boils a protean Aegean to froth. Is this the Ottoman's revenge? Six hundred years of glory ended, but we'll blast you infidels, you miserable, ungrateful Greeks every summer, full-gale force.

Do we have a chance? No life jackets, no lifeboats or rafts, nothing I see that might even float—well, maybe a bale of rotting hay. The skipper, his one-man crew, they suck on their pipes, duck the spray as waves roll over the bow, sweep down the deck, explode against the wheelhouse. They don't bother to get inside with me, the skipper only reaching in from time to time to adjust the frayed lashing to the rickety wheel, shove at what I imagine is the throttle, sip bitter coffee from a filthy cup balanced on the gimbaled stovetop.

Unconcerned, these Greeks! This stinking, rusty coffin barely makes it back to the surface when an angry Turkish wave floods over us. And each time we dive deep into a wall of roiling sea, the stern lifts out, the propellor races in the air, violent shaking, black clouds of smoke from the stack held more or less in place with a few odd bits of wire. Panaghítsa mou!—I've learned that already.

Hésta! We'll sink in a hundred fathoms and no mast to reach up from the waters to mark our ill-earned tomb. No comforting fellow coffins like the Piraeus watery graveyard, a thousand masts and smokestacks rising from the sea. Lighters from our anchored steamer had wound through that ravaged forest—planted with British and German bombs—to get us passengers ashore.

An oil drum breaks loose from its lashings, rolls violently from side to side, clattering across the deck. Will no one stop it? Our valiant crew stays put. I start to move, I look at the skipper, his eyebrows rise, his head nods upwards, the usual click of the tongue is blown quite away—the Greek for no. Thankfully the oil drum soon breaks through a flimsy railing to perish in the sea.

Tethered on the soaking deck astern the wheelhouse, braced against a soggy stack of hay bales, are two donkeys, miraculously dancing with this sorry ship. Their complaints are halfhearted, rusty like this entire disaster.

We're still afloat, we've made it, quite suddenly we're in the lee of Naxos's Mount Zeus, the meltémi savaging the sea astern, windmills churning on the point we've rounded. Here the air is still, a burning sun. We coast in between breakwaters. Engine reversed, laboring, hawsers casually dropped on bollards, we're tied to quayside. All that Grecian drama is just routine.

Already salty dry, I waver down the rough stone quay, sea legs steadying the rolling, lurching land. To a group of battered tables and chairs, a shade of cane leaves on stilts. Barboúni, bright red and scaly, bony, its beard still quite intact, squeeze a lemon on it, fried potatoes, slices of tart tomato, olive oil, their sharp white wine, and grapes with the coffee. A lemon liqueur. —"No no, signore, gratis, libero, no complimenti, per favore." He seems to love to exercise his Italian, picked up during the occupation, I suppose. The liqueur label shows a Roman Catholic convent clinging to Zeus' shoulder—Rome infiltrating Byzantium—and a buxom girl on a ladder plucking lemons from a tree.

My head's a pleasant buzzing. Sharp edges soften on these dazzling cubic shapes, bluish-white along the waterfront. A donkey's hoofs clatter on the quayside—am I dozing?—chisels shaping mythic statues from deep-grained Naxos marble. The laughter of circling seagulls—the mirth of Ariadne in the arms of Dionysus.

I'm startled by a hand laid on my shoulder. Our captain. A slight turn of his head, chin up a tad, like half a no. A Greek yes—it's time to go. I pay, try out my careful thank-you, my mnemonic F-Harry-Stowe—it seems to work. Luckily I never tried to speak the ancient Greek I'd learned to read at Cheltenham and university.

The donkeys, still on board, are chewing on straggling bits of no doubt salty hay. Several of the oil drums are being rolled by laughing dark-eyed boys to a storeroom at the foot of the quay. A final crate is cranked up from the hold on the ship's crane and swung ashore. The hold is battened down, canvas-covered, held in place with wooden wedges pounded in by our sleepy crew of one.

We churn our way astern, turn out slowly, our complaining engine spewing soot. Zeus stands tall, a crowning cloud, his locks streaming down the wind. White cubes pattern his cloak that spreads to the sea. About his feet lie several low islands, children escaped from his protecting cloak. He once lay deep beneath the sea in a mythic land the ancients called Aegeus. Through the eons, his cloak of shells formed over him, turned to marble. His day did come, he rose up from the sea, five thousand meters tall. Then ice, snow, rain, wind, the shaking of the earth, washed much of his cloak back into the sea. Thus his reborn island children cluster round him still. It is to one child, Artémisos, that we are headed.

A sprinkling of fishing boats make reluctant way for us through the placid strait, some are rowboats, others under sail—patched, dirty brown—a few one-lung chug-chuggers, with sails too just in case. Three giant turtles ride sedately on our wake, look up quizzically. Later a shark rolls in our bow wave, glares at us, white belly half up. The donkeys are content now, eyes closed, legs spread to the easy motion of our *Arghó*, streams of piss.

Yes, *Arghó*, that truly is her name. Does that put Tiphys at the helm, does Hercules still lurk about, waiting to do him in, am I Jason, is it my golden fleece that lies ahead? And Medea, does she save me from the dragon's teeth, the king's fiery bulls, is she to be my bride, there, on that little island just ahead? Must I then desert her, my mythic fate?

My golden fleece. I already as good as have it, waiting for me on Artémisos, my three-year fellowship. With a very modest stipend, but quite enough for me, and transportation to and from Greece—in steerage. I was the only competitor for the fellowship, but who am I to… Participation-Observation, a nice fat paper for the anthropology department, that's my commitment. Classics department somewhere in the background too, perhaps somehow a joint paper might do.

The sea picks up now that we've rounded to the east,

coming in abeam, rolling us, sometimes starboard scuppers under, overloaded as we are with God knows what. The evening sun sets ablaze the crown of Zeus—we roll on in his shadow. His favorite daughter, I like to think, Artémisos, is now in sight, Tiphys points her out. My golden fleece awaits me in the dusk.

We round a point, well off it, its beacon is not lit—and maybe hasn't been through the many years of war. A scattering of buildings is silhouetted on a low hilltop against the green-gold sky. Slowing, engine barely turning over, we enter a narrow passage with buoys on both sides. Stunted juniper trees hang on rocky slopes, a tamarisk leans towards us at the edge of the strand, colors fading. The captain kicks and curses a lever into neutral, we're coasting now. A little harbor appears around a bend, a few fishing boats are anchored there, silent in the twilight. We sound a wheezy whistle, sidle to the quay—a few blocks of stone, two rusty bollards, a tiny hut, maybe whitewashed once, but very long ago—hawsers over bollards, engine killed.

Not a sound or soul.

The mate, I suppose you'd call him, tips water in a bucket from a wicker demijohn he's hauled out from the wheelhouse, sets it by the donkeys with a handful or two of hay—they aim routine nips his way, get on with sucking at the bucket, farting, munching. The pipes are lit, the stove prepared, a conical brass pot, spoons of dusty coffee, sugar poured in from a paper bag. They hand me two slabs of dubious bread, a large hunk of rock-hard cheese, pour me some wine in a greasy glass. We settle down for supper and the night. The same routine as the night before—we'd stopped at a lonely island perhaps halfway here—some burlap sacks, a tattered Nazi blanket stinking of rotting fish, boots for a pillow, piss over the rail, curl up in the scuppers for the night.

Dawn comes early, but not early enough for me. I'd escaped the stench, my bed of iron, hours before, stumbled quietly ashore, found a patch of grass in the dark, asked any wandering viper to please stay well away, and slept with my head under a juniper bush.

More coffee—disapproving looks at my escape— a chew of sausage, the rest of the bread. Donkeys are tended, the crane unlashed and cranked down, the hold uncovered. And we wait.

I'm the first to spot him, a ragged boy peering cautiously from behind a rock. I point him out but they merely shrug, get on with sucking at their pipes. The boy scuttles back up the track that must lead to the only village, Chóra. Two goats rise—rumps, then knees—from under a mastic tree, bleat twice, shake off the dust. One is belled, it clangs, not much more than a thud.

Two men appear. They stop at some distance, look us over carefully, especially me. They're wearing patched army jackets, each with a rifle—Enfields, my God!—a bandolier slung over the shoulder. They beckon to the captain, wave him over, fingering their rifle straps, have a few words, heads gesturing my direction. One starts towards us with the captain. The other unslings his rifle, inspects it, sits on a rock, the rifle upright between his knees. He watches me.

After much talk, studying my passport, going piece by piece through my pack, thumbing my two or three books, frisking me carefully with special attention to my crotch, reading and rereading my letter from the new Minister of the Interior—I should have destroyed it, I could see his disdain as he studied it, and I'd been told these islanders were largely communist sympathizers—they do let me land, somehow I passed. But that was no way to begin. They fire a rifle at the wind, two more men arrive. The unloading begins, donkeys and their hay first, then the barrels of diesel, crates from the hold, a slim sack of what must be mail, a shiny brass propellor, bits of machinery. I'm left standing out of the way.

Several children appear, stand silently, hungry-eyed. A woman on a donkey stops at a bend in the track, surveys the scene. Another man appears, walks past her, kicking up dust with his boots. He's a bit different, perhaps better dressed, in his fifties, clean-shaven, a sadness to his eyes and mouth, wool jacket, scarf, beret. He is less wary in his motions as he walks right up to me, holds out his hand. —"I am teacher Lucás, you write, Aléko, you welcome." At least I think that's what he says, Lucás whom I'd written to, calling myself Aléko on a prescient whim.

He picks up my sack, insisting with a gesture. Ignoring the others he leads me up the track. Chóra appears round the bend, perhaps a hundred houses strung along the single road, dazzling white despite the wars.

He takes me to his home. Up three steps, he puts down my sack by a pot of basil in an olive tin in front of a blue door. He opens the top half, calls, a woman appears. He introduces her, Theodóra, his wife. He turns abruptly, and, with the sack on his shoulder, beckons up an outside stair. A pot of geraniums on the landing, another blue door, my room. He traces the rent in drachmas on my palm. My room, my home, for as long as I like.

. . .

Perhaps three months I've been here. My Greek comes along well, it rather much has to, Lucás's smattering of English doesn't get us far. Some villagers have a few words of Italian and like to use them. I was told of the time when Lucás's father hid the Italian who'd been Occupation Army Prosecutor for the Naxos district until Badóglio switched Italy to the Allied side. He hid him in a limestone cave from a squad of revengeful Germans who'd combed the island. They probably speak a bit of German too, but I've never heard a word. And now and then I hear Norwegian, Dutch, this and that, from the men who've been off for a time in the merchant marine.

I open the shutters of my little window, look out over the sea to the sky turning green in the dusk, to the low forms of far islands, Thíra balanced on the horizon, stray pink clouds. The Greece you promised, Yvette, the Greece of your dreams. Your stories to soothe little Aidan. Of satyrs and nymphs and naiads, of shepherds with magical flutes, stories that made you young by the telling, stories of my dreams all these years.

They will only be true for you, Yvette, you who would wander Arcadia when I began boarding at Cheltenham. Your picnic baskets and parasols and donkey caravans, you could see a dryad in every tree, Pan behind every curling mustache, a fallen hero under every asphodel, a temple in every dusty stone. Your Aegean, where the meltémi gives warning with a far-off whistling cry, where every fish is barboúni, and the caíquia sail effortlessly onward to the ever-sweet setting sun. Where everyone speaks English— or should—and is honest and open and good. Where the quail are driven to you, where each dive brings up an amphora, where the fruit just hangs there to be plucked.

Blown to bits, Mother darling, in 1943. No no, in fact, that Greece, it never ever was, nor did that sea ever wash clean. My Greece? No, not likely ever mine. Yet I could still get out of bed, look out of this window, now, this morning, on a scene that seems harmonious.

. . .

I've woken late after a long evening of scribbling my anthro-classics notes. The waves of a dead sirocco flow across my ceiling—pine rafters, whitewashed cane, bits of mud and seaweed showing through—reflections from the morning sun. If I were to rise, step across my tiny room, I'd look out through the crocheted curtain, through the glassless window with its two blue shutters, across Sotíris's flat roof, a broken amphora for a chimney pot and a tin spout aimed at the cistern below. And maybe I'd see, running along the beach that divides the village in half, where the caíquia anchor from the summer winds, running and kicking its heels in the air for joy, a baby donkey, a little boy bareback on its mother, laughing and shouting behind. Or maybe Stamáti on the rocks where the beach begins, hurling an octopus against a ledge to soften it, hear the sharp slap-slap. Or Mários with his bull and cow shuffling through the seaweed on their way for the morning drink of brackish water at the village well.

Or I could step out onto my little balcony, pinch a withered leaf off my geranium, pungent lemony on my fingers, look out into the clarity of the scene, out where the world is burning under the sun, where the whitewash turns blue in the intensity, out to the sand and the dust, the limestone cliffs, the stubble fields, the torn sea in the fresh meltémi racing beyond the headland, where the miller swings the arms of his windmill down, one by one, to reef the sails.

Or if it's night, maybe in the moonlight they'd be pulling a net in to the beach, men swinging at each end to their chanting rhythm, little boys rushing around calling out their guesses at what there'll be in the catch. Or lovers sitting in the shadow of the tamarisk. Beyond them maybe see a white wall behind the church light up, and hear their violin and mandolin practicing for a Sunday night dance.

Yes, such scenes are there still, straight out of Yvette's dreams. I rise, splash my face with water from a jug, its rosy Matterhorn cracked in half. Pull on trousers, a baggy Greek shirt I bought for close to nothing from Lucás, sandals. I fasten the shutters open with their bits of string on a nail. It is there, the Aegean idyll, if that's what you want to see. But the men all carry guns—a sort of, Fuck you, Germans!, now that the Germans have gone, and a defiant communist bravado towards the royalists, the British, and now the Americans with their misdirected Truman Doctrine. Across the Fakoúsa passage there—just yesterday they'd rowed me to that uninhabited island, to a cave where they'd taken the royalist papás from Naxos who'd come over to officiate a marriage, took him there stovepipe hat and all, chained him to an iron mooring ring, left him there to die.

Or the story of EleftheRía and Giánnis.

A day in August, the Day of the Panaghía, a fierce meltémi in the bluest of skies, drifting ochre dust into my window from the fields of stubble. A feast day, which means wine at the kapheneíon, or baking the week's loaves, or staying in pajamas all day if you are the fish dealer. I am free and alone and wandering in the countryside.

Elefthería, standing at her gate, her white stone house lonely in the fields, she watches me as I come up the walled-in track that leads from one end of the island to the other. She wears a smock, faded from black to gray-blue, her head and face are wrapped in white—for the wind and maybe for Mohammed, the Turks still lingering about. She takes me in with her sad gray eyes, one hand comes out from under her apron, and with the palm-down beckon invites me to her home. Her bare feet splay in the dust of the yard, commending the chickens to fly, the goats to back resentfully out of range. We sit under her tamarisk, she brings figs and cistern water and sweet brown wine. She tells me, loudly and carefully so I'd understand, that I am her son. Or that she would never have a son, or even a husband. For she had lived faithfully in sin with Giánnis for twenty years, and was thrown out by her family, permitted into only one of the two kapheneía, and no one would help with their threshing.

She is neither wife nor mother, for Giánnis, whom she loves and called her sweet man, is not a man at all. —"He was born, you see, with a thing like a veined tomato, here, between his legs, where men have what they have. It dribbled and stank and made him hide."

They took him to Athens when he was twenty and they operated. When he came back they loved each other but everyone said it was impossible because a marriage must be taken to bed.

—"But we give each other pleasure, and that's enough. Giánnis, he fishes in his rowboat, dynamiting if the wind's right to blow the sound away, or works where he can if the meltémi brings the sea to a boil, and we've built this house, and that's enough. Except a son."

I stay. When Giánnis comes, we have supper. Fish-head

and lemon soup, twice-baked rusks softened in water till they taste like nuts, and wine and figs and thick coffee. They take me back to Chóra with a torch.

· · ·

And now to my sweet Dímitra—my Medea.

I had walked to the top of the island with an idea of working on my notes, but my notebook stayed in my shoulder bag. The wind and sun were harsh over the white earth—I looked for shelter. I found a sort of tunnel made by goats between a wall and the crowding mastic bush. I swept the droppings aside with a branch of broom. The earth was powdery soft and my wine and black bread were my friends. Peace, the crested larks and greenfinches whirled in for crumbs. I slept.

· · ·

Ah, you have come to us, welcome Dímitra, my sweetest Dímitra, I have thought of you so often through the years. Here, come with us. The scent of the mastic-berry oil you use in your hair, the lemon cologne on your throat, the fruit of your breath. Your almost girlish body that I have covered with kisses, those long nights of our love. Why are you crying? Speak to me, my dear, come back the years, there where first you found me.

### Dímitra

I kick the donkey dung, angry. Stó dhiáolo, all of them! Who's ever heard of Saint Dímitra? And my name day is for Dimítris, not for me. But *Goddess of the Wheat* they shout in the village street, the old men when I pass and they try to pinch my bottom, and they ask me if I've found my daughter Persephóni yet, they'd be glad to help. But at least it's my sister Margaríta whom my babás sends each morning to clean the nets—I'd sooner slaughter goats with Uncle Giánnis—and I am sent to the fields. Who can tell? If I return with the basket full of chicory or figs, if the goats are swollen with milk, if the donkey is loaded well with brush for the weekly baking—the bread. the casseroles, the roasts. Who can tell what else I do?

Old Iríni, maybe she'll be out here today too, picking acorns and mastic berries for her pigs. And she'll tell me more, in her whisper so the goats won't hear, about her magic.

About her curse of impotency, just one look in the bride's eyes while the priest is crossing their wedding crowns, and the groom will be no more that night, or any night, no more than the little boys who run naked on the beach and pee from nowhere. And her parents will say he's a freak and scream till all the village knows and they'll threaten to keep him from her dower house. Or she'll be tight like an unripe fig and he'll throw her from the bed. They'll know, it's Iríni. And they'll buy back the curse and the house will fill with love sighs for the giggling old women in the dark. Or if he knows, he'll wear a dagger at the wedding, a dagger hung from his belt, low, in front, to protect his power against the spell.

Or maybe she'll tell of the Black Ghost, of that night

long ago when she was out for a lambing. Between the groans of the ewe she could hear the footsteps in the thyme behind her, and she turned and he was there, quite close, black and naked, his eyes empty white. For ever so long he stood over her. Guarding, she knew, for the pirates had buried treasure on her hill and had killed a black oarsman, a blade twisted in the stomach so the scream would echo forever and the heart would beat on and his ghost would guard their secret.

Will I find Andónis and Stélla again, like that once in a secret place in the sand dunes, ringed by junipers, when I came on them making love? I almost died with the watching, died as their caresses came to me, melted in my belly though my fingers showed it was not my time.

Here, I'll sit in the splintery shade of this tamarisk tree, a twig to pick my teeth and the breeze blowing cool under my skirt. He who will be my man, when will I find him? Will I ever find him, like magic in my heart—will it ever be?—to see him, with the spell of my inner eye, to hold him, with all the power of my secret soul? He who will be beautiful, he of strong shoulder, of black eye, of a face burned in the sun and lined by the sea. He with pride that lifts him tall, that makes his voice quiet when his eye is on fire. He who will dance alone when the fiddle is warm, one arm curved high to his snapping fingers, the other hand to his inner thigh, close, where the pants pull tight, and the leap and the fierce slap of his hand on the stone floor. The steady look across the dancing room, straight to my eye where I sit by my babá. The hand to my elbow to guide me beyond the lamps, through the lanes and fields and olive trees, through our night of love.

But enough of that.

Those goats there, they shuffle in their hobble ropes, paw at the dusty roots, spray out their black pellet droppings, laugh at me with their evil eye. Soon, though, they'll slide into their midday sleep, there in the shade of the pistachio. I'll close the opening in their wall, push in place the sea mine we use for a gate—rusty iron shell that washed up on our beach after the war and the fishermen had cut a hole in it for the dynamite. I'll crawl in behind the mastic tree, cheese and pomegranate in my pocket, to eat in the secret shade.

The larks are here, hopping in the bush, flying off in a rush. A shape in the darkness, I'm blind from the sun. There, that's better, like the moon from behind a cloud. A bundle, a form—a man. Stretched out, sleeping, his boot heels up in a V, gray pants crumpled across his bottom, khaki shirt rolled high on his splotchy arms, curly hair, his face turned into the dust. He, Aléko, the one who talks in knobby Greek, like his knees.

Parents who'd squawk like chased chickens and the old ones clucking honor and disgrace and never-be-alone-with-a-man. But this lump is not a man—sleep like an anchor rope pulled tight—this bundle. And I've crawled in here and it's mine, not his, and I'll not for anything leave.

So, when I'd scraped the last bit of salty goat cheese

from the rind with my teeth, when I'd dug out the last crimson kernels of fruit and spit the seeds to the larks, I sleep too.

· · ·

Yes, that was how we met, Aléko mou. You'd been with us more than a year, I used to watch you playing backgammon with the men in Andónis's kapheneíon. I knew you were interviewing us villagers one by one, but we had never talked. Would it have been better, Aléko, if we'd never met? Who was I, a fisherman's daughter, and you had traveled the world, had fought the war, beat the hated Germans, on and on? In the end our love drove us both away to separate worlds where we could never meet again. And the child of that love, she was torn from me as a baby.

Did you ever see me run and laugh, Aléko, throw myself in the sand for joy? You've seen the love in my eyes, but have you ever seen the hope, the long look to other islands?

Half of me was held there on our island, wanting the boats back, a good catch, home. Or waiting for the moonless nights when the fish rise to the lights. Or longing for good winter rains, pomegranates as many as I can eat, my bed warmed well by a pot of the evening's embers, straight-boned children to fill my arms and heart. A home, the threshold whitewashed, a lemon-fish soup for my man who plays backgammon in the kapheneíon.

But my other half longed for a different world. The world our men would tell of, come back from the years at sea. Your world. Cities glowing like all the stars piled up from the sea to the sky. Queens and beautiful ladies and parades and men so pale and fine with their hands so soft, like yours. Where bread is cake, wine is a waltz, love is sheets of silk—not the scratchy blankets and hiding in the dark, the scooped half lemon to not have babies, slid in no matter how much it hurts. Not a trestle bed in the night when the sea is too stormy for nets, wool garment tugged open, black forms, the boards creaking, the child in the same bed.

You see me here, now, twenty, twenty-two years old, but fifty, sixty? Look, just watch. This hand of mine, it's strong still, perhaps stronger, but now it is spotted, lined, twisted, the nails broken and black. And these eyes, these empty eyes, eyes you looked into that last day on the beach. No, even then I knew you, though my mind had broken, an urchin dropped by a seagull on the rocks.

But Aléko mou, is it wise, this turning to the past? Only a fool would fish tonight in last night's waters. And only a fool sets sail in a stormy sea—the sea that has no handles.

### AIDAN

Do I have an answer, Dímitra? We met, we loved, yearning so, and the memories are beautiful, however sad. Not morbid nostalgia that drowns. No, no tears for the past that is not the present. Simple memory, accept the pain, embrace the joy, that is all. Come with me, my Dímitra, back to our hidden beach.

· · ·

We stand here hand in hand, where the maquis meets the coral sand. The waning moon is rising to the east, time enough before that final darkening warns of the dawn. Dying waves echo in the caves of the limestone cliffs, whisper in the sand. We spread a ragged blanket in the dry grasses, we kneel. See, this autumn crocus, all whites and blacks in the moonlight, how it reaches for us. You touch your finger to my lips. Slowly, like little children, we undress each other, the night air flowing through us.

Our shoulders glow in the moonlight, tremble to the touch of fingertips. Your lips are drawn apart, your breath is a tiny gasp. Your mouth so sweet, your eyes so closed, your brow drawn, your shivering sigh, your shivering body —be still, my love. You come to my lips, a lingering kiss. Your arms move round me, you come to me, sit gently on my lap, my breath on the curve of your neck. Slowly we rock, slowly we row our enchanted boat among the floating stars. Longings that flow out into the night. No land below us now, no fear to fall, only the still sea with a moon looking up from the depths. We sail in our diamond vessel, free of the floating stars, to the sparkling dome of the sky. Out in that great arc of blinding whiteness, out through the curve of the universe.

To sleep in the honey of the thyme.

· · ·

Would it have been better not to have loved at all?

Sweet memories, my Dímitra, times of contrast, intense, from the sweep of the meltémi, the burning sun, to the silence, the dark behind the mastic tree where I found you. Sweet like the blood-red cherries in their syrup that you serve me when I call on your parents, like the oúzo turning slowly white in the humid night air, the bars of honey and sesame seeds, the black figs you bring me. The smell of the cushioning bracken in the dew of a calm night.

Or perhaps I'm working in my little room, the end of a long day of talk, of trying to fathom village social rules. When the slits of sunlight through my half-open blinds die, when the bells ring vespers, I'll stow my notebooks and go out into the gathering night. I'll gossip and eat fried fish and tomatoes at the kapheneíon, maybe with Cósta who's tired of womenfolk. I'll play a game or two of backgammon and try to speak in proverbs about the uselessness of women. When asked, I'll answer, quite offhand, that my work goes not so badly. They'll shake their heads and leave it at that. I'll scrape my plate onto the floor for their dog. I'll buy a bit of bread and maybe cheese and tinned milk for tomorrow, hard brown oranges.

And I'll leave, I'll linger on the beach, skip stones with the little boys, help draw water at the well. Until it's quite dark and the lamps are burning and the mothers are call-ing their children home.

Or later, that thick darkness that flows about me as I move out naked onto my balcony. Where the midnight stars hang heavy to be plucked, where the seagull's cryings have ceased, where the scops owl sits on my shoulder.

Here under summer's last shooting stars. The world of my darkness, traced in phosphorescence where the waves break on the sand, scented with burned coffee boiled over into the embers, echoing to the lament of a donkey.

Yes, Dímitra, I have my inner darkness too, my succubus that found me, there behind my geraniums and my sea-blue door. I never told you what it was like.

I'd not been well—feverish, depressed, I put myself to bed, telling you and Lucás not to worry, that I had water and that I could not eat. How long I lay there, hours, days, I never knew.

I would study my room with utmost care, cataloguing, cling to each item to resist the fevered sliding. The wooden floor, gray with dust and age, the crocheted curtain, unstirred by the meltémi's attacks. Here, this wall, whitewashed, cool to the skin of my back, stained, I know, where my head rests against it. The ceiling, eleven bare cypress beams, one hundred and ninety-three bamboo canes—sagging with age, with the layers of yellow dirt piled onto the roof to keep off the winter rains, sagging over my table, pressing on the half-dark air, pressing on my skull, sinking me deeper—imp floating in a bottle, press the rubber top and the imp sinks slowly to the bottom.

Fixed objects, everything in its place, except perhaps that chair. Orderly, you see? Fix myself, here, in position, course bearings with my compass on known positions in my room—at least a relative position, for if I'm to be sure that my room itself stays fixed I'd have to open my window and take cross bearings on maybe the windmill and the hilltop and that ledge out to sea where the gluttonous cormorants sit.

But despite my efforts I'm sliding, helpless, thrown across my storm-tossed room. I crawl back, I must retake my bearings, continue cataloguing, be sure just where I am. This table, it sits there quite patiently, seemingly undisturbed by the objects loaded on it. The water pitcher, covered with a doily to keep off the flies, the tumbler turned upside down, the basil in a glass honey jar dutifully releasing its green odors. Soap on a plate, a bowl, my shaving things and comb and toothbrush, books, notebooks, a sketch pad. A wool tablecloth keeping things from sliding in bad weather. And four chairs, sitting politely in place around the table.

That mirror, like a hole hanging on the wall. Flanked by the ancestors, two by two—mustaches, the black shawls, hands heavy on the knees, the fezzes, the solid looks of death. The chest along one wall, silent in the heat of day, its creakings sound at night—unopened, teeth clenched.

Three spikes in the wall, one for my trousers and shirt and towel, one for the paraffin lamp, and one where my duffel bag hangs by the throat. My unyielding bed, its iron bars are painted patriotic blue, chipped and dented from many attacks. The mattress is a sack of straw, the sheet is striped with red lash marks.

I stumble to the window, crack open the shutter, look out on the blinding view, watch the boats scurrying round, the women working on the nets, the donkeys stumbling by with their loads of firewood, a freighter steaming by on the horizon. Run my fingers lightly over the cool wall by the window, feel its bone through its plaster flesh, its steady pulse. Let the curtain brush against my shoulder, the touch of women's fingers in the cotton thread. Put my toe under the edge of the chest, watch the wood dust drop on me piece by piece, a termite passing his days. I go to my painted door, lay my fevered cheek against its wood, warm from the sun outside.

A fresh wind comes in from the west, forces ajar the window shutter against its wobbly catch. The slice of light cuts cruelly, I must go, screw the catch in tighter with my thumbnail, return to my bed, my legs not folding to their proper place. Settle back into darkness, watch the shadows slide on the whitewashed walls, on the powdery floor, shadows that detach, float free to hover over the table. A slit of sunlight through a crack in the door cuts my insubstantial flesh, burns on the face of the chest, smoke wisps from the blackening wood, a flame throbs in the wound.

In the half-light, in the hollows and floating shadows, I sit in balance on my bed. No thoughts to disturb the steady flow of blood and breath, no intrusions. The waves on the beach are silent now, the sun has passed out of reach behind my solid wall of stone, the wind has died to nothing, the seagulls' cries have ceased, the lizards and spiders and beetles rest, their eyes filmed over. There is no water in the sea, the beach is bone dust, the sun is dead in empty outer space. I evaporate into my special death.

. . .

You washed the blood from my lips. Your hair gentle on my cheek. My body was pain, pressure pumped in my hollow head, my nerves scraped on broken bones, my burning eyes, my tongue a swollen wound. Your breath warm on my neck, your caress gentle on my palm.

So it was, Dímitra, you at my bedside, looking for something in my eyes, trying to bring me back to life. For my epilepsy is death, death with warning, red death from which there is no escape. And to lie there again, half living, is only to know it will happen again. Selinissmós, my moon sickness, they call it.

You had opened the window shutter and the top half of the double door. It must have been the next day, or maybe two days later. They'd broken the door in to get to me. All was sunlight and white, you so pale, so beautiful. The chest was covered with the new rug you had been weaving for me. On the table was a vase of asphodels, I was dressed in strange clothes. I heard Lucás outside my door. —"A fit, found naked, bleeding, the girl Dímitra now to nurse him."

In that long calm interlude, when the moon would silently follow the sun across the floor and up the wall to set in the mirror, when the shadows moved peacefully to and fro, faithful to the ordered objects of my room, when I dreamed no more, in that time our tides were as one. Your coming and going so tenderly, your caring, your silence, dark and warm against my white walls.

### Dímitra

Your face is clouded, Aléko, as I had seen it those many years ago. Why? Why, when we were so calm and we loved each other so? I was your Dímitra who cared for you and felt our life strong and sure. You had come through some dreadful test, you had survived. There, I see the scar on your cheekbone, I touch it with my fingertips, lean to kiss you there.

That cheek that had been mine, scarred now, shining with your tears and mine. I weep for those days when your tongue had healed and you could talk again, those days that ended in a bouríni that tore at the sea and left us both shattered.

Your enemy words that would attack me again and again. Darkness, inner voices, unreason, escape, corruptions. Words that made me black when I longed for light, words to shut me in the misery of your theories. And your promises, Aléko, you promised such senseless things, things that hurt the more because you thought they were right for me, your Dímitra, too. You'd give up your studies, crew on a trawler until you learned fishing, and then be your own captain with me to clean and repair your nets. As if for me to want something else from you were wrong.

. . .

Yes, Aléko, so it was. I sit here beside you now, on this bit of sand, hidden from the sun, much as I sat by you on the edge of your iron cot after that bouríni, sat there to help you through your second deathlike fit. That storm was threatening as your words attacked me, when you told me you would never never take me away. We had hurried back to your room. As the storm broke about us, I was seized in a terrible shudder, my head seemed to empty. For just a moment I was again a little girl, sitting in my mother's lap, held tight by her as she was wrenched by a spasm, as she was hurled into her madness. Sitting by you, gripping your hand, my finger nails tearing your palms, it was then that my heart turned to stone, my eye to ice. My mother's madness was mine.

You had stretched out on your cot, I stood over you, remote, looked down on you through the shroud of my hair. You sought my eye, my unknowable raven's eye. Your body stiffened, your head crashed against the wall, you lay bleeding, senseless.

I could still touch you then, still care for you. But love was empty, like me, love could no longer be. How I had loved you, Aléko! Loved you as many times over as all the fish in the sea.

Now, though, in the afternoon shade, your friend there, your Youli, silent, attentive, I can only be with you in memories, let you listen to the past, waves from a long gone wind. The dead sea swell left from the bouríni, it still washes on our shores, the final storm that left me mad—touched by Selene, the moon goddess, I heard them say—the bouríni that carried you, that carried our child away.

### AIDAN

My dear, my sweetest Dímitra. Your island storms—you had told me the signs. When the gulls cry in the evening, not the laughing sunlight cry that knows the calm is coming, the sea like oil and the little fish trembling on the surface, no. When they cry a single cry, when they come to land, hide in the caves and the beach reeds, it is then they forewarn of a bouríni. So you tell me. The fishermen, they've heard, they know, and they'll not set out to sea this night. Their caíquia are in the winter anchorage behind the mole, their souls are safe at home.

The storm was fierce. The explosions of wind were pressures and vacuums, cracking in my skull. Sand hissed against the door and windows, sharp blows of flying debris. Breakers roared on the beach. A night to mourn for those left at sea.

The cold seeped in about my heart. In the faint light of the paraffin lamp I looked for you, sought your eye through the raven's wing of your hair. Your inscrutable eye, your unreachable eye, empty. The room swirled about me, caught in the vortex of the storm—my warning, my helpless falling into death. Oh help me, hold me!

My bed rose up, hurled me against the wall.

They say that you were there with me in my storm-tossed room throughout the night. The next day, when I had climbed in agony out of my darkness, when you had tended to the bandage you'd wrapped round my split skull, you brought a bowl of warm milk, toasted bread sprinkled with olive oil and bits of garlic, figs from the second crop.

As you moved about the room, Dímitra, you seemed carried by the air. Round the table, to the mirror where you waved a strange goodbye to your image, to your empty eyes. Circling, on behind the lamp where I could no longer see you, curtains swinging where the wind slipped in, on round my room. You turned to the table, carried the vase of asphodels to the chest, caressed the table cloth you had woven for me, studying it with your fingertips, lifting it, folding it, tucking it into a pocket of your apron. You took the scarcely touched bowl of milk, carried it to my balcony, bending carefully to leave it for Theodóra's cats. Back to the table, brushing crumbs, returning the vase, reordering objects in a kind of dance, putting a chair back in place, moving on.

That evening, in a beam of moonlight through a crack in the shutter, you were gone. My dearest Dímitra, the seliniasménos, touched by Selene, the moon of the falling ones and of the mad. An urchin crushed against the folly of your Aléko, the moonsickness of your mother. Dreams to dust, swept away.

Later, when the bouríni had long passed and the sea had quite forgotten, when I could walk, but carefully, the bandage pressing me tight, my tongue healing that I had bitten through, I tried to see you. Always they said you were much too sick, a fever. But their eyes would slide away, and I was left to move on and their doors seemed always closed.

Once I saw you, alone on a distant beach. I had been walking, each day farther, to get my strength back, to loosen the knots in my soul. That day I had finally made it to the north end of the island, high on the cliffs where the waves drove in, great sheets foaming at my feet. I came down to the edge of the sea towards the east. As I rounded the headland and onto our beach, our beach with its secret caves and coves, our beach where we would swim together by the light of the moon, where we'd played naked in the green sea with the sun beating in our blood, there I saw you. You were turned from me, kneeling in the sand, your hands stretched out to the afternoon sun. Your black smock was pressed by the wind against your body, your hair blew loose.

I came up slowly, a few paces from you I stopped, I sat, cross-legged, just above where the surf's foam hissed in the sand. What were my thoughts as I sat there, why was there fear in my throat? The sand sifting through my fingers, bits of shells and seaweed, was it myself that I feared?

I watched you with longing, with love, with fear. You had turned from the sun, to the sand to smooth it carefully before you. Were you drawing there, or writing, a driftwood root in your hand? You bowed down your head in prayer, your hands lying still on your thighs. You were calm, the wind had fallen, your hair flowed down on your breast.

You turned on your knees towards me, your hands on the sand. For a moment I believed you were coming to me, that you were here with me, sand cupped in my hands, I would pour you warm on my body, you would cover my eyes with your hair.

Your face that I had so often touched, so often kissed, you were looking at my hands, the sand that trembled, trickled away, dimples, craters in the sand. Your face was dark in the shadow of your hair, your lips drawn back, your vacant empty eyes. Your hands held up a silver stick of driftwood, bending it, snapping it in two. With the pieces crossed towards me, you rose and, bent with your arms high, the cross in the line of our eyes, you backed away. Slowly, your bare feet sliding in the sand, you moved down the curve of the beach. The surf slid up to foam at your feet, washing your footprints from the sand. When you came to the first rocks of the headland, distant now, a scrap of black blown among the boulders, you turned, you flew off through the junipers and thyme, a raven winging off to the sky.

I looked down, my hands were still cupped, empty. And when I rose, I could see in the sand, though your feet had scuffed it and the surf had come to its edge, that you had drawn a cross and had written, I am the Sister of Christ.

. . .

What choice had I then but to leave?

Wherever I went in the village, I carried a wave of silence, eyes slipping elsewhere, even the children stopping their play. Once while walking in the hills I came upon Elefthería. Looking to see that we were alone, she moved up to me, took some dried figs from her pocket and put them in my hand as if to balance her words.

—"I have been waiting for you here, Aléko my son. Many days. Do you know? Our Dímitra, she has been twice touched, a privileged one, Aléko, touched by our goddesses, Selene the Moon and Erinys the Avenging Fury. And she is with child, Aléko. So, yes, you must go. Go with fortune if not with our gods. And remember me, your mother. Go."

When I left it was Cósta who took me. He had come to my door the night before. —"The wind will be right tomorrow, we'll sail when the night is broken." Though I'd said nothing nor made any plans.

His caíqui would be tied to the mole. I could hear his sail flapping nervously in the wind in the last blackness before the dawn. He was unloading his nets, a sign, I knew, that he expected a sea. I swung my duffel to him, he dropped it through the hatch into the fish hold. I squatted on the deck, uncertain what to do or say, cold and fuzzy from sleep. He handed me a coffee that he'd prepared on a spirit lamp in a corner of the cockpit. Somehow that was my only goodbye.

Or perhaps another. As we wore off round the point, I thought I saw, there on the last bit of rock, washed by the mounting sea, a dark form in the dawn, a raven's wing blown in the wind.

# 10

You had left, Aidan, dropped out of my life, your Pooh-stick had floated away. Roselle, I had lost her too. Huge empty spaces in my life. Three years of grinding graduate school ahead for me, three years of this, my permanent spot, books piled up around me in the dusty hush of a university library. Can I make it through?

The page blurs. Distracted, I doodle on a file card, mindless. My doodles are always absurd. A grotesque light bulb emerges, screwed into the North Pole of a tiny globe of the world. It's shedding light in the form of dollar signs. A logo for my father, for me? A logo for General Marshall's Plan? Most of these books, articles, papers seem to say yes, do it with dollars. I wonder. But I'm committed, win those initials after my name and I'll get out there, see what that sort of light can do for the war-scarred world.

. . .

R and R, Sunday, escape the books, a hike in the nearby hills. A windbreaker, a sandwich, an orange in my knapsack, a goatskin of wine slung at my side. Alone, no one out on such a dreary day. Good.

A woodpecker rattles up ahead. The mourning call of a train in the valley, its tone falling as it hurries on. The scrub oaks are thinner here, stunted, twisted by the winds. Rock ledges take over as I near the top. Here, a good spot, mossy, a boulder for a backrest. A bite of sandwich, a squirt of red wine, careful, the regulation handspan from my mouth—and a good bit splashes on my chin. Laughter, a woman, there behind me squatting cross-legged atop my boulder

—"All right for you. Here, let's see you do it better." And she does, perfectly. What can I do but shrug? —"I'm Alison, I've seen you in the library. I'm in archeology."

Man's white shirt, lumpy brown sweater over her shoulders, blue jeans, sneakers. Pert, Irish pretty, touch of the nasal Midwestern voice. Nice. —"You heading down? May I join you?"

Well…

### AIDAN

To be your best man, to leave Greece, come back to the conventions of your America? No, old friend, no more. My world is here, for me I wish no other. So, be well, enjoy what you can of your wedding. Thank you for the photo of your Alison. Nice-looking bird. And here's to a game of Poohsticks in our dreams.

· · ·

We did see each other often in those years, what you called your VIP years. In Washington when I returned from Greece to assault the CIA, in Rome, in Greece several times. You wrote me of your life—what I liked to picture as your part in the rebuilding of that shattered world.

In Rome you and your highly presentable Alison had a villa on the Appian Way, you the favorite acolyte of the lady ambassador, bringing water for the daily test-tubed rose pinned neatly to her breast. You survived Senator McCarthy's hit men sent to ferret out the Reds, burn subversive books. Wagons-lits to Paris every month, conferring with the brass. Special trips to Washington. Put Europe back on her feet, build up their armaments industries, kick the local commies out. Weekend touring, all the sights, dolce vita, concerts, Caracalla opera, skiing at the best resorts. San Remo, your Aunt Alice's villa, a banquet for the remnants of the royal family spared from exile. Forbidden toasts, Viva il Re!

To Bangkok with your cooks and gardeners and ayahs, canoe-taxied to your office on the stinking canal back of your compound. Ministers and princes, costume balls, official cocktail parties, diplomatic corps and government toadies, poolside parties, office parties with a mongoose-cobra fight and a severed tongue to stick back on and ceremonial dancers—temple figures come to life.

Your role in ousting your greedy ambassador. He was bent on getting Brownie points for persuading Washington to double unneeded economic aid—you fed him to *Time* magazine, they quickly gobbled him up, spat him out on a full-page spread. Terminated. Well done, old boy.

Bamboo rafting down from Chiang Mai in convoy for a week, ostensibly to sample soil and water in preparation for a dam which will wipe out all that countryside. CIA types using silly covers, U.S. aid to train traffic cops disguising commando buildups, commie dangers, Vietnam hotting up.

To Ceylon with a team of self-styled experts to devise a plan of aid. Elephants and temples and tea planters' hill-station retreat, kites by the thousands in front of your hotel. Ceylonese officials after pieces of the pie. And Taipei, Manila, Vientiane, planning, pushing progress, economic development—stop the commies, demand our products, our successes, be like the U S of A.

To Washington, same agenda, progress ready-mix. You were praised, often promoted, in your early thirties and already near the top.

And yet. Power-addicted, you'd ask yourself, important, doing good, fixing up the world? What were we doing, what world did we truly want, what was this all about? A missile race, preemptive strike, fire storms and nuclear winter, war to end us all, leave the cockroaches in charge? Bomb shelters with machine guns and minefields to keep your desperate neighbors out? Escalating populations, pollutions, corruptions, severe depletions, fifty wars at once. The air-conditioned nightmare of our consumption-driven lives. A wealth of luxuries for a few. For the overwhelming rest, dwindling glimmers of a promised land, impossible expectations, commitments never met. Is this the world we want?

In the end, you opted out—so much for the shattered world. Was that resignation an anyman's choice, an easy call? Gutsy, I'd say, an act of courage. And quite effective,

I should add, in upending your dear old dad.

You got yourself taken out of *Who's Who*—a middle finger gesture for the coveted line of Brewster VIPs. Took Alison off to Italy, a Tyrrhenian island stone hut, alone in the terraced vineyards above the sea, one room, one loft, no electricity, a trickle of water. Your study was a stone tool shed hidden in the gorse. Later, the two of you moved to a shabby mildewed would-be villa in the Tuscan hills. You got yourself on lecture tours, your cranked out articles of protest.

. . .

Alison, you've come to join the story? I trust that time has removed the sting, that to sit here beside Joel will not distress you.

### ALISON

Aidan, I'm sure I'll manage. Joel, no need, I trust, for further ado. For starters, I'll go back to grad-school days. You were, yes, I must admit, quite the handsomest around, and obviously on the rise—those friends you had at grad school, that Brewster name, even a girl like me from the Midwest knew something about that name, or so I thought. And I was game, ready to keep up, in fact I really enjoyed the prestige, the cachet of it all—married to you and to your career.

You seemed well-informed, to know a lot. It was only later I learned how much was merely your manner, your name, your various degrees. No no, do not interrupt,

Aidan. Yes, I'm still angry with you, Joel, and at myself for buying into it. I'll stop there, though, I swore I would keep up the façade.

However maladroit I was at first in that world of VIPs, diplomats, I was game, you must admit. And for me, unlike your mother, it was no hardship. In fact it had become my world well before you suddenly and cruelly switched allegiance, snatched it all away—the homes as we moved around the globe, the glamour of your jobs, the interesting people that came your way.

Why, what happened to you? You turned away from success, from friends and family—and me. From your role as a helper and a healer of a damaged world to that of an isolated critic. And you were bent on imposing an austerity on your life and on mine. Thank God we had no children. A stone hut on a cliff for a home! Yet I went along for a time, hoping for catharsis.

It didn't happen.

You seemed not to even mind when I turned to the lawyers and divorce. Distracted by your flurry of articles attacking the arms race, the bomb shelters, the cynical competition for allies, however tyrannical they may be? Or had you simply given up on us, fallen out of what at least I thought was love?

No, don't try to answer.

I had to end it. You were generous in our divorce. There was none of the usual bile and greed. And I survived, I married again, I was content.

Well, páce, Joel, yes, I'm ready for that. You've done good things with your life, and I'm told that you found a good wife. Until that awful accident!

# 11

From Artémisos I made my way to Athens. I stumbled through my tears in unfamiliar Athenian alleys, burdened by my loss, my duffel, my life that I had turned to lead. I came on a sign, Room for Rent.

Third floor, sagging bed, a condom curled up under it, a table and chair, paraffin lamp, basin in the hall, a privy in the tiny patio. Stink of exhausts, sewage, rotting garbage in the street below, stale bodies. The dust-streaked window rattles mercilessly—a motorbike roaring by. A street vendor cries out for knives to sharpen. Close the outside shutters, stretch out here on the bed. Weep.

My Dímitra, the caress of her raven hair, her naked body in the moonlit waves, the magic voyage in our diamond vessel. Her loving eyes—her empty eyes. Gone. My home, my Artémisos, the slap of the octopus, the creak and thud-thud of the windmill, the clatter of a donkey's hooves, the laugh of a child and a gull. Gone. Me, here in this noxious, baking hell.

I must leave.

I am up by early dawn, pay the furtive landlady, and simply walk away. Close to the eastern edge of the city is Hymettós, a low mountain rising through the smog. I had climbed it once before while I was waiting for *Arghó*, the rusty tub that was to carry me to Artémisos. I head there, escaping the stink of the city. Only a few blocks, and I'm in the cluster of communities, villages of displaced islanders, their smells of baking bread and roasting coffee and donkey droppings. Soon I'm in orchards and vegetable gardens, then higher to groves of olives, forests, to prickly pear with its orange fruit, fig trees, bee hives everywhere. Higher, into thyme and bracken, and finally to a small monastery, the Kaisarianí, on the site of an ancient curative spring. I hold my head under the splash of water from a ram's head.

. . .

For months I wander a bitter Greece, torn by civil war, communists against royalists, village against village, brother against brother. By buses, trains when the warring factions would let them through, trucks, carts, and mostly on foot. Often I glimpse Dímitra on the path ahead, guiding me through the bloodshed to new vistas. She turns back, takes me by the hand, laughs in her delight, adventures just round the corner—a snow slope to glissade, a mountain lake for a wash and swim, a goatherd's hut for a bowl of milk and a crust of bread, village music under the arms of their plátanos tree, a castle fort, a bed in the riverside grass.

I manage a pretense of research—innovative, fresh point of view—and the stipend keeps coming, Poste Restante several towns ahead. Talking, nonstop talking, scribbling, over endless cups of coffee, sips of oúzo, salty rock-hard chickpeas, an egg, fried potatoes, twice-baked bread to dunk in their retsína wine with its pine-tar and goatskin tastes. More talk, long pauses, outrageous assertions quickly affirmed, or denied, violent disagreements. Backgammon pieces clapping, players cursing, a radio blaring a football match to groans and cheers, the sizzle of burning fat—in the murk of reeking smoke.

I learn from a shepherd—half blind, missing most of one leg in a skirmish with royalists—to play the floghéra. We make one together from a section of cane, burn the holes with a red-hot ice pick. I help him with the herd—his royalist uncle had cut his sheepdog's throat. Throwing pebbles at the strays, flapping my arms, yelling the way he did.

That floghéra serves me well. In village after village I play, a few gather, the talking begins. In a Peloponnesian town, an old fellow sits down near me on the pavement to play his santoúri, hat beside him for the odd drachma. He hammers its strings, sings of bitter lost love. He asked me accompany him, and for weeks we played together from tavern to tavern, street corners, name days, a wedding.

I learn something of what it means to be that kind of Greek. To be born in those blood-soaked mountains, to be fierce and proud and crafty, suspicious, yet overwhelmingly generous in the face of ever-present death. Death lurking with every gun unslung and propped against a knee, every flourish of a grafting knife, every visitor from the city, every turn in every path, with every brother. Revenge and death.

Always the flood of stories, but, Joel, they are more than memory should have to bear. There's one, though, I cannot put aside. It was told to me by a soldier in a kapheneíon, a town under royalist control, close to a communist stronghold. We were playing backgammon—I lost.

He smiled, leaned forward.

—"You're British, no? Hear this story. My family lived in Athens throughout the war. They hid three British soldiers from the Germans in a shed in their patio for more than two years. When Greece was liberated, as you say, by the British, those three returned to England. The war had ended. Then communists came, shot my mother, my father, two sisters, my little brother because they had hidden the hated British. I wrote to those three. They never answered.

"I guard the jail here, they bring in communist prisoners, I kill them, that's the payment, that is all. Once it was my wife's brother, I shot him, that is all."

Honor and dishonor inseparable. My sympathies are largely with the communists, but the horrors come from every side. One thing I'm sure of, though. The British, then the Americans with their Truman Doctrine, are wrong. Corruption and tyranny are fostered, generosity squandered, abused, rechanneled to private Swiss bank accounts. All the old tricks of a ruthless, state taking largesse from thoughtless benefactors.

Is this a crumbling civilization, is this the womb of the Western world?

So...I have a mission. I ship myself to Washington, I'll go back there, put things right. I stay with you. You, and your pretty wife. You put me in the attic. I'd hear your stirrings just below—me in the grip, so often, of a secret petit mal.

I call it my gumshoe period. Some government department would, must, want me—my inside knowledge of what's going on in Greece, of what's needed, of what we're doing wrong. One of my targets was the CIA. I even get as far as one of their psychological tests, see what kind of a cloak and dagger would fit.

They lead me into a blacked-out barn, directing me by loudspeaker. —"Move ahead, left a little, reach out now, both hands, six inches farther, that's a rope ladder, climb up it till we tell you to stop." I climb maybe twenty steps, swinging wildly around.

—"Stop there, turn around, your back to the ladder, good, reach out with your right hand, left two inches, now, just in that direction. Six inches out is a hanging rope, no, you can't reach it, we want you to get ready, lean out, let go the ladder, seize the rope with both hands, of course, and let yourself down to the ground."

I won't, I don't. What does that make me? Rebellious, shrewd, trusting no one? Whatever the reason, they turn me down, all of Washington turns me down, and it is sobering to learn how many government agencies have their fingers in that pie, particularly now that it has become so tasty. They never learn of my falling sickness. It didn't get to the point of a detailed physical, and of course I lied on all my applications.

There were good times, being with you and Alison. Your sympathy helped when I heard from Eleftería about the birth of Érsi, my daughter whom I might never see. And somehow you managed to justify for me your attachment, your positive devotion, disregarding your usual skepticism, to General Marshall's famous Plan and all that foreign aid you were involved with. There was a glitter about your jobs that was hard even for me—a skeptic too—to resist. Success became you.

There were bad times too, being with you those weeks, excruciating times. Do you remember, Joel, one evening, you and I, an evening walk in Rock Creek Park, Alison off with her book group? A long summer evening, the light lingers, cool now, down here by the brook, cool among the magnolias, the giant rhododendrons. A couple lying in embrace on that mossy bank—murmurings, slow searchings. A whippoorwill calling for a mate. We sit on a grassy bit at the base of a granite outcropping. We sip from your flask of brandy, lean against the warm rock.

I tell of my sweet sad time with Dimitra. Of my wanderings in the war-torn heartland of Greece. Of a chance encounter with a shepherd boy. Noontime heat, he's sitting in the shade of a fig tree, the flock asleep. We play our floghéra pipes, chasing each other in improvised duets.

Our duet finished, its echo mocks us from a far cliff. We eat black figs, he drinks from my battered canteen, hands it back. I have spilt some on my chin. He reaches to me, wipes the drops off with his thumb, his hand stays on my cheek. We kiss, we lie together.

I say no more. You are silent, Joel, your eyes, are they on my lips, my eyes? They linger for a moment, you turn away. You rise, you offer me your helping hand, we walk back. Silent still.

.   .   .

Well, I am deeply grateful that the agencies of government were astute enough to realize that to employ me would be to introduce a mole, a whistle-blower, a troublemaker, into their midst. For the next chapter of my life took on a hopeful look.

I moved to New York, Yvette put me up, we were on reasonable terms by then, and The Admiral had died. I got some work done on my anthropology–classics artifice—it really was that, I'd be the first to admit. I settled in at the Public Library.

I took in the odd cocktail party. Boring chatter, gossip, posturing, I was good at all that once. No more, I seemed to have lost the will and the skill. No one showed the least interest in my adventures, my opinions, my knobby knees were no longer on display. I'd chucked the bagpipes long before. Then Cornelia happened.

Across that vacuous room, through the circulating trays of drinks and canapés, I glimpse a young woman. Alone, sitting in a window seat, obviously bored or uncomfortable with the scene. Dressed in white, nice to look at, slight, long silky hair, light brown, more blue eyes, though a bit close together.

I go over and introduce myself. We chat for a time. She is different, definitely different. A poet, and something about her seems seeking to escape. That's for me. I drop whatever manners I still had, sit down beside her, announce that she and I would shortly be husband and wife.

No, it wasn't a line, not at all, I'd never said anything like it before—or since, for which I am most thankful. She must have thought that novel, even charming, given the setting, for we were married a few weeks later, as soon as her divorce had been sorted out, the custody of her two young children awarded to her.

It's hard for me, impossible, to recapture the feelings, the romance that must have been there. I slide easily into the sweet moments with my sweetest June, Dímitra on our moonlit beach, others. But with Cornelia memory doesn't do it, not this time round. Too much has happened since, too much bitter bile, venom spat from both directions, too much lasting damage.

· · ·

She listened, really listened, in those early weeks—choice bits of my story, my Grecian passion, told con amore. Cornelia had some money—divorce or family, maybe both—enough to provide a living, as one might say. Enough to get us and her children to Greece.

We sailed forthwith, a few farewells, climbed aboard a smallish liner, waved dutifully to Yvette on the pier, and sailed. Middle class this time, no more steerage, not for us. The ship stopped in Gibraltar, anchored off the town, lightered a handful of passengers ashore. The children amused themselves throwing coins over the side to diving boys. Cornelia and I sat in deck chairs sipping beef bouillon. I told her more of my story there, of The Admiral, Amos, and Yvette, the Gibraltar apes, our final escape.

On to Sicily, Palermo, its gracious bay, Monte Pellegrino topping things off. Braving Scylla and Charybdis, two slowly whirling dimples in the sea off Messina. Then Corfu, Ithaca, Patras, the spectacular Corinthian Gulf, Parnasus, Delphi. Acrocorinth hanging its ruins over the town, the canal with its towering walls of limestone, impossibly narrow. Piraeus teeming with yachts, ferries, fishing boats, the forest of sunken ships' masts now gone, the Parthenon distant in the smog, foreboding.

. . .

While staying in New York I had become friends with a leathery shriveled woman who sat in a kiosk—newspapers, girly magazines, postcards, maps, that sort of thing—on the Lower East Side. She had come twenty years ago from an Aegean island, Rekalía. She still wore the gray smock and the scarf round her head. Her Greek at first was hard for me to understand—her English worse. But I picked up the cadence, the dialect, and the random scattering of English words. Her grandson often took charge of the kiosk. Twice I took her to a Greek restaurant squashed in between two tenements. We'd munch, she with some difficulty, slices of sizzling entrails, kokorétsi, off the vertical spit, pita bread, bottles of beer, and baklavá.

She spoke fondly of her island, pointed to it on her map with her twisted newsprint-blackened finger. Within easy sight of hated Turkey, it was far beyond Artémisos, beyond the reach of my past. Remote, yet it once was the center of her world. She'd rattle on, its mountains and monasteries, its bustling little port, the fishing boats, the tipped-up fields of wheat and vineyards and olive trees, the taverna with weekly entertainment from a slithery-noted clarinet or a bouzoúki or both. She dictated to me a letter—a niece who was still there, a sort of introduction. She could not read or write—just as well, given the wares she peddled.

That was where we were headed.

. . .

We spend three days in Piraeus, a flyspecked hotel room, waiting for the weekly ferry. By the time we get to Rekalía every passenger is violently seasick. The smell is horrible. Not a good beginning, and, by Cornelia's measure, things get worse.

Our home is a stone cottage in the heather a short walk from town. We enroll the children in the only school. I had a desultory idea of starting another research project, this time for a degree. Bad idea, I'd write something closer to my heart. And I am ready again for the Participation part of my renewed academic scam, ready to engage in this island community.

I learn a lot about fishing, particularly with sticks of dynamite. We sneak out when the local police are well into their oúzo, rowing, no motors, knowing just where and when to heave the dynamite—two arms, an eye, a hand were missing in the village. Or Pános and I would go along in the string of dories towed behind the grigrí. And there was the night fishing, the acetylene lamps roaring, glaring into the depths, befuddling the fish, you hope.

And much time spent in the kapheneíon making friends.

. . .

Cornelia, my dear, you've chosen to join us. Here, there's plenty of room. Yes, right, I'll just dig this sandy sitzbad a bit wider for those hips. You're looking, ah… your not-a-year-over-thirty-five look, my dear, the London look, shapeless gown, and that ghastly royal-Windsor-family hat, really, do take it off. You know Joel, of course.

### CORNELIA

Joel, it is nice to see you again…I think. Aidan, courteous as ever. I must say I'm not at all sure that I should be here. I do feel quite outnumbered. Defensive? Oh no, Aidan, you should know me better than that. Maybe less venom now, though I sense you're not running near empty, but the facts are still clearly at my command.

Let's get it straight about that Rekalía idyll. You took us there in the dead of winter. Our home was a goatherd's hut thirty-five dangerous minutes up a precipitous rocky track. We had plastic sheets for windows, and the roof was just rusty tin on an occasional sagging beam. We fed our one-plate ovenless stove with twigs, bracken and bits of wood when you chose to scrounge some, and we'd splurge on a bucket of charcoal once a week, which lasted at best two days. And that was all there was to keep us so-called warm and to so-called cook. Our light was a single lamp, stinking and sputtering on watery paraffin.

Water, well, you forgot about that. Winters, there was a trickle ten minutes' bucolic walk through the miserable gorse. We could scoop from it with a cup into leaky plastic pails. Or we could catch, in a variety of pots, the drips aimed at our beds—that saved some trips if we didn't mind flakes of crunchy rust in our mush. Summers I had to bring water up in German petrol cans on a donkey. Laundry? No, we can't ask the village women for help, pay them to do it, that's too classist, undemocratic, we'll just do it ourselves. Your *we* meant me.

That was the peace I'd said I'd dreamed of—my embroidery, my books, my poetry, contact my Muse. And you with your feet up on someone else's stove, picking someone else's fish from your teeth, enjoying their wine, their stories, their admiration of your Greek. Which, by the way, I worked hard on, became proficient myself, though you never seemed to notice. And the children. Remember them? We had them to deal with, no? School, language, friends. Not exactly comforting.

The litany could continue, but perhaps that's enough.

The children lasted through the summer—yes, it finally came round—but faced with school and winter again they simply opted out, went home to their father in New York. Would that I had gone with them.

It was cruel. Westchester to Rekalía? Really, Aidan, what were you thinking? What was I, for that matter? Oh, I was fond of you. You were glamorous, your stories of your Greece, your romantic vision, your common touch—yes, I did have some romantic inclinations left in me back then, but not for long—and I did, it's true, want out. Swept away, shining-armored knight, the whole bit. Merde! Skatá!

We did finally move to Athens. High on Lykavittós just below the park, a genuine farmhouse in the heart of Athens, still the remnant of an orchard in the yard with lemons, figs, almonds, a pistachio tree. There was a privy—we used it in the frequent emergencies, but the house had all the mod cons, and it was well out of reach of the Kolonáki diplomatic upper-crusty set, whom I too abhorred.

It was comfortable enough to get my children back, at least for a time. And we even produced two of our own. What could I have been thinking?

You did love our two, yes, I'll give you that, loved them ferociously in your exaggerated way. Timon, Alexia —they do work in English, those names, as I'd insisted. But Timon the Skeptic, Alexia the Protector of Men, as I later learned? You put one over on me after all.

I did feel sorry for you, Aidan, bridle if you will. Your fits were frequent, and one or two grand mals, frightening. You were good, I'll grant you, about trying not to ask me for money, though a regular job was clearly out of reach. You taught English now and then, lectured, sold some articles you'd written, and you were still working on that book of your adventures in the Civil War. You collected around you interesting intellectuals, usually Greek. The expatriates, on the contrary, even those who'd been there for years and I thought wrote well of Greece, you scorned as staying carefully on the surface, as ignoring any of the undercurrents, the darker side, inventing romance where there was none, cheapening originals in their translations, kowtowing to the ruthless sycophants of the gullible roy-alists in power.

The children—ours, for mine had gone back to their father for good by then—you'd have them barefoot, snotty-nosed, playing your ridiculous Poohsticks in the muddy gutter. I didn't disagree with your leftist political views, your sense of social justice, your sympathy for the brutalized people of Greece. I too loved them. But your deliberate exaggerated deprivation of our children, that was way beyond the point you wished to make.

You, Joel, and your wife—Alison, yes?—you joined us for a week. You were vacationing in Europe. I liked you, Joel, you seemed modest, open, a good listener, not well educated but ready to admit it, though I couldn't quite understand the close connection to our Aidan. And there did seem to be some weight pressing on you, a kind of despair, I'd say, but entirely unacknowledged. Alison? Well, nice enough, but forever trying to be something she wasn't. Ah well, so long ago.

You came alone to Lykavittós some years later, Joel. I remember trying to hide from you the growing anger between Aidan and me, avoid the plate throwings, the torn shirts and raw scratches, the terrorizing of our children.

The two of you, you and Aidan, went off to walk over the Northern Píndos range together. I was suspicious. I knew of your night together at that hotel in Innsbrück at the end of the war.

No no, the both of you, be still! I have the floor.

The children clearly were distraught, their education was poor and getting poorer. Anger and fear and loss, our endless warfare—I was exhausted. It was time we left, the children and I, left you, Aidan, to your Greece and whatever else might be your inclination. The only safe way to avoid your rage was to wait until you were off on one of your side trips to your peasant friends. Yes, we just packed up and left, the children screaming, the house a mess, I half deranged.

*AIDAN*

The bitch, the bloody bleeding bitch!

My wife, my children, they just aren't there, packed up, gone, took to the hills. Good riddance—the naggings, the miseries, prissy manners, clamor, the demands, their we-don't-belongs. Took to the hills? No, mountains, glaciers. Ice them in, deafen them with the cuckooing clocks, blind them in their picture-perfect paradise. The whole bit—cows and bells and goats and hanging pastures, Heidis round every hayrick, toy trains yodeling across unlikely chasms. Switzerland. Smug and highly profitable neutrality, venality, depository of deceit, dirty money—and my children.

To hell with you. Gone.

Good riddance?

I am bereft, left desolate to hurtle into private chasms. My golden children are no more, torn from me, my heart left shriveled, cold.

With a bit of bread and cheese in my pocket, a skin of water, I walk across the city, cursing love, beckoning death. Distraught, I wander through the stink of Omónia Square—the rancid sizzling of kokorétsi entrails turning on the upright butane grill, urine puddling from every convenient recess, diesel smoke, footprints of shit, rotting fish heads swarming with flies on a torn bit of newsprint—I retch in the gutter, a snotty face peering down at me, a small dirty hand held out.

I stumble up the sloping edge of the city, toward Hymettós. The city climbs with me for a way, then gives up. And just there, where I stop, wipe my eyes with my shirt sleeve, leaning against a fence post, a sow and piglets squealing abuse at me, just there... Hymettós rises over me, throws me down, buries me in my darkness.

Gone.

# 12

JOEL

Not that I'd pretend to match your dramas, Aidan, but...
my Alison...it must have been shortly before your loss...
no children, though...she too had gone.

We had moved from our hut off the coast of Tuscany
to the countryside south of Florence, a dirt-cheap-un-
heated-rundown-nondescript-nineteenth-century-farm-
house-cum-poorman's-villa, with a regulation palm tree
and an aphid-infested rosebush. Spectacular view, though,
Giotto, Brunelleschi in the distance beyond the nearby
farmhouses, the vineyards, orchards, olive trees, avenues
of cypress, villages, bell towers.

We seemed to be doing well. Alison, she grumbles,
but.... I'm in my stony studio much of the time—my
sheepdog, the lizards and spiders and ants to keep me
company—working up some notes for my lecture tour.
We've enough to live on, thanks to generous government
salaries and retirement pay and the sweat of underpaid
Asian labor making light bulbs. We even have a car, a
two-cylinder Topolino. What more could one want?

A winter's evening, we're sitting huddled close to the
meager fire in our terra-cotta fireplace. Our rickety rush-
bottoms—the chair-makers from the mountains still come
door-to-door, bicycles piled with bundled rush and chest-
nut staves—not exactly comfortable, but the wine is good,

the fiasco on the floor between us is emptying. It's been blizzarding all day, snow knee deep. Tuscany!

I listen with my earphones to the body-count news from Vietnam. Alison seems fidgety. She turns to me, takes the earphones off my head, and with, a strained and unnecessarily loud voice, announces,

—"Joel, I have decided I must leave, here and you. I... the American consul found a lawyer for me. I can't go on like this. It means nothing to me, all this austerity and protesting and...you leave me out of it, entirely. I don't know what's happened to us, I..."

I...Christ, Ali! Why? I didn't know, nothing...

—"Yes, Joel, that's just the point. And you never will, at least not about me, about us. You take me for granted. I guess that worked all right when we were out there in what you now sneeringly call your VIP mode. Not now, not here in this vacuum. Your despair, your extremes, I can't... Jesus! Sometimes I even wonder if you're mad. What's the matter with comfort? You can afford it. Who else cares if you live like a hermit? What's the point?"

My protests, my distress, my asking for time, for help, my explanations and arguments—they make no difference. —"That's all just words, Joel." I try to pull her to me in bed. Nothing.

Three days, packed up, gone.

· · ·

Your Cornelia, my Alison, they had a good bit in common, I'd say. Strong women, ready to move on when they perceived failure. But for me there was no Hymettós to throw me down, to bury me. No screams of rage at my perfidious wife, no children to lose. My distress turned inward. We deserved what we got, Aidan. It hurt when she walked out on me, hurt plenty. But I knew even then that it was my obtuseness, my fear, my failure to express, the unspoken demands I made on her that bore a large part of the blame.

. . .

I'm soon back on this Tyrrhenian island where we, Alison and I, first lived when we moved to Italy. Our dear friends Beppe and Ede are dead. Their ancestors built this stone hut—abandoned now—in their vineyards, their fig and olive trees, always ready to flee to their fortress of a village if pirates were sighted, the village church bell sounding its frantic warning.

Sitting on the whitewashed vaulted roof, hanging over the crimson sea, wrinkled in the evening breeze, the sun a ripe persimmon setting behind Monte Cristo. Crackers, cheese, Giuseppe's wine—the fiasco Ottavio had given me when he met me at the ferry landing. My return to visit their graves, to be with old friends, to sort things out, to deal calmly with Alison's j'accuse.

And just to play old tunes on my cranky harmonica. Timeworn tunes, modest renditions, amusing if anyone were listening. Shall I ever find my Uncle-Charlie song again? I wander in the notes, try out a few sharps and flats, searching for it. A bar or two, a hint? But still, no, it stays lost. And will there be a song for me one day when the gene has found me out?

Dawn, the dark sky turning green behind their hilltop village on Monte Pagano far above. A drink from Beppe's trickle of a spring, cupped hands, a splash on my stubbly face. A fig, a bunch of yellow grapes. Now the long climb in the new sunshine.

A donkey trail I know, a twisting path worn knee-deep in the rock and the dust by the clamberings of centuries. The sweet smell of donkey dung drying in the sun. The resinous olive and rosemary smoke from the last of the fig ovens, the domes of the many abandoned ones merely white dots in the yellowing leaves of the vines, the pale pink granite of the terracing walls that stretch out to the far end of the island. Blue rosemary blossoms, yellow dragonhead flowers of the broom, a nightingale jug-jugs from a copse of dwarfed umbrella pines, the squawk and thumping of a pheasant, a cuckoo clucking in a medlar tree. Frightened lizards, a black snake twists away.

Yes, I'm back.

I ask Ede's brother, Ottavio the island bus driver, for the key to the cemetery. He chuckles. —"Quelli che sono dentro vogliono star fuori, e quelli che sono fuori non vogliono star dentro." Those inside want out, those outside don't want in. His hands lift, palms out, mouth down, eyebrows up, a wry that's-it gesture. No lock.

Two headstones side by side, names and dates, the loving children, the oval photos. Ede, huge—always ready with her sarcastic loving quips, her enormous pots of spaghetti and stews. Giuseppe, hacked out in granite—sledge-hammering ledges into dust he'd mix with humus to make more earth for his vineyards. In the photo his hair is still that unmanageable shock. He's holding his guitar, there's a line of music cut into the stone, one of the dreadful songs of his he'd sing to us.

I did love those two.

I wander outside the massive walls—portcullis and all. Livia, picking snails off her lettuce, readying chard and artichokes for the winter, cutting off clumps of little tomatoes to hang from the rafters with special bunches of grapes—they'd sometimes last through the winter—straightening from time to time to ease her back, pulling caper berries off the vines clinging to the crevices in the outer walls. Kerchief, woolen shawl and stockings in the autumn sun—the chill of old age.

Is all this less valid than an Embassy costume ball in Bangkok? Will you some day understand, Alison, wherever you may be? Yet I asked too much, I know. You were a comforting presence, Alison. True, I was inattentive, I know that, and, yes, I did swing between extremes and expected you to follow along. The stance that I chose in our last years together—the lone protest, the frugality in the face of consumerism. Alison, was I a monk praying in his cell to speed all worthy souls through purgatory, was I seeking a butterfly effect, one lone prayer, one tiny act to vibrate throughout the world?

It is time now to head down for the evening ferry. The sun has been drawing up great clouds, arranged along the eastern horizon, mounds of bleaching wool on dark columns. The villagers watch these storms carefully, instinctively. They can sweep down fast, break on their figs or grapes or chick-peas spread out on the ledges to dry.

Shadows fade into gloom, the olives turn silver and the sea is swept dark purple. Heavy drops slap steaming on the rocks, set random twigs of the rosemary jumping, make dust-plumed craters in the earth. They'll be out tonight, the torchlight hunt in the rocks and weeds for their luscious snails—cooked in oil and garlic, plucked out with a barbed sliver of cane, popped in the mouth.

I hurry on down another donkey path. Silvers, grays, blacks—many of the vines have been abandoned on this side of the island, dying, crippled elbows in the mounting wind. Far below, a group of tourists, here for the last bit of autumn sun, hurry through the searchlight beam of the ferry, the steady rain.

## 13

*AIDAN*

The swineherd found me, carried me in a wheelbarrow to a stinking hospital. My recovery, digging out from my darkness, was brutal and slow, with many petits mals to further confound the one doctor the hospital could produce.

When I at last could manage it, I wrote to you in Tuscany. I said I needed medical attention, that I'd heard of a Harley Street clinic where they specialized in epilepsy. I gave you an address in London—Marta, a friend—where I'd be staying. You wired me cash anonymously but I knew it was you. I spent it on a Shetland jacket lined in red silk—Jermyn Street, no less.

No, not cash, dear fool, and begging's not my style. It's quite something else I have wanted so long.

The doctors said my brain had sprung a leak, short-circuited itself, mildly fried, other colorful metaphors. Nothing new there. Lots of *there-there*s, a few discreet and clearly insincere *it-could-be-worse*s. More pills. And one of the experts speculated about blood disorders too, blood sugar, daily nibblings to keep things balanced—balance, was that what I'd want?

I tried a Jungian wise man—penetrating, uneasy thoughts. And also ballet lessons, a kind of afterthought. They said I was extraordinarily good, could have been a primo, well, at least the chorus, if I'd not waited till I was forty-five.

You did write, though, saying you'd be in London soon to help someone through a messy divorce. Was that mere excuse? Did you really come to rescue me, could I hope, dare I? Or were you completely unaware?

Your first day there, I take you to watch me at my ballet routine. There are only three or four of us men and our gorgeous teacher, all of us in the regulation tights. I'm sure I'm by far the best student, and the Adonis of the lot. Or so it seems in the mirrors. Mirrors, barres, the somnolent pianist, the sweat, the skinny girls waiting their turn in the background, the whole bit.

There, did you like it? You smile across the room, thumbs up. I shower, emerge as I slip into my splendid jacket. You bought it for me, Joel, yes—an odd number of pounds and pence arrived, but it would have been an exact three hundred dollars. Who else but you? You're offended, an extravagance when you thought your generosity was saving me from the poorhouse?

Back to Chelsea, Marta's basement guest quarters.

—"Only one bed, boys, emperor size though, hope it will do you two. Stocked fridge—milk and butter—electric kettle. Stay as long as you like. Bridey comes in to Hoover once a week. I'll knock you up for morning tea, send down fresh rolls. Marmalade and jams on the shelf over the sink."

Early traffic rumbles on the cobbles, ceiling shadows

passing by, household stirrings far above. You curl peacefully into sleep, I lie beside you, my arms that would embrace you if only you'd ask. But then the warning, a split second, no escape, my world is finished yet again.

Climbing painfully from deep chasms—I am lost, where are you? All is backward, need you have changed things about? Yet you still are sleeping. My compass, it's lost its bearing, magnetic forces all askew.

. . .

That night, so many nights, so many despairing nights. Those nights together in the Píndos. That was years before our London encounter. My memory does slide about. A digression, but indulge me.

The first night—we'd rattled off from Athens in a bus, free of Cornelia's venom—we're in a flophouse on the outskirts of Tríkala. The fleas and a horrible smell, both of us restless throughout the night. The next morning we find a pile of filthy socks under your bed. The loo is unspeakable. We escape, here, to the mountains before dawn, hitchhiking to a farmhouse at the end of the dwindling road.

Then today, hours, up through beech forests and pastures, springs trickling into stone basins, an aluminium mug for the passerby. A tiny shrine to the Panaghía, on the shelf by her feet is a glass jar of green olive oil, a thistle-head wick floating in it.

Mountains close in on us, the track leads into a defile between rock walls, opens into a small hanging valley—

pastureland, a plot roughly ploughed, a thread of a stream through a walled-in orchard and garden of vegetables and flowers and herbs. One side of the valley ends against the mountain's slope, the other is edged by a man-made wall, beyond it a void. At the far corner, backed against a cliff, is a monastery—gray stone, whitewash gone, a fortification, no windows on this side. I bang with the knocker on the heavy, weathered door.

The door creaks open, a monk signs us with the cross, silently shows us in, leads us to the row of cells. There's one for each of us. A pallet bed, a pillow of straw, a Royal Army blanket, regulation gray, Property of His Majesty's Government. Dim light from a window slit looking over the gorge, a waterfall blood-red in the setting sun. He shows us the toilet, an overhang in the outer wall, a seat, a hole to drop your bowels into the void. We wash under a trickle channeled from the stream into a stone basin. They have already eaten, but he brings us bowls of soup ladled over bits of black bread.

An ancient monk sounds the bell hanging from a scaffold near the entrance to the church. We are invited to attend their vespers. Five monks shuffle silently to the choir screen hiding the altar, their Byzantine chanting begins—resonant bass voices float in the smoke of lavender and rosemary incense.

We're awakened by frequent prayers through the night, by the chanting of matins at cock's crow. Still dark, we're brought, each to his cell, a hot bowl of coffee and goat's milk. We leave a coin, receive their blessings, we're on our way.

Up through beech forests again, to stands of fir, to summer pastures. We cross a ridge, the track winds steeply down to the gorge of the savage Ahelóös, the home of the river gods. It is crossed by a hanging bridge just wide enough for a laden donkey—for their hay, firewood, sacks of grain, carcasses, the bodies of royalist and communist soldiers. Swaying with each step, you cling to the railing, you never look down, and once across you collapse.

You're acrophobic! I'm sorry, my dear Joel, I didn't know. But here, just at the end of the bridge where it doesn't sway or bounce, Poohsticks, we must. Twigs of rosemary, ready? With the bridge so narrow, the current fast, let's make it down to that rock. Now! You win—I hug you, swing you in a dance.

By sundown we find a tiny chapel just at tree line, an erimoklíssi. It's roof is half gone, but there is a door still, closed, so goat droppings are not a problem. It's just big enough for the two of us and the spiders and the lizards. Our supper is a can of sardines, bread, cheese, your canteen of wine. As the sky turns pale green behind the mountains, the stars come out one by one. Sleeping bags, side by side, exhausted, in the holy dust. You sleep. Through my tears I count the stars as they appear.

On we climb, a long day, high pastures, down into forests again. Sheep and goats, a lone herder with his dog. He beckons us over to a stone hut, a thread of smoke rises through a blackened hole in the slate roof. He hands us bowls of hot milk, bits of cheese. By twilight we get to a village, the only village since we were dropped off at the end of the road. It sits under the final crest of the range. Donkeys, mules, ponies, women, sometimes even goats, sheep, dogs are the burden carriers—no wheeled vehicle has ever been here.

Children are still playing in the half dark round the village plane tree, a rhythmic chanting game. The kapheneíon is crowded—a roaring petrol pressure lamp, a football game on the transistor, backgammon, one shaky table vacated for us despite my protests. The men are all in browns and blacks. The only woman is pouring wine and oúzo behind a sort of bar. Goatswool capes steam off the afternoon rain squall. I must work my way through their cautious curiosity and suspicions if we are to eat and sleep. Slowly, hunger mounting, hesitant to interrupt the process with interpretations for you, I succeed. First, a small plate of dried chickpeas, two oúzos and water appear, then eggs, potatoes, wine, a sort of salami. Then candied fruit in syrup, thimbles of coffee. With a few tunes on my floghéra, politics are avoided. They show us to the empty schoolroom for the night. You beside me, sleeping soundly on the dirt floor through the night.

We are up before dawn, the kapheneíon is already busy—coffee, the usual rusks to soak in bowls of milk. We buy bread, more sardines and cheese, candy suckers. You fill your canteen with their black wine.

Over the top today, Joel, a long day for sure, to the first village on the western side. Climbing on, through heather and bracken, pastures sprinkled with tiny flowers, marmots whistling at us, ravens in noisy flocks, an eagle wheeling over a snowfield. On to the ridge just below the highest peak.

You need a rest? Here, Joel, some of these suckers, or more if you're hungry. I won't be long, but I have a need to scale that peak. No, I see a route, no need for rope work.

An hour later I'm back.

Are you ready, Joel? No, I'm quite rested enough. Just beyond the ridge it's all downhill. First, there's a bit of rock work I could see from above. I'll show you how to do it, talk you down as I did so often with Yvette.

You look grim with terror.

A mass of black cloud is moving fast towards us from the west, could be dangerous in rain or sleet or snow. But it holds off until we get to the talus. Then rain and sleet, torrents, freezing quickly on the rocks above. We're soaked through in seconds. No shelter, no friendly cave, nothing for it but to race, slither, down the talus, lunging, throwing ourselves down the mountainside to get warm. We glissade a snowfield in a thick cloud, praying its ending is not a cliff. Down to pastureland again, we find a faint trail through the gloom. Goat bells clank in the fog, the goatherd crouches nearby under his conical wool cape, his crook beside him stuck in the mushy sod. He greets us, casually of course, waves us on our way. —"No, not far."

Hours later, night is on us, we finally stumble into the village. We cause some commotion. A dignified fellow in baggy old-fashioned knee breeches—must be a village elder—takes us under his wing, no questions, no suspicions voiced, though several of the men are carrying guns. Our sorry state seems to serve as at least a temporary laissez-passer. He takes us to his home—a fire in their indoor bread oven, its stone slab door open to warm us, enormous earthen bowls of mutton soup, wine, fresh bread, and our beds of heaps of goatswool blankets.

The next day the guns are gone. We're invited into other households, attend a mass. It's a welcoming village, clinging here to the edge of a great chasm that splits the mountain. Stone houses, slate roofs, the church, two kapheneía, rivals across the square. Goats and sheep and donkeys and chickens. A fountain with a dozen jets—they splash for a week, they tell us, on newly woven goatswool materials to soften them.

We stay for three days, then a punishing fourteen-hour hike out to Ioánnina. A hotel, long hot baths, a stroll in the twilight, throngs of girls and young men eyeing each other, and the swooping clouds of starlings over the plane trees. The bats take over, squealing as they dive in the moonlight. We find a proper restaurant—fresh fish from Ighoumenítsa .

Our last supper, our last night together. My dreams, my longings for you, still unanswered. You sleep through my petits mals.

Goodbye, old friend, go with God.

. . .

Not long after our time together in London, you came to me, Joel, to my empty little home in Athens. I wrote. —"Join me, another hike, Mount Olympus this time."

The evening of your arrival I take you to a local restaurant, shabby but good retsína and spanakópita. Afterwards we go to Iáson's, a friend, a poet—not one of the Anglo-Saxon Grecophiles, the colonizers, who insist on seeing Greece as only romantic, Byronesque—though that's a misnomer, he was well aware of a dark, tormented Greece. No, Iáson is a hard-edged poet of cruel realities.

He plies us with whiskey, which only improves the English he was managing for you, but pretty well muddles the two of us. We wander home, fumble about in the kitchen for oúzo, water, a plate of salty pumpkin seeds, sprawl on your bed, pillows against the wall, our tray between us. We carefully tip our shot glasses of oúzo into our tumblers. The drops of the liqueur hitting the water, turning milky as they sank—deliciously suggestive to me. I plunge tipsily ahead.

About how gender didn't matter in the fullness of love, about the times we have slept together chastely—Innsbrück, London, our mountain hikes. I blunder on with a tangled and no doubt hilarious discourse on the ancient origins of male-to-male love. About how I'm quite repelled, though, by the loose-wristed flouncing throw-it-in-your-face ways. And something about the Zorbá way, however much I disliked Kazandjákis and his pretentious *Odíssa*. I taper off in mid paragraph.

I kiss you, just a touch of lips. You don't resist, but there is no spark. Yet I muddle on—to disaster. I stumble off to my room, angry, shamed, leaving you with the shambles. I scribble a note for you, something like,

*Among other things, our proposed hike is a victim of my misused and now abandoned love.*

Ridiculous, whiny note. Distraught, unable to face you, I escape into the night and am struck down by a grand mal. Someone came across me in the gutter, bleeding, comatose, got me to a hospital. I was there for weeks. When I did get back to my home you had left no word.

# 14

JOEL

Alison gone, dropped clean out of my life. Depressed, her parting words endlessly circling in my mind—blind, weak, failed. I keep busy for a time, a book of my protesting essays published, book-signings, another lecture tour. I return to the house in Tuscany. But I need change. The rent is high—I'd been paying for that distant view of the stones of Florence—memories were sad. It seems a sullen place now, it leaves me quite morose.

I buy a much-used, thirty-foot, sleeps-four sailboat in Viareggio. I spruce her up, christen her *Arianna*, and sail her down the coast. With some exploring, I settle on Porto Santo Stefano as a pleasant place to stay. A good harbor, electric and telephone hookup on the quay. My new home. Comfortable, everything I need. A good place to get on with my work.

It is a pleasant enough life. Work goes well. I make friends with the harbor master and his large family. A grape harvest banquet at his brother's farm on the slopes of Monte Argentario. A noisy Christmas. Their chimney-sweep pageant, the blocks of sugar disguised as chunks of coal in the children's stockings for their oh-so-bad behavior.

. . .

It's spring, time to uncurl. Santo Stefano to Rome is not far by train or bus. Four of those VIP years of mine

I had spent in Rome. A painter—abstract landscapes in acrylic, portraits for the money—Lorenzo Graziadio, and his journalist wife Anna had become close friends to Alison and me. I will visit them.

. . .

Lorenzo, Anna, I thank you, I toast you with your grappa, alla vostra salute! Dio buono! A hundred proof, no less. Your Hot Abraham grappa named for that Lincoln penny, an American penny? I see it there in that bubbling bit of glass tubing, shiny Old Abe faceup. A vital part, no doubt, of your apparatus, your ridiculous still. Whatever it is, this grappa—cosí detto, more like straight alcohol—does emancipate or at least hot up the soul. Vostra salute di nuovo!

Your home is my home? Well, I did pitch in back then. Tufa blocks, mortar, a mason's hammer—and I'm rewarded with this smashed and still numb fingertip—it got in the way. But thank you, it is good to be here. No, please, no more toasts or I'll not make it out to your vineyard, Anna. The spring pruning, spading the vegetable garden for the seeding.

I'm not to be trusted for the pruning. Digging, though, I manage. Hot work, I stretch, mop the sweat with my sleeve. Hillsides across the valley, golden with the gorse, sheep bleating, I can just make out their shepherd, his black-and-white dog. A ghost of St. Peter's dome in the city smog, maybe thirty kilometers away.

A sad landscape, battered by the lava, the earthquakes,

the floods, the axes and goats and sheep—no forests left. The legions of wars—the Hannibals and Alarics, the Caesars' hordes, the Popes and Duces and Führers, the Kesselrings and Clarks, the nibbling consuming suburbs. The whole sorry lot, encouraging entropy to hurry on.

Yet here, on Monte d'Arca, their wondrous miracle, it thrives, defies this wasted landscape, grows green and lush about us. Pines and eucalyptus, young olives, a grove of bamboo, flowers, an orchard, a well. They've hacked holes in the tufa for each tree, each flower, each vine. Composted kitchen- and garden-wastes into humus, imported the bees, fenced out the marauding hordes. Their cow, their chickens, their guardian peacock-and-hen, their doves, mewing in their newly-built cote. Glad flocks of birds have made this home. Their studios, their house, a bread oven outside the door, a tower of tufa for water tanks.

This oasis, these lives renewed—and mine.

They insist that I stay for a time. They put me in the little room in the base of the water tower. A tiny door, a barred window, a table, a chair, hooks on the wall, a shelf for books, a canvas cot, a kerosene mantle lamp, the smallest of stoves with its pipe sticking out through the wall. I bus back to *Arianna* for books, manuscripts, my Olivetti typewriter. Back the same day, I settle in.

· · ·

Through my little window, a lizard on the sill, I see Lorenzo by their grape arbor. He's fiddling with his pipe, tapping out the ashes on a pergola pole. A bear, like his mother I met in Ravenna years ago—cleaning her caked paint brushes with a hammer, truly—he too can growl like a bear, Russian-peasant-like. She was a Russian exile, his father a Ravenna judge. Broad face, hair black and short and stiff—your bear again—eyes brown that see too much and rarely smile except for children. Strong hands, long fingers for the piano or the paint brushes or typing his poems and letters.

Enough, back to my typewriter, my slowly evolving book on American misadventures in Southeast Asia—emotional stuff for me. A tentative tap on my door. It's Anna, her long dark hair tied back, always her warm smile, her quiet manner, work skirt and cotton jacket, she's drying her hands on a very faded apron.

—"Forgive the interruption, but perhaps it's time for a break? We're hoping you could join us, Lorenzo's new student and her little son, from England, for tea. I just pulled my bread from the oven. Our honey, butter I churned this morning. Do come."

Yes.

. . .

—"Casilda, yes, that's right. It is a strange name, right from the Latin, dwelling place. My mother found it. She was tired of the usual names in our families."

Do you have a nickname, Casilda? I always ask that, perhaps because no one's had much luck with Joel. Cas? No, that's not great. May I call you Silda? Good.

And who is this? That lovely lady with the curly hair,

is she your mummy? Your name? Andréas, a nice name, a manly name, I like it.

Blond, the blue eyes, all knees and elbows, chasing a butterfly. You're five? He carefully pulls up four fingers from a fist. I walk with them to her car. She's pretty, unusual, lively, much younger, dare I find her attractive?

—"I came to Rome on an au pair job, but it didn't work out. Logistics problems with Andréas. I waitress now at that American bar-cum-restaurant—lounge, pub, whatever—on via Veneto. They like to have a Brit on the staff, maybe our poshy talk—I can really lay it on—and a four-year-old seems an asset in a Roman bar. Come try us out."

. . .

Two or three expatriates and one rather natty local, slouched at the bar, no one at all in the restaurant section. Casilda and an Irish woman who seems to be in charge. I'm greeted, introduced around. Regulars, I assume. They're pushing drinks, olives, ashtrays, desultory conversation. I dutifully join in as best I can, not much good at this sort of thing.

Half an hour passes, when, through the smoke from a dangling cigarette, I'm asked in an Irish lilt, —"Dinner, Joel? We're not set up for much, things are slow as you can see, but... Casilda, put something together for Joel. I don't need you at the bar for now."

She shows me to a table. I watch her as she busies about preparing and bringing in her special salade niçoise.

Tight curly hair, gray-green eyes with specks of gold. A chartreuse flowered shirt with baggy sleeves, blue jeans—a gorgeous bum. I'm not one for bums usually, it's breasts for me—lovely there too, this Silda. Her bum, though, sensational. She serves me, humorously, with mock deference.

Won't you sit here with me, Silda, have a bite?

Her laughter, her BBC voice. Her face lovely, expressive, ever varying, ever responding to the emotions she sees before her. A touch of olive, not the usual British peaches and cream. Her easy independence, no help from Papá. Making do, and gladly, whatever the many jobs she finds. An attractive young woman, and me the stereotype of the older man. Beware, Joel, but still, she's fun—bright, fresh air.

. . .

Now...

My book is finished, the manuscript sent off today to my eager publisher—lucky timing with the Vietnam involvement becoming clear, with disaster in sight.

Letting go—the deadline pressure, the horrors of their war. Their war—once my war, Aidan's. The bloated bodies, empty helmets, shattered rifles among the spring flowers, a piano with a shell hole through its heart, the stench of death in the cities we had crushed. Hatred, the lust to destroy, a child tearing off a butterfly's wings—is this our species?

I wander out into the bracken and gorse, down to the borro—barely a trickle—moss, Christmas roses, watercress, low willows fenced off from the sheep and the goats. Sitting in the dry grasses, I lean against a rotting fence post, watch a frog licking up bugs, a water spider dimpling a pool. Faint far notes—a Beethoven bagatelle.

I doze.

A presence, a shadow, the tapping of Lorenzo's pipe on his boot heel—he sits there, on a rock across the borro. Beret, dark olive corduroys—quizzical.

Ah! I was sleeping.

—"Did I wake you? May I join you? I come here often. Peaceful, little else is.

"Look there, Joel, down the valley, the distant cranes hoisting up their high-rises. Beyond, St. Peter dying in the smog. Man's tenure on this Earth is drawing to a close, it should be, we are managing to destroy all that was bequeathed to us.

"I must get back. A new student will be waiting."

You turn, climb slowly, shoulders bent, up through the gorse and rockrose toward your home. My spider walks across his puddle, climbs up on a rock, dries his feet carefully, jumps, and disappears.

. . .

I saw Silda several times in the next three weeks. I would hop the local train to Rome, catch her in her off hours. Walks, the three of us, picnics, once to the Ostia beaches, bundled in the wintry winds. She invited me to her tiny walk-up flat in Trastevere, she'd prepared a kind of smorgasbord, many goodies.

It was a delight to be with her.

At Monte d'Arca, Lorenzo's sense of doom, of humanity's self-destruction, seemed only to soften when he turned his passions to his painting, his etching, a Chopin nocturne. Anna's gentle smile, her quiet wisdom, had no effect. That gloomy climate—though brilliantly argued, backed with keen intelligence and knowledge, it was oppressive. It revealed for me the negativity that I came to realize was the foundation of my own life—my dissents and rebellions.

This gloom lifted in the presence of this joyful woman, in the wondrous energy and curiosity of Andréas. They simply would have none of it, and let me know directly. Silda would challenge my judgments mercilessly. Andréas would pinch me whenever he saw my face turn gloomy. We had quickly become fond friends.

. . .

I will miss them, Silda and Andréas. They are off to England for two or three months. Silda's sister is having a baby, needs help with her household, her two toddlers, a husband who often must travel. The via Veneto bar has given her leave.

*Arianna* and I, we are sailing to Greece.

I'd been writing articles, op-eds, letters to the editors about the military coup in Greece. Not that I knew more about it than anyone combing the media, but a few did get published. Hand-wringing stuff, probably quite useless, mostly just *I-told-you-so*s. And the media had little idea of what was really going on. Censorship was obviously very tight and...I did have one piece of what you might call inside information. The American ambassador had been one of my bosses from the VIP days—an unprincipled egomaniac who would have joined those colonels' Junta if he could. Another obstacle to truth. So, maybe... Aidan no doubt was somewhere in the thick of it, a part of the underground resistance. Perhaps he has reportage I could smuggle out. Or maybe he just needs a friend.

# 15

A day of dreams. Sometimes half awake, stirring, to munch a bit of orange, to settle back into those dreams. But now I am here. The shadows reach out over that outstretched finger of rock. The figure in flowing white, the dark figure on the headland's edge, they disappear in the dusk. The calm sea fills with evening stars.

. . .

Back to the village, to the kapheneíon, to chew on bits of octopus grilled over embers in a rusty iron drum, to down a beer. A television on a table by the back wall flickers with a soccer match, the roar of the crowd, the frenzied voice of the announcer. A dozen or so, mostly men, are watching, silent, smoking—their side is three goals behind. A bouzouki tries out some movie music, switches to an island dance. A clarinet joins in, sliding through the notes, the island way, almost a woman's wailing. A half-crippled old fellow stumbles into a few dance steps, waves the usual handkerchief, but no one joins.

. . .

The game is over, the kapheneíon slowly empties, I'm left almost alone. The black and the white, those figures by the sea, were they gone, were they gone forever? Fantasies, were they ever there?

The village is dark, the air oppressive. I stumble up the alley to my bed. A seagull whimpers in the dark.

### AIDAN

From London I came back to Athens, my silk-lined jacket of no comfort to my disintegrating brain, my friendship with you, Joel, is it destroyed by drops of oúzo in a glass?

Black times they are.

The jackboots march again in Constitution Square, the Parthenon looking down on it all with yet another aesthetic shrug. And this time the boots are made in Greece. Colonel Papadópoulous and his crowd of tyrants, they've pulled off a coup d'état. The dissident rubble is swept up clean, or so they seemed to think, sent off to torture chambers, to certain death. Their tanks roll on the feeble protesters, in so-called democracy's putative place of birth.

But bear with me, Joel, I must back up a bit.

• • •

My Érsi, my sweet daughter. She'll be here soon, with me in my decaying little home, 69 painted crudely on the lintel, an apt and useful street number for the likes of me. She's always prompt—for tea, to read some poetry with her reclusive babá, to chat. She rooms with university friends now. Enough of the fusty austerity which had become my way. Ten years she'd been with me, my sunshine.

• • •

When I came to Washington for my joust with the CIA, a letter from Elefteria was waiting for me, forwarded to your home, Joel. Elefteria was my only contact with Artémisos, and we kept it secret.

Dímitra had given birth to a beautiful girl. The Artemisiótes honor the moon-touched ones, but they'd had to take the baby from her mother. Dímitra was too far lost in her own private world, and her parents—dishonored, shamed—had disappeared. The child was given over to Lucás and Theodóra.

It was Lucás who named her Persephóni, Érsi for short. Lucás with his passion for mythology—he loved to teach it in his little school. Granddaughter of Zeus and Demeter, here on Artémisos, in the shadow of Zeus's Naxos, of course, and he pictured her, Persephóni with the Cock, the herald of new life, renewal. And yes, that unerringly makes me a son of Zeus, no less.

Years later, I sat at my typewriter, the postman tapped at my dusty window, waved an envelope at me. Lucás and Theodóra had died. Eleftería, my only confidante, her scrawly handwriting did not say when. They'd gone fishing, they never returned, their boat found floating bottom up two days later. The child was taken by an orphanage in Athens. She gave the address.

I found Érsi that same morning. It was no trouble to convince them that I was her father, to take her from them—charity only stretched so far.

Ten years, my only joy, my delight. About her mother, I told her only that she was beautiful, a mountain goddess, that she had died in my arms. I could not bear to say her name. And from the moment she came to me I was her dear babá.

She has begun university studies now—art history, painting, restoration. Our visits are our weekly tea times.

## Érsi

Babá mou! No no, wait, quiet, listen to me! I have such lovely news! Giórgios. He's a lecturer at the university. We are engaged. Quiet, black eyes that never waver, not the usual mustache, a worried forehead—with good reason—intense. You'll love him, I know you will.

A Marxist, babá moú, like all of us, or really communist like you. You'll be the best of friends, you'll chatter on forever about poetry—Seféris, your tragic-predicament-of-man grandiosities. I know you two. He and Seféris, they're namesakes. Giórgios likes that, he even met him once. He has a lovely smile, just like yours—now!

. . .

There, a hug, kisses, both cheeks, for my Babá. My newest news, no, it just can't wait. Here, you must be sitting too. Ready? So. Giórgios, he and I, we are married! Last night, well, the civil one. The church—the crowns of flowers, the circling, the mumbled ancient Greek—we'll do all that when things settle a bit, all this commotion between Papandréou and the King and the Army. Will you give me away then? Oh do, dear Babá, do!.

And we're off on a wedding trip next week, Giórgios is free for a bit, to an island he knows. He fished with a crew there three summers. Out beyond Naxos, Artémisos it's called. Perhaps you know it. You never spoke of your island past, of where you lived, of my mother. Only that she died when I was tiny, that to say more, to return to that past, it would weigh too heavily on your heart.

. . .

And here we are back, our mínas tou mélitos, our month of honey, though it was barely two weeks. Yes, Giórgios is coming too, he just stopped to buy a paper. Are those tears, your hard old heart?

The Army, we're worried, everybody is at the university, something's going on. Their papers screaming, Commie Papandréou out! And our wavering fascist Glücksburg king threatening an election.

Literary talk, Seféris, that will clearly have to wait.

Babá mou, I must tell you. One day on Artémisos my Giórgios was off fishing with the men on the grigrí. I went for a walk on a beach at the far end of the island. I met a wild and wonderful woman, Dímitra. Very special, fey and blessed. After that we often picnicked together, explored caves in the cliffs on the edge of the sea. Pink caves with floors of coral sand, and we'd wade into them, and once we scared an enormous octopus who'd been sucking on a clam. And we even swam together once, naked in the winter sun. She called me her daughter, kóri mou. I was so touched.

. . .

Is this me, a little Érsi in her dusty home, her babás helping with her aorist passive verb forms? That ugly sound, is it the knife grinder propped on his bicycle outside our door, sharpening an ax?

Is it?

No, no. Here, me, Athens…

My city, my people, where are you, why do you hide? Empty streets, the terror of silence, sucked away, hollowed by a distant grinding sound. A gathering sound, the street hears it now and trembles. I, Persephóni—Érsi—with life stirring and protesting in my belly, my heart stops, I can no longer breathe. Around the corner they come, one, two of their tanks crawling down the line of sickly palm trees, down this ugly avenue, gun turrets slowly turning. Evil insects crawling on this corpse, searching with their antennae for shreds of rotting meat. Sherman tanks, made in the U S of A.

They ignore me, alone with my bag of books and paints and paraphernalia. I was stupid to stay at the library so long, knowing by now their routine of early-evening terror. Forgive me, my baby, Mélantha—your name, have you learned it yet? We'll sit here for a minute with the pigeons, on this battered bench, rest our hearts. It's not curfew, just an everyday reminder in case we had not heard the screams of the tortured. Made in the U S of A.

Mélantha mou, will you ever know the joy of dancing with your father, of our picnics high on the shoulders of Hymettós, will you ever dream to the song of the floghéra, as I did when we'd rest for a time in the shade of a juniper, when dear Babá would dig his reed pipe out of his rucksack, play an island song? Has tyranny left any room for joy?

A gritty yellow cloud gusts up the avenue. Tatters of their posters—we still dare to rip them off our walls— dance gaily, unconcerned. As the growling of their tanks dies, a ragged old fellow appears from nowhere, sits on the next bench. He pulls a floghéra from his pocket. With trembling hands he plays a lively tune.

Through the grit and the stink of their engines, the Parthenon, golden in the dying day, sits smugly on its cliff top above our tawdry, evil city, complacent, immune to treachery and persecution—nothing new. People, a few, appear in their doorways, look cautiously about, hurry off. It's time for us too, Mélantha and me, for our bit of shopping and home, to get there before Giórgios, get supper started.

We keep to the side streets where we can—they seem safer. Some shops are opening in hopes of evening trade. Check the windows, Érsi mou, for reflections, for the furtive unemployables now recruited as informers. That scraggly derelict face floating in the glass above the piles of fake antiquities. He's out of place in this supposedly classy district. Is he the one who was waiting at the gates of the university as I left, who seemed to start out after me? There is always a group of them ready to turn in a student who may have been, or more likely was not, heard saying something subversive like, What a shitty day! And there are the phony students in the hallways, heedless of the bells and the rush from class to class, listening, note-books in hand. Am I perhaps a special target, the wife of the notorious leftist poet? And every day I worry, it gnaws on my heart, will he be all right, will he say nothing, write nothing, do nothing, will I lie in his arms tonight?

Hurry on, and perhaps he's already home. Something special, what shall it be, garídhes in a tomato and féta sauce, or a hirinó steak? First the baker's, now we're out of the city center, here where Athens's myriad of neighborhoods are scattered, villages, each from its own part of Greece and Smyrna. No plate glass here. We know what's in each shop, no need to be told, and ominous reflections by now are quite unlikely.

Leonídas gives me our usual loaf. Your hand on my belly? Yes, of course, and may it bring us all luck. A block or two farther, friendly villagers smile, make blessing signs at my baby girl. I'm proud of my leaning-back pregnant stride. Stamáti's fish are gleaming in their beds of ice. He wraps my garídhes in newspaper, Papadópoulous on the front page. Now to get a bottle of Giórgios's favorite wine—and tobacco for his pipe.

On to our tiny home behind its flaking blue door—I whitewashed the threshold just yesterday. I hang my coat on the rack, peek into Giórgios's studio, no, not here yet, just books and his monstrous typewriter and his slippers on the goatskin rug. The bedroom is empty, our kitchen too—it smells of charcoal and thyme and cheese and bread—but it's still quite early. I put the féta into the evaporation cooler on the windowsill, fan life into the charcoal burner, peel the garídhes, onions to sauté in olive oil. Salad, bread, and cheese. Candle on the table, his pipe, tobacco, slippers, there, all's ready. Don't be too late, aghápi mou, we want you here, and yes, we're hungry too.

I step out to our back porch, to our tiny patio—just room there for one fig tree, the bougainvillea, and the privy. Please, Giórgios, please come soon. Your office must be closed by now, it's not a long walk, it's dark. I know, there's no curfew tonight, but, but…. Oh please come soon, no, now, my dearest.

But…now…

No, no, no!

I know you never will, never never come. Never will I lie in your arms, never will our Mélantha dance with her babáka. Oh God! such a dreadful word, that never. A knock on the door? He wouldn't knock, he'd use his key, call out cheerily. Have *they* come? I rush through the kitchen to the study. No car, though, nothing to be seen through my secret crack in the shutter.

Babáka mou, it is you. Oh, I know by my heart, I know by your face, I know by your jacket shoulder, sprinkled with bits of heather, with our tears. I know, and my world turns thin and bitter cold, the only warmth left me lies quiet in my womb, listening.

You lead me to my kitchen, seat me on a stool, mumble about how I must eat. You fan at the charcoal, put the prawns to simmer with the onions. I can only stare. I hear a muddle of your words, a story, nothing to do with me.

### AIDAN

Two unmarked cars and a van waiting for him outside his office...dark by then so no one could identify them... many eyes, always watching...to ESÁ, their house of horror...he's gone, best not to hope...here, a handkerchief... you must eat first...pack a few things, go, I'll help you, danger, they'll be after you soon, a rucksack, a duffel, less suspicious...one of ours is on the corner, reading a newspaper by the streetlight...another by the gate in the alley stretched out, drunk...two in the kapheneíon, ready to lurch out, stumble, if there's any sign of danger, warn the taxi...taxi in the alley, you in the boot, Rafína...unlikely direction, no major shipping or border or airport...

Joel Brewster—have I spoken of him?...a friend from the past...he's come from Italy in his sailboat...wants to help the Resistance...he'll take you to Italy...some of my writings too, smuggle to the European press...no no, I'm needed here...I shall never leave Greece again...here, the handkerchief, and you must eat, my dear.

### ÉRSI

Hold me, hold me tight again, my Babá. Yes, for Mélantha, I know, I know.

An airless taxi boot, it stinks of dog shit and oil and rubber. We creep into the night. Hours and hours, and finally we arrive. In this blackest of nights, stumbling, we feel our way through the crates and nets of Rafína's harbor, my babás and the driver on each side to hold me.

They lift me on board this *Arianna*, my babákas's hand to my cheek, to my tears.

A whispered, —"I'm Joel, Érsi, come below." I've heard very little English since school. He puts a finger to my lips. No light, he leads me down what seems to be a ladder, no sound but the murmur of ripples on her hull, forward to a tiny compartment, the fo'c'sle he calls it, to my bunk. —"Stay here, quiet, sleep."

I hear the careful casting off, feel their push to set us free, the motion as the sails—they must have been already hoisted—catch a lightest breeze. No motor, only a slight heeling, a rolling as we pass the breakwater, I guess, head into the Gulf of Petalíon. I curl tight under this pile of blankets that only presses deeper the trembling cold of my soul. I cannot sleep, I must not sleep, sleep would be forever.

I slept. Mélantha wakes me with her morning nudge. I am warm, the sun slides gently to and fro through a little window in what looks like a trapdoor over my bunk. Joel's posted instructions help me through the mysteries of the toilet. I start up steep steps to go on deck. Through the companionway I see him in the cockpit, hand on the tiller. He stops me, tosses a sailor's cap to me.

—"Wait! Good morning, my dear, but you must stay below until we're out of Greek waters, two days I reckon. If you have to come on deck, an emergency, tuck your hair into the cap, put on that oilskin, that yellow jacket hanging beside you. A mug of tea?"

Disguised as his potbellied buddy, just in case, that's me.

He goes on about this and that—is he just distracting me, this pleasant American? The sails, the course...light wind, drift without the motor or any lights for a time, Soúnion not before noon...Corinth Canal late to sneak through in the dark...hide you in a sail bag in case they board us for an inspection.

He hooks some lines onto the tiller, comes below to put the kettle on. He points out Cape Soúnion's temple through the porthole. Somehow I'm holding a mug of tea now, externals slide by me, meaningless, despair. A voice drones on, unaware.

—"Aidan—Aléko, your father—he and Giórgios and I, we planned all this days ago, just in case... *Arianna* ready to smuggle you out, others too if needed...Giórgios would never go himself...We're getting you to Italy, we could have gone around the Pelopónnisos, but the sooner we get out of Greek waters the better. They may start nosing around, looking for you, though Aidan told me that he had arranged for a friend to go daily to your house with a doctor's kit, let himself in as if you were there but ill, and stop by at your kapheneíon, offhandedly let it be known that you have a bit of flu, contagious, best not to visit. And if they do come, they'll see the note that your father tacked up while you poked at the prawns, a note from you to Giórgios, typed on his typewriter, saying you hoped his trip went well, that you had an urgent message from Naxos, from the papás who had gone there to telephone that your friend Dímitra was very ill and calling for you. That you had the flu, had waited some time—we kept that vague—for him, but then, with the fever gone, decided to catch the weekly ferry to Naxos, find a fisherman to take you on to Artémisos. With no police there, no phone, it would give us an extra two days, maybe three, for them to get out there and back with the truth."

Joel tells me of our progress.

We swing to the west, rounding the cape, stay well clear of Saronicós, work our way toward the head of the gulf, the mouth of the canal. We only just make out the shoreline far ahead as the sun sets off our bow. He starts the motor, lowers the sails, turns on the red and green lights, hooks up something that seems to keep us going straight automatically. He comes below to have me try out the sail-bag routine—forward of my bunk with the other sail bags.

It is a starry middle of the night when we approach the canal entrance. I burrow into my bag, Joel shoves us forward. —"I'll let you know, Érsi, how things are going." I hear the motor killed, voices calling from shore, and Joel had told me that there was some system of lights to instruct you how to proceed. I hear Joel's clumsy, —"Endáxi, okay." Then his quiet, —"Érsi, can you hear me? They want me to wait till a freighter comes through the other way, don't worry, all seems normal."

After maybe half an hour I begin to hear, no, more like feel, the heavy throb of the freighter's prop. A whistle blast, Joel's answering toot, our motor starts up. The music of the ripples on our bow, only inches from my head, the gentle heave and roll as I imagine we pass through the freighter's wake. And soon Joel calls down, —"Safe now, Érsi, no lights below, mind, but you can move around, peek out. This canal, it's astounding."

We're squeezed by vertical walls—one hundred, one fifty meters?—spectacular, reaching upward to a narrow strip of stars. Our lights, on the left blood-red on the limestone, the right a gangrenous green. A slice into the flesh of the earth. And those bridges against the starlit sky, are they stitches of a wound that doesn't heal? Peloponnisos set adrift?

Through the canal now, well out into the Gulf of Corinth. Still careful not to be seen, I move from porthole to porthole. The snow tip of Mount Parnassós, far ahead off to the right, it bleeds in the dawn. We come up on a fishing boat as they turn off the twin acetylene lights, a night's work done of luring shrimp up from the depths. I find Joel's food supplies and make toast on the rack over the alcohol burner, poach three eggs, brew black coffee, hand it up to him. He's slouched over, catnapping.

I struggle to pay attention to my breakfast, blurred by tears. There is no hope, no one escapes, no one survives their interrogations, their horrors, their disposals. We know, word gets to us by a note thrown through a barred window, a boasting guard, the screams that die into silence, our spies.

A light wind from behind us takes the glaze off the sea, a sea that had been ládhi, as the Artemisiótes would say, like oil. Joel hauls up the sails. They barely fill. Behind, to the southeast the sky has lost its brilliant blue to a faintest touch of yellow. Joel studies the sky, hooks up that self-steering thing, and ducks below. He taps the barometer, puts on earphones.

—"It's the English weather forecast, Érsi, an African scirocco making up somewhere near Crete, unusual for this time of year, we'll be sailing with it, keep ahead of it for perhaps a day. It should catch us beyond Ithaca. This forerunner breeze, it will pick up a bit later today, you'll see."

By nightfall we're off Pátras. The wind has increased, Joel kills the motor. We sail well before the southeasterly, the sea choppy but short, as we're still protected by the mountains of Akhaía. We've managed some canned salmon, wedges of tomatoes, bread. Joel pulls on rain gear, climbs on deck, harnesses himself with an umbilical cord, which he hooks to lines rigged along the deck. He fiddles with something he's dangling over the side, he says it will measure our distance. He switches on our red and green lights... —"No, better leave them off." And the light for the compass is dim.

On into the night, on toward Ithaca. The seas are longer now that we're not close under the land, the wind is moderate, quite warm, and we're sailing almost with it. —"It should be safe now, Érsi, to come on deck."

Sitting here on the lower side, I watch the bow wave, surging as we ride down a following wave, splashing a foam of bubbles, a dazzle of phosphorescence, a sizzling as the foam slips by.

By midnight we can see a scattering of lights on Cephalonia off to the left, the black bulk of mountainous Ithaca, no lights to be seen, ahead to the right. We're headed for the Ithaca Channel between the two islands. The harbor lights of Argostóli port blink faintly. Between them the brighter lights of a boat appear.

—"Too fast for a fishing boat, Érsi, and they're headed right at us. You know that when you can see both their red and green lights at the same time." Their searchlight flashes at us, trouble. It stops for a time, green light only, rolling, then begins to follow us slowly. Trouble, official trouble. Waiting to see if we're leaving Greek waters?

I climb again into my bag. My trouble becomes yours, Joel—skatá! shit! shit! He shoves me behind some other gear. Curled tight around my Mélantha, an embryo within an embryo, we tremble in this canvas womb. I hear the throb of their engines, my ear pressed against the hull. The flash of their searchlight, dim through the canvas. A megaphone, good English, they must have seen our American ensign.

—"Heave to, Captain, drop your sails, we board you."

Ach, Théë mou! And these are *my* people? I hear Joel clambering about, the sails rattle down, the thump and lurch of their patrol boat, the heeling as one, two, I think, board. They've come below, a cabin light through the canvas.

—"You are headed out of Greek waters, Captain, middle of a stormy night. I see you don't deny it. No running lights, no exit papers? We must search you." English, a pleasant voice, heavy accent. Then in Greek, —"Seaman Dimítri, I'll do the cabin, you search topsides, start in the stern, the cockpit, lockers, lazarette."

A careful thorough search, I can tell. He is working his way forward. From the galley, now the main cabin. The clatter of floorboards—that would be a favorite, I suppose. Joel had told me that he had hidden Aléko's writings about the Junta there, but in a waterproof envelope taped up to the bottom side of a fixed floorboard. No words, nothing, thank the gods. But me? He's poking around among the sail bags now. Christós kaí Panaghía! Melantháki mou, I do love you so. He drags out one bag. Tugging mine, too solid, too heavy.

I hear him call up to the seaman, —"Nothing there, Dimítri? Go back on board to mind the cutter. I'll be there soon."

Then, —"What do we have here, Captain? Out of there, Despinís mou, stand up. Oh, I see, you're with child, right? Naí, you said? You are Greek, then, yes, Kiría? No papers, of course. You are Persephóni Koutsoyánnou, yes? We, they, are looking for you, wife of Giórgios.

—"Captain, let me see the ship's papers, whatever you have. Yes, you seem to have entered correctly. Now. I shall exit you. Here, fill this in. Sign here, I do too. No, no, no comments, no questions. Keep on your way. This sorókos storm will be good cover for you, out of Greek waters by sunup. Rough, very rough, as the seas build up away from land. So, be careful, Captain. And put your lights on now, you're cleared.

"Speak to no one of this. The usual formalities, nothing more. Take care, good care, of Kiría Persephóni. We need—yes, we, there are many many of us—we need all our heroes, all our heroines. I shall report to our comrades that she is safe. Here, I would shake your hand, Captain. And Kiría Persephóni, I kiss your hand, and I wish you the speed of God."

Unbearably handsome in his naval uniform, close-clipped black mustache and pointed beard, the flash of his eyes in the dim light, fiercely proud, but I see in the tightness of his forehead, the burden of constant fear. He clicks his heels, bows over my quivering hand, lifts it to his lips. He straightens, tall. I rest my hands on his shoulders, on the tips of my toes I reach up to him, my belly bumps against him, I kiss him, kiss him full on the lips.

They're gone.

These too are my people.

We roll in the cradling sea. I weep in your arms, dear Joel, my tears on your cheek, my sobs, I can't help it. Oúzo? He left it here for us, this wee bottle? Just a thimbleful—Mélantha, you know. To my Captain, to my people. Yiá sás!

You touch away my tears, gently, with your thumbs.
—"Stay here below, Érsi, you two need sleep. I'm fine
alone on deck. Straightforward now, up the channel, north,
and soon we're out into the Ionian Sea, well out of Greek
waters. The storm will be heavy, it seems. Already picking up. Force ten before it's over. Rock you to sleep, my
dear. Never fear."

He's gone, closed the hatch for the wind that would be
driving into the cabin when we turn before it. I already feel
the grit of the Sahara in my teeth. There's banging on deck,
the wild roar of a storm sail. No bigger than a handkerchief,
he said. It catches the wind, we heel sharply, the rolling
becomes a twisting surging motion. We're on our way.

The sea sings of release, of grief. Beneath the roar of
the wind there is a gentle moaning that Joel has told me
is the wind blowing across a drain hole in the sail's hollow boom—*Arianna*'s Aeolian organ pipe. The waves are
mounting, longer. We seem to surf down each one for
minutes, then almost wallow out of the wind until the
next one catches us up, lifts us back into the power of
the sorókos. On my ever tossing berth, I'm best off in an
embryo position. It gives me some stability. And even in
my sleep I seem to be hanging on with one hand to this
board. Sometimes I wake enough to see Joel studying the
chart under a tiny red light, glancing at a compass built
into the table. And somehow I feel, for the first time since
that dreadful afternoon in Athens, a strange comforting
sort of peace, consoled by the boundlessness and inevi-

tability of my life, of all life. I say a prayer for Giórgios. I hold him in my heart, in my belly.

The kettle whistles me awake. The hatch is open now, there is a faint yellow lightening of the sky outlining Joel's form as he lowers himself into the cabin, careful of the heaves and rolls of our tiny ship.

—"You're awake, my dear? A mug of tea, and I'll make a bit of toast. Honey, jam? You've been mostly asleep when I've checked during the night. We're well out of Greek waters, wind's down some. Headed north now for Italy. I found a fat mackerel washed up in the scuppers this morning. I'll clean it for lunch."

The hot mug warms my fingers. I prop it in the table rack, climb half up the steps for a look and to blow the cobwebs away. A dark sea rises high over our stern, curling green, white at the crest, slapping angrily on our stern, half filling the cockpit. Lifting us, carrying us in a rush and hiss of our wake. Wild, frightening.

I turn forward, hair whipping about, gritty when I clench my teeth. The sail—I never heard him hoist it back up—mud-splashed where spray has hit it, the horizonless sky mixes with the sea close in around us. We are cradled in tumult.

By midmorning the wind is dying. Soon we're rolling, sails and ropes and things slapping, in a dirty almost-calm. With the motor on now, the exhaust stinks linger on our stern. An hour or so later there's a faint new breeze, freshening, northeasterly.

He cuts the motor, pulls in the sails. The seas are confused, new messages, and finally blue, blue with fresh cool skies. Dolphins leap about us, celebrating, playing with our bow wave, diving back and forth under our keel, turning up to wink at us, to beckon us on.

We race now, graceful, leaping through the dancing sea, the wind a force five, he says, whatever that means. There, far on the eastern horizon, are the ragged tips of the Píndos. Somewhere off our bow will be Italy.

Italy, it must be, it will be our home, Mélantha mou, until our people discard the Junta. May we learn from the Italians their warmth, their amused dismissal of things political. May we take that with us back to the ferocity and pride and intensity of our countrymen. Greece, where politics pervades the very soul, often seeming to overwhelm the humanity of our past. Have we given so much to the rest of the world over the millennia that we have little left for ourselves? Yet I yearn for that wild gaiety and vigor and generosity and wry wisdom—there is so much of your father, Mélantha, in that bitter land.

We race through the sparkling day, far from any land, the three of us. This dear man, Mélantha, and me—and brave *Arianna*. Our sweet hero, our Captain Joel, manages to prepare something hot for supper—*Arianna* ever skittish, bouncing about. We sail on into the twilight, into the night, under a sky that fades from sapphire to emerald to jet, a jet now dazzling with a million million stars. We charge the seas, slap into the crests, the spray washing away the Saharan mud. Often the tip of a wave will sneak over the side and dump into the cockpit, dousing us. Or we sense it coming, turn quickly to catch it on slickered backs.

We do watches, four hours on, four off, the inscrutable self-steerer doing the work. It's my watch now. He'd said, —"Keep an eye to the northwest for landfall, ahead, a bit to the left, a lighthouse, Érsi." I bend down often to peer under the sail. Finally I see it, a faint flashing. Land ho, Captain, Italy! Joel climbs clumsily on deck, ducks down to peer. He busies about, excited—compass bearings, speed, calculations.

There is a fading of the stars to the east, a softening of the jet black. Dawn flows toward us, jewels from the orient, amethyst to ruby to coral to lapis. He tells me more about our plans. We shall bypass the tip of Italy's heel with its lighthouse, sail on for perhaps two more days to Peschici, a fishing village on the north side of the Gargano, the spur on Italy's boot.

The lighthouse is on Santa Maria di Leuca, Joel says. Leuca, lefkós—white, of course, like the white cliffs of our Ionian island, Lefkás. Magna Grecia, the ancient Greek empire spread over the Mediterranean. On the chart I see names like Sibari, the colony of the Sybarites, and Kalimera, good morning—I remember hearing that they still speak a sort of Greek in parts of Italy's Puglia.

Bit by bit I learn of the plan they, mostly Joel, have for me and my baby. When we land, Joel will telephone his old friend, Lorenzo Graziadio, a painter, who will come from Rome by overnight train. He has papers for me just in case. He'll take me to his farmhouse outside Rome. He has arranged an apprenticeship for me in art restoration for after Mélantha is born.

Joel will mail his and Aléko's manuscripts to journalist contacts. He will stay with *Arianna*, sail back to the other side of Italy, his port near Rome, near Lorenzo's. He'll no doubt see me, us, there.

. . .

Babá moú, listen to me, this me. I know, this phoning's dangerous. Quick. Yes, I'm twenty-one, but I'm haggard, nothing short of really haggard, and my dress dangles as if I were a wire hanger. I have neither the knack nor the will to look chic like the women of Rome. And there's no way to hide my grief. Whatever beauty there might have been is now with my daughter. She's walking now, she chatters nonstop in Italian. I try never to speak Greek to her, it's safer that way. Will you ever come to see us in Rome, to see my Mélantha, leave your evil Athens? You like her name? I found it in a poem. Mélantha, my dark flower.

## 16

JOEL

We've made it, Silda, Andréas, *Arianna,* and I, here, moored to the Rock of Gibraltar. A long summer sail, Porto Santo Stefano to the farthest corner of the Mediterranean, back along the coast of Turkey, Cyprus, Rhodes, the Aegean.

. . .

This beauteous fickle sea, this womb of our western world. Fierce winds, sheltering ports, coral sands, umbrella pines, snow peaks far to the north. Anchored off a sickle of sheltering beach, a picnic, a swim. A naked dive from *Arianna* into a clear blue sea. The rush of bubbles, the rippled sand, a skate waving fins through turtle-grass, fingerlings nipping toes, the lovely form of Silda in honey dance. Ashore for a meal, a moonlight dance. An idyllic time.

A stopover in Athens, an excruciating time. When I had asked Silda to join me with Andréas, it was to be for a month or two, a romantic summer sail, ending back in Rome. My hope, though, my unformed dream, had been that they would continue on with me, on to Gibraltar. That we would sail out into the Atlantic to the Canaries, that I would sail solo across the Atlantic, that they would fly to join me, discover a new America together, our partnership never to end.

It was not an idle dream, this solo sail, this return to my country. I had told no one of it, but...

I had left my country long ago, a wasteland always on the brink—weapons, bomb shelters, so many useless things. Arrogant power, impoverished in its might and wealth. Yet it is a land of beauty, of idealism, of generosity. Can there not be hope? The last of my years in the government, and now this time in Europe, it had for me been a time of dissent, of largely ineffective censure. I had listened to Lorenzo with concern, there by the brook below Monte d'Arca, his despair. I had watched that wee spider dry his feet, leap off his rock, go on. That tiny act, that miracle of being alive, was that not the answer to despair? My time too, my time to go?

Our cruise, the three of us—could that be my leap off the rock? To be in the presence of those sunny two, to sail on westward with them, to leave despair, to seize each day, to build on hope?

Our Athens stopover, there in Piraeus harbor. It is time, I must tell her—my secret dream, my hope, my leap—will she, can she too? But I could not bring myself to ask. My heart wept that I could lose her, lose those two. My head—no, Joel, you are not ready, your loss of Alison, you are wounded still. A suicidal sail, a Quixotic quest, to ask a woman and her child to join their lives with this you? You must not.

We had moored to the yacht harbor quay in the evening. We would stay over a day, I said. I had business to attend to in Athens, I'd be back for a farewell lobster dinner on board, a lantern hanging from the boom.

I'll go to Aidan. Since that evening debacle years before, our few meetings have been stiff. Perhaps that can change, perhaps there is a wound to be healed. And perhaps he can help me through this paralysis of will.

. . .

I knock on his faded blue door. Yes, it's Joel, may I come in? It is good to see you, I need your help. He looks deep into me for a long moment, a quizzical eyebrow. He turns, —"Of course, come in, here, in back."

The kitchen smells of potato-and-onion soup. On his workbench are torn bits of kefalotíri cheese and black bread, a strip of thick leather, a copper medallion in the vise. He makes coffee in a tiny long-handled brass pot. It foams over, he tips it into our thimble cups. We sip at it, thick with sugar. Cool water in tumblers made of cut-down retsína bottles, he pours it from a wine jug wrapped in terry cloth. The jug sits on the windowsill to cool in a bowl of water.

I tell him of Casilda and Andréas, of our summer to-gether on *Arianna*, my dreams, my dilemma. When I have finished, he looks at me, silent, fingering his coffee cup.

His eyes that had been fixed on me turn white, the blue slipping quite away. He twists, a spasm upsets his coffee onto a sketch pad scribbled with jewelry designs, then he's rigid, frozen. A minute, maybe two, a release. He turns back, looks about, bewildered, his hand, palm up, drops into the puddle of dregs. He sees the mess, wipes his hand reflexively on his pants. His eyes wander, as if searching for some landmark. In the end they find me. Soft now, suffering, still unfocused, the blue but a thin rim around immense pupils.

A slight shake of his head, —"It is time, I think, for you to go." There's an edge in his voice, a bitterness. I reach to him, my hand on his for a moment, seeking peace. He flinches, but our hands do meet.

—"Wait, Joel, one word." He holds his head, his face, in his hands, elbows on the workbench. A tear, two, drop through his fingers onto copper dust. He raises his head, looks out to the fig tree in his yard, a bird pecking at the fruit. He turns to me. —"Your way is not mine, Joel. I do not ask or give forgiveness. I know my way, I do not know yours. I will not say more. I am bone weary, you must go. And Joel, travel well." He stands, unsteady. An awkward embrace.

. . .

I stride the dusty streets that lead down to the bus station. Somehow I am ready. I hurry to my *Arianna*, to Silda. Andréas asleep in his berth, we sit on deck. A bouzoúki is playing in a quayside taverna. I tell her in some detail of the many books and articles that I had recently read, their descriptions of a new awakening in western culture, especially in Britain and America, a counterculture. A seeking for new ways, alternatives to the wars and riots and materialistic degradation of our world. Of my hope to explore that path, to sail to America, see where it leads.

She looks away, touches the back of a hand to a cheek, moves to stand up.

Silda, look at me, my eyes. Will you join me, my love, will you be the center of my life? My lovely bird, come with me, adventure with me, you and Andréas, yes?

A long, an unbearably long pause, then, —"This is scary, oh, but yes!"

### AIDAN

Did I lose you, Joel, did I win you, those parting words of mine? Distraught, my bitter tears, drained by that seizure, by your dream—I did not know.

. . .

To Rafína.

My Érsi, with Joel, gone into the night. I'll take the taxi back to Athens. —"No, no extra charge, comrade, I'm driving back anyhow, solidarity, comrade, solidarity, and may your daughter return soon to us, to our Greece delivered from the fucking colonels. Here, my handkerchief, it's clean, comrade."

We rattle on through the dark, the scents of thyme and goats and diesel exhaust heavy in the dew, swerving often to avoid the potholes. By dawn we clatter into Méts, my neighborhood. It still has its own identity from the rural roots of its people, but the swallowing up has begun. Joel told me only yesterday, when he was picking up my manuscripts—not at my house, too dangerous, in the swarm of tourists on the steps of the Acropolis—told me of a visit he made to a penthouse on the top of an otherwise nondescript block of flats near my home. A schoolmate of his, Peter something, and his gay architect partner, he'd poured some of the proceeds Daddy passed on to him from the Teapot Dome bonanza into creating a kind of all-male harem. Tents of Persian rugs, date palms, monkeys, a stuffed and unmistakably male camel, two peacocks showing off to each other, an oasis-style pond with egrets strutting about, mint tea, turbaned servants forever bowing.

Blood in the alleys, disappearances, screams in the night? Of no concern.

We'll stop now, here, this bakery. Bags of today's loaves are being loaded onto a sort of cargo sidecar of an idling motorcycle. Sweet alcohol odors come downwind from the open ovens. They serve coffee for the early risers. Here, this bit of a metal table, dented, rusty, loose-jointed chairs on the damp pavement, smell of wet dust from the morning sloshing of mop-up water. The baker puts on a record, island music, sad Arabic slitherings of a clarinet. We join the cheerful chatter of an old couple at the other table, she with her toothless laughter, a bit of mustache, chin hairs, he with hat pulled down almost to his eyebrows, managing to tend to his pipe and clack his worry beads at the same time. The baker brings coffees, triangles of baklavá in glass saucers filled with Hymettós honey, sprinkled with cinnamon.

—"No, no, no, for my honored guests, my pleasure."

Two, three thousand years of oppression, savage civil wars, tyranny, extreme suffering, yet this generosity and pride and spirit. I ask myself, Is this why I live here, beyond the edge of Europe? When my children begged me to leave this benighted dangerous land, my children who'd been stolen from me, I wrote to them. I said something like,

*I cannot leave, I cannot explain my choice.*

*This place of crass banality, stupidity, brutality, of treachery and venality, and of overwhelming humanity and love. Here where semen flows in the streets, here where love and hate sleep together, where much of beauty and wisdom was born, and was shat on.*

*I long to have you with me. I cannot leave.*

We drive on to my home, much like Érsi's and Giórgios's, squeezed in a row with six others on my block, whitewashed, doors and the one or two windows for each house painted shades of blue and green and brown and yellow, each with a box of flowers, an olive-oil can of basil—sprouted from the drops of Christ's blood, vasilikós, Lord of Heaven. Terra-cotta roofs, mossy, sprouting bits of grass and weeds.

I'm weary. I'll hack at a bit of jewelry, heat up something for lunch. There's a thumping on my door, urgent. I hurry down my bit of hallway, loud whispers.

—"Aléko! Aléko! We're friends! A rally at the Polytechneíon. Student power! Fuck the colonels! Káto the curfews! The barricades, Aléko, come!"

We rush, we shout. Mostly students—and middle-aged

me, game though, angry, elated. Gathering crowds, churning, police, tanks roaring towards us. Káto the Hoúnta! A raised billy club... brilliant blue of the sky, a swirl of swallows... gone, void, I float over death.

A shrilling, a shocking pain, blood black on grimy stone. A threshold, the door cracks open, I'm dragged inside, a violent slam of the door...a return to the void.

Crumpled greasy sheets, stinks of piss and shit, pain beating in my skull, murmurs and moans, an orderly sits on a stool by my bedside, filthy white smock, his voice thin, far behind the pulsating veil that surrounds me.

—"Aidan Allard? We have your name from your wallet. American? The police will come through the hospital again soon. No hiding you, nor all the others here. Stupid useless riots. Perhaps your embassy can help. Shall I notify them?"

Fuck the embassy, *their* tanks, *their* billy clubs! I sink again into emptiness.

Are those my screams that split me open, are those my hands, the wedges driven under three fingernails? Hands strapped, wedges tapped, tapped deeper.

—"Talk, Allard, names, places. American eh? You'd be a criminal there too, enemy of the state. Americans, they put us here, they need us to stamp out what's left of you fucking commies."

Tap, tapping, and a knee slams my groin.

Blackness, cold slimy concrete, moans and weeping and shit stink. Hysterical laughter, retching, vomit stink.

Distant, though. I am not, I shall not be, part of that.

I am weightless, I am a boy flying over treetops in a magic bathrobe. I float to my little kitchen, to my table, jewelry tools pushed aside, lips around a fig, sticky white sap, sweet red juice, lick my fingers. It tastes of blood. I hear my neighbor's kitten licking at the plate of sour milk I'd put out for her.

In a faintest finger of light from—is it the moon?—I see a rat nibbling at my coagulating blood.

It's dimmer now, then blackness, drifting on waves of pain, faint daylight again, light to dark cycling, endless cycling. My mouth, my tongue, swollen so that I can only force down water drop by drop, water that someone has shoved to me. I cannot talk, but through the terrible ringing in my head I do begin to hear voices around me, cries for help, for death, for mother.

Jackboots clatter on the concrete.

—"There, Allard, the epileptic, over there in that pool of piss. No use to us, he just pulls off a seizure instead of talking. Get him out of here. American, dangerous."

I'm dragged, stumbling on my knees, through several barred doors, dropped on the pavement. Yes, here, outside ESÁ, the house of the muffled screams, not far from the poshest of hotels and the Embassy of the U S of A.

Pain, relief, the agony of my adopted country. I cannot walk, I cannot think ahead, I can only weep. Yet soon there are gentle hands, soft words, I am picked up, put into the sidecar of a motorcycle, propped with some sort of padding, though I cannot lift my dangling throbbing head.

—"We'll get you to a hospital, far from here, new name, new documents in case they change their minds. Sorry about this sidecar, best we could do, and it helps to show you off, to show the world what they do in there to the few that do survive. We'll make sure to drive you past the American Embassy and the Hilton. We're always here, waiting, on watch, mostly to try to count the dead, try to identify them through stories of the survivors, glimpses of the bodies. That's how we knew they'd killed Giórgios. It was your good fortune that they must not have known of your connection with him, found nothing in your house, just that you were there at the demonstration—and being American helps. We shall keep in touch with you, see what you can tell us when you're better. Now, go, stó kaló, comrade, ó Theós mazí sou."

· · ·

This shabby dusty hospital, it's quiet, it must be well out of the city. Long-termers we are, so they say.

—"More than the damage they did to you, we must work on the seizures. Your epilepsy has nearly killed you. Medications, weeks of rest, we've learned more about it by corresponding with our colleagues who escaped to Europe. There are warnings, ways to cope, new medicines. And diet—there may be some blood disorder too, hypoglycemia, or something similar, so some treat these unidentified seizures a bit like diabetes, watching blood sugar, the right intake of carbohydrates, usually frequent small amounts, but cautiously, not with big doses of sugars, something more like nuts. We'll see what we can work out. We apologize for our hospital. It's the best we can do."

Hadn't they told me something like that in London? And I'd paid little attention to it at the time.

Is this ward to be my home? Two long rows of beds, packed close, everyone overworked, minimum hygiene, flies, dust, heat, slow with the bedpans. They do what they can, we are grateful. Tuberculosis, epilepsy, gangrene gone too far, failing hearts, wasting diseases—for most of us it looks like the last stop.

In the bed next to me is a boy, a young man, with the haunted look of the tubercular. Sweet Leftéri—we reach out to each other. A few words, and we are friends, we are gentle lovers.

Fleeting moments.

. . .

Ah, Leftéri mou, come to me, one last embrace before they send you away. Months, maybe a year or two, they say, but there's nothing more to do, let him die at home. Will you write me? May I come to you if they ever let me out of here?

# Part Three

# 17

A bell sounds—*Arianna's*? has our voyage begun? Again and again, it commands—the voice of a punishing God. Their morning mass, my morning bath.

. . .

At the edge of the village, where the alley becomes a donkey track, I turn, look back over the church. Its bell hangs from the branch of a plane tree, silent now in the still air. An air of auspice, the sea silver-flat, the sky a gray opening to scraps of blue. A day to turn inward, back into the hills, their hidden valleys, their shrines to the past.

A solitary day, a contemplative day, a day of fasting. With my harmonica and a bottle of water in my ragged knapsack. In my pockets, that heart-shaped fossil, my ancient coin in its leather frame.

I head upward—maquis, half-abandoned terraces. A plot of chick peas, a few still-surviving grape vines, olive trees, figs unpruned for years, an abandoned goat corral of limestone slabs, the milk shed's roof collapsed, thistles luxurious in the manure.

Higher, the hillsides are barren, dry stalks of asphodel—*khería*, candles to the dead, the islanders say. Here a dip, a cleavage. A bit of grass, still green, periwinkels, sage, the tiny blue flowers of the barbary nuts. Just above, a flat rock has been half buried into the moist bank, collecting on its mossy surface, a slow drip drip into a pond made of a rusty iron half-globe, a German mine, no doubt, salvaged by the fishermen and cut in half. Christmas rose, water cress lean over the edge, spiders scurry the surface. A swallow darts through our little glen, scooping bugs, twisting, skimming the spring for a sip A place for me, my reveries. I settle to the soothing drip drip drip.

Quiet now, inward, ask.

Childhoods, fathers, college, young men at war. Girls, mothers—revelations, dedications. Failures, damage, madness, loss. Perséphoni, Mélantha, Aidan's torture—their renewals, their escapes. Released from madness, an open path—I find my Silda, my sunshine.

I had finished my bottle of water. I lean over the pool, catch a few drops from the mossy stone slab on my tongue. A tiny frog moves back from the rusty edge of the mine to hide under the Christmas rose. My face looks up at me from the surface, I catch it in a sunny smile, a smile to carry with me through the quiet day.

. . .

The sun has found its way through the clouds, a winter sun, low now to the southwest, scratched by the needles of a juniper bush as it sinks behind a hilltop. An hour till dark.

### CASILDA

Joel, my dearest, you have called me, an almost daily delight, wherever it may be—a walk up our Eagle Bluff, a sail in *Arianna*, pillows on the rug before our hearth, our bed, your dreams. I'll just sit here by you, by the drip drip of this tiny spring, watch the spiders, their water-walking dance, the dragon flies scooping water on the wing.

Aidan, you've come, of course, at last we meet. Here my kiss for you, both cheeks. Join us, here, I'll sit between you two.

Joel, love, I see you have your fossiled stone and your ancient coin, laid neatly on the moss. I'm touched. Offerings are they, there by the holy water, this shrine? Talismans, I've heard you say, protections, but from what? That you wouldn't say. From yourself, your self-perceived inadequacies, your fears? All that nonsense about your family genes? Crazy, you know it is, you researched all that yourself—the probabilities are barely north of zero. Come on! Worse than nonsense—you've let it keep you all these years from having children of your own.

Inadequacies? Yes, when first we met I suppose you were in your head mostly—your work, your protests, your rebellions. But right off, there at Lorenzo and Anna's, I knew. You looked me in the eye, you smiled and a kind of grimness just dropped away. You were so sweet with little Andréas. You jumped right into my heart, my love. I knew just then who you really are.

A talisman is an excuse, relying on something else, someone else to provide what you thought you lacked within yourself. You have your own sunshine, my love. Dance in it, you can, you do, I know. We have danced together through our years, danced as one. We have shared each other's sunshine. Dance on, my love, in your own bright smiling sun.

This fob of leather with its coin, it speaks for Aidan's love, but have you let it stand as well for his intolerance, his denunciations, his despairing path? Yes, you have told me of your admiration for his disciplined determination, the unbending rigor of his convictions, but did they not lead to his nihilistic end? Did Aidan ever impose his path on you? Given how you have successfully maneuvered your rebellions, your styles, your responses to a changing world, that may be a big part of your attraction. And vice versa, my dear?

True, he wanted from you his own expression of love, so be it, but it was not yours. You refused to follow. Why blame yourself for not meeting that measure? There was a bitterness to his response, but he gave his daughter, her unborn child, into your safe-keeping. He gave you that token lying there with mine.

Different measures, different paths.

· · ·

Now Aidan, what's your sign? Let me guess. Taurus, stubborn and blunt, yes, that fits. I'm right, yes? I know a lot about you. But no birth time, no rising sign? We'll get by without. And none of your skeptical grimaces, Joel.

Aidan Allard, alleged son of The Admiral—yes, I do know about that. Taurian, skeptical no doubt, like Joel, maybe a bit of the Aquarian in there too, denying yourself the fun of intuition, insight, dimensions beyond the rational—and, some would add, beyond the succor of faith. Voodoo you'd call it, all that. Astrology, homeopathy, afterlife, UFOs, prophesying, the millennium, black cats, broken mirrors, ESP, Ouija boards, religion, the lot. Your Orthodoxy, I imagine that at bottom you're in it because it's Greek, but I'd guess there's faith in there too. Just to become Greek must have taken a large leap of faith and a considerable dollop of the romantic. Faith, I hear you would grab onto a Tibetan thunderbolt, your dorje, to inspire your writing—there you have it, ha!. Well, I collect sage—or I did—whenever I was out in the American desert, and I'd bundle it and set it smoking to smudge a room or friends or me. Cleansing bad stuff, evil washed away. It works, try it. I was once with a tribal medicine man when he...

### AIDAN

Wait, Casilda, I must interrupt, jump in before Joel beats me to it. You've hit a nerve or two, your aim or your luck is impeccable.

I make no apologies for my convictions or my anger. Skeptical, Casilda, is a totally inadequate word for me, romantic even more so. Remember, Greece is my home, my chosen country that has given me—however ironically, with the knowing lift of the eyebrow—citizenship, for God's sake. Know something of my country if you are to understand something of me. It is a place of brutal reality—hidden, like as not, for the benefit of the new money and the tourists—but a place of treachery, informers, unlimited greed for power, a country that has throughout most of its history lived with a knife in its back, with revenge in its heart, with pride and honor at any price. Its romance is an illusion, tricked out for the foreigners, the invading literati. Read our own poets, with notable exceptions like Kazandjákis, and you'll smell and taste—and probably run from—our reality. A Greece tricked out for the numb-minded, the blind, the school children, the new classes hiding behind the illusion of their money and power.

I have no way of explaining why I have never left. Greece has fed me, given me endurance, and, yes, a beauty that resides somewhere deep in her fiber, unrelated to landscapes and monuments and icons and history. My Orthodoxy is a part of that, my dear, and has nothing to do with faith.

Do not presume to know me, woman, however white your hair. Do not!

Cornelia, our children, yes I did withdraw my love, love that I once gave extravagantly. And I asked no forgiveness. For what, for being Greek, for being me? It is they who left, they whose courage failed, who resorted to banal convention. They have been taken in, fallen for it, accepted deception. Reality will someday shred them.

Forgiveness is a lie, the truth is in our fearless response to desire, in our willingness to give ourselves. Only death can forgive. And if we forget this we are extinguished. Justice is a whore, only solitary freedom is pure, freedom that gives infinite space for our devotions, all honor to our souls.

### JOEL

Casilda, your smile, a sort of I-told-you-so smile, no? Our Aidan is nothing if not outspoken.

I have listened to you carefully, my love, I always have. Our dance, my dance...soon, yes, soon. But that rock out there, that Khímaera...there's something yet to be done.

And many journeys to bring us here.

. . .

So, that sail from Piraeus to Gibraltar. Silda by my side, our hands together on the tiller, Andréas floating woodchips in the scuppers—to Aidan's birthplace. Silda, there, a plaque to Aidan's father, Admiral Allard. We climb up to the terraces—are jumped on by flea-bitten smelly apes. Strange place, Gibraltar, tacky, military still, Gibraltarians rather unattractive. Even the restaurants seem cobbled together and rudely serviced—their customers are transients, one-offs, no need to entice them to return.

Preparations for our sail to the Canaries, my Atlantic solo, they'll take time. New running sails to rig, life raft to check and repack, ocean charts, celestial navigation tables, the trade routes to study—avoid the dangers of modern routes, follow the experience of sailing-ship days. Provisions to bring in, stow, plenty of non-perishable reserves. And time for ourselves.

We take a room in the poshest hotel for too few days.

It's really a suite with a small room for Andréas. Off our bedroom is a large balcony all our own. It looks out over the restaurant's terrace, the harbor, westward to the Atlantic. We splurge on a lavish room-service dinner.

First, there's a something for Andréas. When he's finished, I carry him on my hip like a bag of cement—that always calls forth a giggle—drop him onto his cot, tell him a story about a frog and a Kleenex box. He's asleep before the end.

Dark by now, the candles steady in still air, the bats trilling in the moonlight. Desserts done, the wine bottle empty, the table cleared. Cognac snifters now. I reminisce about that stopover in Piraeus. My dilemma—to ask you, Silda, your Andréas, to join my dream, or to sail on quite alone. My visit with Aidan, his bitter and cryptic acceptance of my dream, my decision. Your *Yes!*

The light is dim, is that a frown? You turn away, the candle light glows on your bare shoulder. You are silent. Why?

### CASILDA

Yes, my silence, my shoulder to you. How much of your life is yours, Joel, your dissents and rebellions, how much relies on, obeys, another's measure—this Aidan's? Or mine for that matter—I am not your sunshine, I have mine, you must have yours. Would I commit myself, my child, to one who marches to another's orders? Must a life with you be clouded by doubt and reproach? I turn my back. There's still time, must I leave the dream?

Was it permission you sought from Aidan, or advice and love from a friend? Am I... I turn, your lips are open, they move as if to form a word, a slightest shake of your head, silence. I look into your eyes, your worried eyes, a frown.

I go to the edge of the balcony, lean on the railing. Three couples are dancing on the terrace below—slow, sweet music. Several freighters are anchored beyond the docks. The sea stretches out into the dark. Is that the direction for Andréas and me? This man, there's much I do not know about him, but of one thing I feel sure. He learns, he does not give up. His rebellions, his principles, his measures—with time he'll learn that they're fully his. And this other thing, this sunshine thing, perhaps I can help a bit with that.

I turn back. You are standing by the table.

Joel love, yes, I am still here. My thumb to touch your tears. I am still here.

Listen, that music. Let me show you a dance. Will you?

No no, drop that sheepish look. Come, out here in the starlight. Now first we both must strip, yes really strip, nothing left but what we really are. Come on, it's truly private.

That's better, good. No, there's nothing to hide. When will you drop all that?

Now, a few pointers. Let's see, how to put it... The music must come first, the lyrics can follow—the body, the heart first, then the mind if need be. Does that make sense? It's a must for a dance, maybe also for a life? Drop out of that lofty mind of yours, down into your belly, yes, right here, that hairy belly of yours. You're still embarrassed! Now close your eyes, let the music move into that belly, then just do what it says. The belly's in control.

A bit of jazz, good. Yes, your head too, your arms, those sexy legs. Just don't let that body disappear into the mind. Here, take my hands, let us move together.

A waltz now, Chopin. Come, hold me, kiss me. We are each other, we move as one.

## JOEL

A sunny morning, white caps out there off Algeciras. Time to set sail, my Silda. Westward ho! But no brass bands to send us off, no signals flown at *Victory*'s maintop, no *England Expects That Every Man Will Do His Duty.*

Up sails and off, the wind is easterly, the sea with a bit of a chop, *Arianna* taking no heed, though the westerly Atlantic swells roll in as we pass Trafalgar at dusk. *Engage In Close Action*, the French fleet has sailed out from Cadiz. Innocent *Arianna* engaging rusty freighters and the endless tankers of Arabian oil. We turn south to cross the ship lanes quickly, get on our private way to the Canaries. We reduce sail for the night, dead-reckon our position with cross-bearings from lighthouses. Running lights on, the self-steerer checked. Make up the bunk for you, Casilda. You look sleepy, my love, a bit subdued. I still can't believe the miracle of you being here.

### CASILDA

Yes, but hang on there. You can't just sail on, hoping to avoid my plight. Subdued, you said I was, out there in a cockleshell on that endless rolling sea? *Seasick*, that's what I was, Joel, as you well know, and drugged with Dramamine. It was one thing in the Mediterranean, bashing against the meltémi for a couple of hours between islands. Out there in the Atlantic you had us for ten days without respite, rolling violently in what was left of a major storm somewhere—off to the northwest, you said.

Heavy winds, rain, then one morning when I struggled on deck we were in a flat calm—still rolling horribly, though—the air thick yellow, no horizon, no sun, no sky, the sails streaked with mud. Hundreds of miles off the African coast yet here we were in a Saharan dust storm, mud storm, and you seemingly unconcerned, balancing up on the cabin top listening to the radio with earphones, for God's sake. I know, I know, you were trying to get radio bearings. Still, it struck me as downright crazy, the whole scene.

And we did get there, Tenerífe, I know, and it was a sweet time, Joel, those few days. Driving around the island, beaches, skinny-dipping—chilly, though we were down to the twenty-eighth parallel, you said, but it was March. A climb up the volcano Teíde, way above tree line—Andréas really loved that bit.

A week later you put us on a plane to England. You'd wanted to solo the Atlantic, the hero thing it looked like, though you did downplay it—just an inner psychic trip, the easy route, the benign season. And you'd not wanted us at risk, and we knew I'd have been miserable with weeks in the rolling seas. Fair enough. You were to sail the next day.

Then silence, no word. An awful month of silence. You had no radio transmitter.

### *Joel*

A toast, Rioja from my demijohn, to our volcano, its snowy pink tip sinking in the sunset. Here, sliding through these southern seas, swirling, foaming, never silent seas. The song of the wind in *Arianna's* aeolian rigging, tackle slatting, the slap of a choppy sea, the surge and fall of the bow wave as we're carried on the immense swell of that endless sea. And, lying here below on our open bunk, curled around a book, the insistent murmur of girlish voices, wisps of voices—I can't quite catch what they say.

Fair winds, a tropical rainstorm in the hot morning sun, naked in the cockpit with a bar of soap—naked all the way, why not? Flopping of flying fish on the deck above my head, three dead this morning.,

Sun setting just off the bow, catch the green flash. Pump up the pressure on my Tilly lamp, fry the morning's fish, a clump of bean sprouts—they're growing faster than I would eat them. To sleep, curled tight in my rolling, ever rolling home.

Fear, always this nagging fear—a tanker steaming blind through the night. I've slept through my staggered oven timers, I rush on deck—no nothing to be seen. And that struggle, through one long night, on deck in my umbilical harness—fucking twinsail frayed loose, wrapped around the keel.

A noon sight, every day a noon sight, propped up here in the companionway. I'm getting really good. But this calm, dead calm, two days of it, rolling, really rolling in this giant swell, sails, rigging, everything below decks slamming about, stayed-out boom dipping in the water.

Birds now, distant clouds collecting over the hills of Barbados. Porpoises playing in our bow wave—lead us in, my friends. Grenada, sailing into Saint George's, no brass band, nobody noticed, just Paul Simon crooning *Fifty Ways to Leave Your Lover,* beer and peanuts in the local bar in celebration. And Casilda's sweetest voice.

. . .

All night, now all day, steady heavy rain on my pup tent, pitched in a hurry in this forest of Allegheny oak and azaleas. My notebook, a pencil, a love letter, a really heavy duty love letter to Casilda. Do come soon my love. We'll explore this land together, see what comes our way. I've a tiny home on wheels now, ready for us three.

### CASILDA

Me, in London struggling with an anal American Embassy bloke about a visa. Guarantees? Your fiancée? A five-thousand-dollar bond. What kind of a country is this, this America? Spiritual intentional communities he wants to investigate, what's that all about? A fiftyish latter-day hippie, seems to have money from his light bulb stock and some saved from his posh government service—which he doesn't bother to talk about—and a pension already of some sort. Me a thirtyish working-girl, close to penniless, gladly working my buns off at whatever comes my way. What am I doing? Bonkers, bloody bonkers.

. . .

Here, cruising the continent in our funky little home on wheels. It turns out to be our home for four years. All the mod cons, amazing. Stopovers at your so-called intentional spiritual communities—hippie drop-out communes, some would say. It is not the movie America I knew, though with perhaps a touch of *Easy Rider.*

Many surprises. A community of CIA escapees, turned Sikhs. Their hair, even their beards, are tucked into turbans except when they bathe or swim with us in their weedy pond—de rigeur in the nude, hair down to the waist, all of them, parents, daughter, son-in-law, grandson.

At another community, we hang out for a few days of tomato canning, pepper picking, helping assemble citizen-band radios, listening to folksy Sunday sermonizing from a homegrown guru type. Or that one where they are all sproutarians, nothing else, nothing cooked, just sprouted seeds. Or the one where they do nothing but meditate and experiment with smelly composting toilets.

I sound judgmental. In truth, I am moved by the hopeful innocence of it all, I'm often caught up in their social experiments. And it is a country of such amazing land-scapes, so varied, immense, a huge country, thousands of miles, I had no idea. At first, we park for the night in places like shopping-centers, parking lots, cemeteries, hospitals, friends' backyards. As we get farther west we find spectacular spots in their national forests—clean air, clear nights, stars through our back window, maybe coyotes chattering nearby.

On to a hippie wedding in the Bay Area, Mount Tam, leis and look-like-togas and Buddhas and chants of *Aummmm* and Joel baked them a loaf as a wedding present, ah well, ah well. But yes, I do get into it, new, experimenting, kind of fun, and every now and then something very deep and moving and personal happens.

We stay for several months at a center for what they call appropriate technology—organic gardening, solar ovens, more composting toilets, carpentry, welding, animal husbandry, beam barn-raising construction, that kind of thing. I get into gardening, veggies, flowers, orchard, the works, my passion ever since. Andréas walks, rain or shine, to school with his new dad.

And finally, when I had almost given up, had readied myself to return to Europe, you say it. —"Will you marry me, dear Silda?"

We marry in a snowstorm, an antique ring from a pawn shop, the town sheriff quoting Khalil Gibran, dinner afterwards with turbaned friends, lotus position—or what we could manage—round a reed mat. A carved rosewood prayer table only inches high—Buddhist, I'd guess, never mind, eclectic as we are

Finally we park for good, it seems, on an island on the British Columbia coast. A run-down farm, homesteaded, to be cared for by stewards. Stewards, that's us, our community that we set about forming, a kind of commune, I guess. Twinflower Farm, we call it, the twinflower, its tiny pink twin flowers.

Hundreds of stories to tell, probably never will. Cows to milk, milk to bottle, endless bottle-scrubbing, the milk delivery route. The gardening, the orchards, the haying, the bailing. Horses to sell that came with the homestead.

A school we start for the island children, Andréas leads the pack. An apprentice farming program. A pea-patch garden for islanders to use. Solar ovens for cooking, for drying our fruits and veggies. A composting toilet. Organic farming, horse-power, man-power wherever we can. The grumpy former owner, —"Damn hippies!"—friendly, though, bemused.

Joel, he gets fired up to get land put into trust, wherever. We begin to travel, help make these land trusts happen, many of them, Europe as well. Articles, lecture tours— land trusts, community life-styles, the pros and cons. Our interminable meetings, how communal living can work. Exasperating, sometimes they drive me up the wall.

The moments of release. Swimming in our lake or in the sea nearby. Picnics, hikes up our Eagle Bluff. Once we had a musical funeral there for one of us who was killed when her ancient tractor lost a wheel, rolled over. We spread her ashes on the moss to a gay tune from a French horn. Simple Christmases, parties of a sort, canoeing by moonlight, skating on the lake, island celebrations. Our little Andréas is in a permanent state of elation.

With time, the islanders—loggers, fishermen, a dozen Indian families on their reserve, other hippies—we are well accepted. Our school is overflowing. One of us is elected mayor.

How would your parents have taken all this? I wonder. That time when you'd gone across the continent to your mother's eightieth birthday. He took you aside and laid into you nonstop about your misused life. Bloooody 'ell! I've had that man up to here. We live our lives, not his.

### JOEL

Yes, our lives, not his. It took many years, many rebellions, several confrontations, but finally I was out from under his shadow. No longer that hovering presence, judging, pulling strings. He'll not come to Khería, Silda, no fear. By the end, he had some sense of the hurt he had inflicted, he would not wish to relive it. And if he were here I would have to open old wounds.

Tucked in my memory is a lecturing I got from him on a visit toward the end of his life. I had come back to their home from an afternoon walk with my mother. He was alone, sitting in his usual chair, dozing. As I reached into that ornate silver box for a fistful of nuts, he jerked awake. Peering over his half-moon horn-rims, he began.

—"Joel, my boy, I'd like you to come see us more often. Your mother misses you...Still the subsistence farmer, are you?...Sure to be a dead end, that place of yours...All that education, your promising career?...You've dropped your friends, your colleagues, your contacts with people who really count...To get yourself removed from *Who's Who*, what were you thinking?—offensive, insulting to the family name...That talk of acid rain at dinner last night, nonsense, a few lake fish might suffer, but the acid is good fertilizer, good for the soy and grains...You should get a haircut, my boy, and that beard, you embarrass us, you know...Fix yourself up, I'll find you a spot in the Company where you can do some good...I'd like to not be disappointed in you, my boy."

He went on and on like that. Rebuttals were impossible, useless. It became fascinating, verging on the pathetic. But when I see him now in recent memory, his eyes have an embattled look, fear and doubt. Tolerance and love, too. If only I had seen that long before, might we have understood each other better, been able to show our love?

And my mother. My last time with her, she's in a hospital, a private room high over the city. Pleasant nurses bustling about, the usual stinks of hospitals kept largely at bay. They've wheeled her over near the window, propped her up a bit so that she can just see, almost hidden among the skyscrapers, her home on The Hill, the oldest part of town—there, that street of slate roofs, brick buildings, there back of the golden dome of the capitol. —"We wheel us over here to have a look 'most every morning, don't we, dearie?"

Rare to be alone with her, rare too a lucid time.

Her ravaged face, her sweet smile. —"Joel, dear, come, a kiss, sit here." With effort, her hand seeks mine. —"I am dying, you know. Yes, you know. The others, friends, the nurses, the doctors—they all deny it. So silly! But we know, you and I. What is it, death? God, heaven, an afterlife? I don't know. Churches, prayers? It is exciting, though. I am happy, Joelly.

"There is something I wish to tell you about your father. But wait, sorry, I must collect myself. Steady, Jorie, steady. There, that's better. Silly me.

"Your father, I was with him when he died, was it ages ago? He was not a happy man. He was hard on you, I know, dear, you were so different, I know. He was a good man, though, and I never stopped loving him. My water, there, just hold the straw, my mouth gets so dry. Yes, a Kleenex, my eyes just water all the time.

"He fought almost to the end. Poor dear, tubes and wires, tears of pain. Mostly he couldn't talk. But, those last words, I leaned over, could hear his whisper, *But life, my dear, is beautiful withal.*"

Her eyes close, drifting into sleep. I pull the curtains, switch off the light. I'll sit with her for a time, here, her hand in mine. Quiet, just a hint of distant city rumble. And... Ever so faint, a wisp of sound, a high clear note, a song, a little boy tucked in, lights out, prayers said, our special song, please Mummy. A boy, older, by a bedside, his Uncle Charlie, that song, that crystal voice. Fading, quiet, lost.

. . .

A cow bell, a buoy, the Reverend Boas's little church? Peaceful here—well, there are these pesky ants, they insist on a careful inspection of my book. Here, the mossy ledges of Eagle Bluff, my retreat. The bothers—the meetings, the relentless milkings and weedings and…. All of that, Casilda and I, we seem to have withdrawn, the community getting on famously without our constant care. That *bong!*, of course, our new school bell, they put it up this morning. Recess time.

My notebook, scribbling, the outline of an article, a doodle of an angry ant, the schedule for my Asian trip. Travelers now, we are. Silda, she's off soon, London to check in with Amnesty International, Oxford to collaborate on an article about an indigenous people threatened by a dam. Me, I leave soon for Mongolia.

# 18

While you're milking cows, dealing with the weeds, I'm in my dusty home, banging on my ancient Olivetti, tugging at the jammed keys, diligent with the carbon paper, the onionskin copies, inking the ribbon—and my whiteouts. Or I'm resting under my lemon tree, a pull on my gurgling pipe. Or I heat up some chickpea soup, gulp down the damnable medications, then pocket a handful of peanuts to be nibbled in an hour or so, keep the carbohydrates dribbling in.

Those experiments with me in the hospital, they really seemed to work, it got so that I could judge the when and the how-much. The bloke in London speculated it was a blood disorder, told me to keep up the dribble of carbos, can't do any harm. Remember? Medicos tell me now that's rubbish, some quack from the distant past. —"Gumdrops might do it if you're hypoglycemic. Peanuts? Awfully slow." Still, they seem to do the job for me, no grand mal unless I forget. The crafty psychosoma at work, pulling off its tricks? Well, so be it, if that's what it takes.

The Colonels and their Junta have gone, stored away for good on a very unpleasant island. The bourgeoisie plague has taken over. Socialism, communism, they have retreated, from all I can see, to the occasional salon of a few weary aging intellectuals, artists, the dangling politician—is that all that's left of the so-called proletariat? Fascists, royalists? Never existed. And the American hegemony rolls on.

There's some relief, though. Listen.

. . .

I'm back in my beloved Píndos, alone, but content. The Ahelóös races by under the same precarious bridge you and I, Joel, had crossed years before, though a goatherd told me yesterday that German youths show up here now, not the Sturmabteilung troopers that roared in when old Metaxás said No to Mussolini—tyrant to hero overnight.

—"They come now with some kind of soft boat that slithers over the waves. A snake over sheep dung. Float down my river." Strange image, that.

Here the track is steeper, and it is still the only way to get to the village. No lorries or jeeps or carts, just mules for bringing provisions, for carrying out the logs they cut in the government's forests. On, up, to sleep in the same chapel shrine where you and I lay side by side through my tormented night. What was left of the roof when we were there is gone. Stars in the moonless mountain sky, I drift among them till dawn.

Through the empty doorway of our chapel I look up at black peaks, pink snow in the rising sun over the Aegean. An Alpine marmot whistles, I see him standing guard for his colony, competition with the goats for the few blades of grass.

Above the forests, almost to the timberline, our village

appears, dogs screaming at me—it's enough to reach for a stone, they cower, yipping away—the kapheneíon, the same somber men at their backgammon, children playing round the plane tree, the single room of the schoolhouse where you and I had slept. I sling off my pack by a vacant kapheneíon table, settle with a flask of oúzo, a tumbler of water scooped from a pail a ragged boy had brought from the brook, a little plate of the usual dried chickpeas. Rock music on the transistor, slaps of the backgammon pieces, shouts of success, talk as they collect around me casually.

—"Oddly familiar, this stranger, from the other side of the range? Can't tell from how he talks, maybe Tríkala."

Here in my Greece.

. . .

Bittersweet, Joel, that return.

Back now to Méts, my Athenian neighborhood, what's left of it. My life turns ever more inward. There is a sweet gift, though, Persephóni—Érsi—and her daughter Mélantha. With the Junta gone, they had come back from Rome and are often with me. Beautiful, my daughter, my only child by then, constant, steady, true Greek. Mélantha, joyous and loving to this old bit of flotsam who had washed up here long ago.

Érsi had moved quickly into a job, leaving art restoration behind, intent now on this new Greece. She finds a staff position to one of the few remaining communists-socialists in Parliament. A determined woman, living on very little. She livens up whatever group she joins, even the has-beens' intellectual soirées I occasionally get to.

And one day...

. . .

I must have been dreaming. My neck is stiff, cracking, the keys of my typewriter are jammed together, my head must have lain there. A loud knocking at my door, it woke me. My God, it's Joel, and somebody else, Christé mou, I had no idea.

Come in, come in.

Introductions, small talk—something about being en route to Mongolia, plane delayed, address but no phone number, Walter, a colleague and collaborator.

Some tea, wine? Here, do come back here, my workshop and kitchen. Tea, bits of toast, Walter is effusive about my marmalade of lemons from my little tree. He asks a few good questions, which I answer in my usual oblique and obscure way. Soon he leaves. —"I'd like to go for a walk, we have three hours still, I'll be back in two." Tactful, discreet, bored? I'm not sure. Had Joel told him of our...?

I heat up some potato soup—was it that the last time too?—fetch my earthenware wine jug, cheese, more toast. At first, our talk is careful. Children, mutual friends, my writing, my jewelry, my dear Érsi, her daughter.

Joel's Casilda had flown with him as far as London. She had appointments to attend to, would visit family and friends. He seems nervous, his eyes meet mine for moments only, wander on about the room—uncertain. Cautious, I am too. Though we'd seen each other a few times since our disastrous drunken night too long ago, unease remained between us. Even during the Junta years, when we were planning Joel's heroic rescue of Érsi, his trips to smuggle out my manuscripts, even then our relationship was wary. No rivers, no bridges to cross, no Poohsticks.

I clear the table, rinse things in the stone sink, return to my stool. With no forethought, I reach for the tin box at the far end of the workbench table. It's half full with jewelry items I'd finished.

Joel, I'd like you to have this. It's a watch fob—I don't suppose they use them anymore, but perhaps for a bracelet, round your neck, a key chain, a keepsake? I found this ancient coin quite improbably near the summit of Mount Olympus—yes, I did get there finally, without you. The leather surround is from my finally defeated mountain boots, the copper for the rivets I found in a junk yard. I'd like you to have it.

He takes it, examining, touching the worn faces of the bronze coin, the rough leather with its braided tail. He looks up at the whitewashed wall with its racks of tools, a photo of Mélantha funny-facing the camera. He drops my offering in his shirt pocket. His hand reaches to mine, lying by the jewelry vise in the copper filings.

I can't hold on, the room swirls about me, torn from my grip. A blaze of light, searing—then.... How much later? Why am I looking at this blank bit of wall, where am I—ai, my tongue!—is this blood on my chin? Who is this? Ah yes, Joel is it? Sorry, sorry. Is that your friend at the door? Yes, perhaps it is time that you go. I am all right now. Be safe.

. . .

Floating about in memories, my magic carpet. Up from my kitchen terrace, over the lemon tree, the absurd roof oasis of Joel's architect friend, over the cemetery in a swarm of bourgeois ghosts, the Acropolis melting in the smog, Constitution Square crawling with its parasites, Omónia Square, the stink of last year's deep-fry fat. Lykavittós, posh apartment block where my farmhouse home once was—yes, Kolonáki has quite taken over. Higher, swing over to the east, my Hymettós, honey colors, still rising above the smog, glide lower, goats, yellow gorse, heather's white buds, settle to that patch of grass by an olive. To rest.

What comes?

. . .

Diesel stinks, violent shaking, pounding through what's left of the meltémi, Cósta's caíqui, painted only once, from the looks of it, since that dawn when he took me to Naxos, on into exile.

There'll be no Dímitra, no raven's-wing greeting, nothing left of youth. No young boy cart-wheeling behind his team of donkeys as they circle and circle on the worn limestone, threshing the golden wheat with their dainty hooves. Approaching Artémisos, the first landmark I see is the windmill, no sails now—new arms, obviously fake, each painted a different color, and there is a large sign on its conical roof, aimed at the incoming tourists, in Roman lettering.

### !!*DISCO*!!

There, now, over the rise behind the village, distant still across the calm sea, is a small procession on the track to the cemetery, faint discordant notes of the death march, the village trumpeter, the same one, doubtless, the miller, who'd boast of his days of glory trumpeting the attack for Metaxás to drive Benito's cowards back into Albania. Who has died? I cannot ask Cósta, though. I'm no longer that distraught exile. I'm full-bearded now, glasses, dodgey hearing, rudimentary Greek, natty clothes, and a city suitcase. Full disguise.

Am I quite mad, succumbing like this to some urge, risking being recognized as the seducer of Dímitra the Moonstricken? Some strange compulsion to revisit… what? What is it—the birthplace of Aléko the Greek, the scene of disaster, the masochistic urge, the risk, or just the smell of that sea, the cry of those gulls, the song of the wind in the tamarisks, the caress of her raven hair? Romantic fool, where is the cynical, driven ideologue, the unsung and evidently almost unsingable writer of contorted obscurity, the converted and legislated and Orthodoxed Greek who hates this country with the twisted passion of a rejected lover?

I walk those hills, escaped from the flimsy new hotel on the beach, the plastic litter on the rocks where still a boy slap-slapped an octopus this morning early, on and on. Escaped these villagers, measuring me, my wallet, my innocence. How many did I know, the stooped and stumbling ones, their juniper-branch canes, the papás, his white hair in a bun, his cross dangling on a chain, his mildewed stovepipe hat with a crust of sweat-salt on its hatband? Who bore those screaming children, still rolling hoops down the lane, still snotty, still with their arrogant pride and their scornful outstretched hands?

The village beach is taken over by new hotels, flimsy, rectilinear, cheapest possible construction but for a few ornamental arches and skinny useless columns. Three cars are evident, a policeman standing next to me says, one eyebrow raised, —"Cars now, yes, but no roads." I pretend I don't understand. Donkeys are all but extinct, the outdoor ovens are stuffed with trash. High, up the walled lanes, the hilltop, to look back on the village stretched white against the sea, caíquia swinging at their summer anchorage, and three, four yachts. Most of the caíquia have striped awnings on them now, tourist-ready. On the hill's far side, ringed by rockrose and rosemary, in the meager shade of a low juniper tree, is a white, curved bench, quite new. A startled viper curls off the sunny seat, disappears in the grass. The bench looks out to the east, over stony fields, a goat or two, stretches of maquis—juniper, aromatic mints, laurels, mastic, myrtles, wild figs, olives bent southward, dwarfed and crippled by the meltémi. Out over cliffs and caves and coral beaches. Out to far islands.

I turn to the north, where the etesian winds drive the

open seas to foam on the coral sand. There, where Dímitra and I would scoop sea salt from dried puddles in the
limestone, there where we would dance on the burning
sand, swim in the burning sea, suck ripe figs in the shade
of a shallow cave, play naked in the moonlit waves, lie in
each other's arms. Nevermore, lost love, nevermore. The
beach is crawling with bathers, more coming in three
caíquia, umbrellas, towels spread about, a man selling pop
from his boat hauled up on the sand.

I take my evening meal on the hotel terrace—tired
fish, limp salad, a foul wine. I'll scare up more clichés
about that atrocious meal for this postcard to Érsi. I'll
mail it in Naxos, thieving eyes mustn't see that I write
her in Greek. I'll leave tomorrow. Artémisos, me, skewed,
gone sour. I'll spend a few days in a mountain village
on Naxos I'd heard of, up where Ariadne had her fling
with Dionysus.

The evening stroll begins along the one street, continues out onto the beach. Some seem to have the leisure for it
now, not when I'd lived here. Canned music blares into the
night from the hotel terrace, the usual, the interminable six
or eight numbers from the touristed tavernas of Athens'
Pláka—when the wind was right I could hear them from
my Méts home—their corruptions of traditional island
songs. I escape to the beach, walk to the end, perch on
a ledge. I look back at the crowd on the hotel terrace. A
woman, a tourist I'd guess from her dress, is dancing with
a young islander, stamping about on the usual debris of

broken plates, the twisted handkerchief, the slaps, the head flung back.

I move away from this scene, wander on to the edge of the village, on in the moonlight, up a familiar lane between stone walls leading out into fields of thistles. Here the wall on one side divides, circles around two fig trees, a small enclosure, maybe once a garden plot. Between the figs are the rotting timbers of an old caíqui, dragged there I can't say why. Dímitra and I would slip out here sometimes in the dark, sit where the timbers make a sort of low bench, trade kisses and secrets—a sweet place.

A woman is sitting there, hair streaming white in the moonlight, crooning an ancient song that I often play on my floghéra. I stop in the shadow to listen, watch over the wall as she begins to braid her hair. She turns as she reaches behind her head, sees me, stops her braiding, continues her singing, stares. She fits *Aghápi mou, Aléko mou* into her song, braids on.

That was my last night on Artémisos, I could bear no more.

# 19

That trilling, is it a woman's voice? The scuffle of foot-steps, Aidan's? No, I half sit up, propped on my elbows, legs stretching by their own will, boots scuffling in a gravelly patch, neck cracking back in place. Bats are at the bug-scooping now, trilling, squeaking, flickering against what's left of the sky. And what's left I hope is enough to get me back to whatever the kapheneíon offers.

Careful, the path is rough, the light is all but gone. Thoughts can trip one too.

. . .

An oúzo tipped into a tumbler of water, grilled red mullet. —"The cheeks are the best part, kyrio, just pull off the whiskers first." And slices of tomato, that's it. Then bed... But no. This, my last night, I'll pay up for my stay at the inn. I'll take blankets, a pillow, I'll sleep on my ledge, out there under the stars.

My bed on the warm rock is ready. I stand by a ju-niper bush, still in the waiting night. Before me, the sea stretches out to Khímaera. Behind, the land rises through the maquis to the sky. A low call spreads out over the hillside, rippling, a pebble in a pond. A call and a silken rustle. No more than a stone's throw, there in a brake of heather, there on a pedestal of stone, stands a white owl shining in the starlight. Goddess of the night.

I reach for the harmonica in my pocket, warm with

Silda's red stone, with Aidan's coin fob. I play my song to her. You, my dearest Silda, you who showed me the sunshine—yours, then mine. This is your song, lest I forget, your gift to me. You gave me joy and love—they need never die.

I turn to my waiting bed. The white owl calls again.

### CASILDA

My Joel, he's off to Mongolia, a Quixotic adventure, with Walter. Me, I've come to England, leaving Andréas happy in our busy communal home. I've left my gardens for their winter rest, our Twinflower Farm will hardly know we are gone. To England, my motherland, to the pleasure of being alone, the pleasure of places, of friends from the past. And a dollop of creature comfort far from cows and weeds and cook stoves, rusty farm equipment, leaky roofs, horse wormings, red-necked abuse, the tedium of communal meetings and meetings and meetings.

Here, in this private London hotel, private meaning expensive, posh, ostentatiously unostentatious with just a street number for a name—flowers and fruit, a half liter of port, chocolate truffles by my bedside. Light-bulb-licensed luxury, what the hell. A jazz club with cousin Peter. A Stoppard play, late dinner at The Ivy with… it doesn't matter. And now to indulge my rather huge addiction, a shopping spree—well, mostly through the shop windows, no? The Burlington Arcade, a napkin ring for a friend's new baby. On to New Bond Street, a scarf for me, a silk stock for Joel to offset his farmer image.

I'll just catch a taxi for Harrods, they've got a full-grown albino elephant for sale, what else could one want? Crowded Piccadilly pavement, I'm at the head of the taxi queue, waving. A Bentley speeds towards us, something hard and heavy pokes me from behind, I'm falling, a hand grabs me as the silver wing of the car bangs my hip.

I'm okay, quite all right, but bloody hell! And thank you, Sir. He tips his rather ragged bowler. —"Glad to be of service, M'lady." Who knocked me? —"Didn't see, Mum."

Whoever...damn, it really hurts.

Bruised, two days and still a bit of a limp, but I must get to my luncheon with the Amnesty people. I'm taking the tube, it's quicker in this traffic. It's crowded even here at the arrival end of the platform. Body smells, electric ozone smells, a rat hurries along a rail, stops to drop a turd. Have a Good Rum for Your Money. And Drinka Pinta—milk, not rum. We jostle for position, guessing where the carriage doors will be. I stand mostly on one leg to ease the pain. A blast of foul air, the roar and rattle of the District train. The crowd is shoving...my sore hip collapsing...

Help me, hold me! My loves, my loves, no no!

My bed of flowers.

. . .

## JOEL

A caravan of camels stirring up yellow dust at a disputed Mongolian border. Maybe we've helped, Walter and I, working as private citizens with the local communities on each side, helped find some resolution. But my attempts to telephone Casilda, either in London or at our Twinflower home, have failed. No word for weeks. And now the series of flights back, one fluorescent airport after another, tight connections, no time to phone.

Home, my community greets me, strangely somber. The reports are there waiting for me—faxes on my machine, phone calls, telegrams, FedExes. A confused sequence—condolences, call urgently, an accident, serious condition, send instructions.

Gone, my dearest Silda, gone.

Lightless, a vacuum, soundless. Only the reluctant flush of blood in my shriveled heart. No breath to sob, no tears to cry, no strength for anger. Gone. I find my way to Eagle Bluff, to the summit, I lie in the moss, my arms are cold and empty. No stars, no hope in the cry of a loon, in the measured tolling of a buoy's bell.

It cannot be.

# 20

*AIDAN*

My visit to Artémisos, deeply depressing. The Athens I returned to was catching up with the consumption-mad Western world—brutally crass, corrupt, a mindless destruction of my country's soul.

Holed up with my Olivetti, my books, my workbench, my lemons and figs, filling notebooks. I did go occasionally to small gatherings at one or another friend's house, if they were within walking distance—I loathed the public transportation, it set me on edge—at least tolerating the quieter neighborhoods of this abominable city. We were writers—journalists, poets, critics, novelists—an occasional politician surviving from the Left, a composer sometimes.

At one of these, well, salons, a handful of us sitting around, wine, pipes, a poet reading verses he is trying out, there's a newcomer, a young woman, beautiful in a quiet, understated way. She's listening, taking notes, playing with a golden cigarette. I'd never seen a golden cigarette. She catches me studying her, or rather the cigarette, smiles slightly, goes back to her notebook. Leaning forward as she writes, her dark hair glows in the subdued light of a lamp beyond her. I'd not been introduced—our host knew well my aversion to small talk. Afterwards, she introduces herself, Gióia Toccacielo. She speaks understandable Greek, slurring over the points of grammar she clearly doesn't comprehend, but she doesn't grope for words and she has a reasonable accent with just a touch of the Italian lilt, the trilled *rrr*, the drawn-out double consonants.

She speaks with low-keyed admiration of my published works, says she is a poet looking for someone to help her in improving her Greek, as she had decided to stay in Greece after the dissolution of an unhappy relationship with a Greek poet. They had lived for a time on the island of Mílou. She wonders if I would consent to be her teacher, she names what seemed an extravagant figure for what she says is the going hourly rate. I'm taken aback. I am protective of my privacy. Do I want anything new in my melancholy routine? I am inclined to say no, but I've been half starving for want of cash. Cornelia sends me a small monthly sum—guilt money—but it is never enough, my royalties are trickles, drying up, and my articles and poems for the dailies and quarterlies bring in pennies.

Well, yes, perhaps I can be of some help, though you already do very well. Greek is not my mother tongue, you know, but they tell me I know and use it without a flaw. We'd have to meet in a place other than my house, that just wouldn't do, I'm a very private person.

She names a kapheneíon not far from my home, I know it, a good choice. We meet there, the lessons go well. She is conscientious in working between sessions and is making progress. Once or twice she brings poems she had written in Italian. I find them quite good, tell her so, which produces a kiss on my cheek.

I do find her attractive. Quiet, modest, soberly dressed, a warm smile. She has a way of dealing unobtrusively with my epilepsy, my petit mals—I seem to have the grand mals under control with the medications and, absurdly I suppose, the nibbles of peanuts. She shows me a short poem in Greek she'd been working on. It is surprisingly competent, one or two minor mistakes in her demotic orthography, but most Greeks have trouble with their vowels.

Two months pass, our lessons continue twice a week. Neither of us says much about ourselves, our pasts, we stay in the present. She describes in Greek things and events around us. Despite the verse she showed me, her knowledge of poetry and of literature in general seems limited. But this is not an examination, I don't probe. She has a knack for listening and picking up on certain opinions I let out, embellishing them, questioning them modestly, then wryly adopting them herself.

We begin taking walks together, bus rides away from the city. We climb Hymettós, a strenuous climb, but Gióia is game, radiant when we get to the top and can look out over the smog to far islands. We picnic. A pleasant day, a relief from my tired typewriter. Yes, she is an attractive woman, though nothing physical happens between us. The sexual juices are past. Just as well, I am far too drained by epilepsy and age and malaise. Still, Gióia is nice to be around.

One day, our lesson finished—glasses of retsína, a plate of olives, on our rusty metal table.

—"Aidan, I have been thinking of taking a break, going off for a few days. Do you know the island of Khería? No? A friend told me it is quite special, well off the usual tourist circuit. She told me of a fishing village on the southern tip of the island, and gave me the name of the only hotel, very cheap. Would you join me? My treat. Please forgive me if this sounds perhaps forward of me, but it could do you a lot of good. You have been looking peaked, this Athens air is bad. No, don't shake your head, think about it. In fact I have already booked two rooms in case you might join me on my little adventure, and perhaps to show you that this is not just an idle idea. Do say yes, Aidan, or at least not no. Will you?"

I am quite content with the routine of my life, its simple pattern, which keeps to a bearable level my exposure to the dissolution of my Greece—no doubt of the rest of the world too. Except for the walks I take with Gióia, I manage to avoid even looking out over the city—its smog, its din, its glare of billboards, its melting monuments to an unhappy and brutal past. Glorious birthplace of Western culture—hésta! My horizon is my neighborhood, still holding off the claws of the monster. Gióia is seeking companionship, lonely? Am I too, is loyal Olivetti my only companion? Very well, I'll let the routine lapse for a time, all the more welcome on my return. Untouched islands, are there any left? I have no expectations, but... Well, what the hell. Just go, leave your precious self—Aidan the Aesthete, worshipper of that which you claim exists no more—for once just take what comes your way.

We find a ferry, an overnight to a commercial port not far from Khería. Two cabins, decent dining room, passable meal, excellent wine, spared the usual saccharine piped-in music. It is luxurious, and to my bemusement I enjoy it.

We arrive at the port early the next morning, breakfast on the waterfront. We pick out a likely boatman by his ancient captain's hat, arrange for a ride to Khería. Smooth seas, familiar stink of fish and diesel, shattering noise and vibration, shouts of conversation—I become quite nostalgic, even sentimental. Me!

It seems a promising island, one of the few I'd missed in past wanderings. There are no sand beaches, they tell us, perhaps that's what has so far saved it from the tourist plague. There is only the one bit of pebbly shingle at the head of a small cove beyond the harbor. Several caíquia are winched up there out of reach of the sea, one is being painted.

The little harbor is enclosed in the two arms of a breakwater. Nets are stretched on the stone quay, three or four men and women squatting by them to knot in repairs. The village is the usual white cubic jumble above the harbor, crowding down the hillside to the quay. The one kapheneíon has three or four tables on the quay under a shading mat of cane. A few villagers hereabouts—bits of conversation, long silences, the tapping of cups on the rusty table tops. Even the music from inside is the clarinet of island tradition. The children are as snot-nosed as ever. The hotel, I'd call it an inn at most, is a few steps up an alley, six or seven rooms, bare and simple.

It does seem a picture from the past, suggestions of the Greece I once so loved. Illusions, of course, deceptions. No doubt the fisherfolk were as eager as the rest of the world to escape to the next McDonald's.

Gióia, though—at the end of the day she luxuriates in her bath, dons a flowery dress, a broad hat produced from her rather battered suitcase. No longer the subdued poetess—slacks, plain shirt, utilitarian hat if needed, book bag, a poem to read, an appropriate addition to the salon denizens. Here, she is an attractive woman quite ready to be admired for her beauty.

I am startled, I find it charming. That there can still be grace and beauty touches in me a sweet sadness, a vague longing, memories. Yet it makes all the more bitter what may remain of the life that I have chosen.

The next morning, I'm up early, step down to the harbor for a coffee. A small boy brings it to my table. He pulls a short stick and a pocket knife from his pocket, plops down on the other chair, and starts to whittle. He chatters, I tease him. I take my little bag of peanuts from my shirt pocket, today's ration, and give it to him.

Gióia joins us. Today she wears a long white dress buttoned high around her pale neck, sleeves down to the trim of lace around her wrists. The same hat, trimmed now with a wreath of wild flowers.

After breakfast, we walk a short way up a path behind the village, turning back when it threatens to lead along a cliff's edge. We read for a time on our balconies, still in the shade.

In the midafternoon, we start out for a picnic by the sea. Goat cheese, bread, oranges, a flask of wine from the local store. We scramble out onto a rocky finger beyond the cove, Gióia in her Renoir hat. The flow of air through the web of her dress caresses her pale ankles, plays tricks with shadows on her flesh. We wade in tide pools, her dress hitched up. We swim. She is the first to strip—unhesitating, with natural grace. We dive off the rocks, short swims. We picnic in a shallow cave, our feet in a tidal pool—her pale ankles, the tipped head so her hair in the breeze would tickle me.

Still naked, we nap for a time on the blanket she had brought, cooler now in the late sun. I open my eyes to the curve of her thigh, the allure of dark fur.

To a damnable petit mal.

. . .

A tiny spider makes his way over the ridges and valleys of black rock. On a smoother spot he casts a long shadow. Still dizzy, muddled, I sit up, turn to find this woman, this Gióia.

—"It's chilly, Aidan, I'll just dress. You are looking out there, out to the sea. Are you still determined, your evening swim to that Khímaera? So far, soon dark, the wind is making up. I beg you, do not go. You must? But please, my dear, a short swim only. Wave to me from out there, come back soon, my love."

Still naked, I leap into the sea.

The sting, the cold. Striking out against the waves—mounting waves, wind tearing off their crests. My head is clearer now—fear, excitement too, down in my belly. I swim on, determined, a Jason, into the angry sea.

Three kilometers, I've done more than that, yes, many times. Khímaera, black there against a dying sky, twin peaks rising from the sea. A horned daemon, lurking, a flash of fire. Or might there be a cave there, a warm rock to lie on, perhaps a trickling spring, a hidden valley, a bit of meadow, a copse of pine, goats long since given up for lost? My woman in white, my Aphrodite, born from the foaming sea?

Mad illusions, leave them, leave this tortured body, this tormented soul, this hateful land, leave for the uncaring sea. Give myself to the plus grand mal of them all.

I am tiring, each breath is wrested from the stinging acrid sea. I pause, tread water. A cresting wave lifts me, I look to dark mountains off to the west, distant against a dying sea. I raise a fist.

Oh bitter, ravaged Greece, my life, my grief, my chimeras. My Dimitra—my Medea lost in madness. My misplaced love—a Joel that could never be.

My curse—*Ai ghamisou!*

Gentle, here beneath the waves, the jealous grasping waves, bubbles rising to the fading sky. Subside, familiar darkness, forever still.

# 21

Nearby, here in the gorse and the juniper, a gull murmurs in her sleep, rustles her feathers. The winter air is cool, still, the stars brilliant in a damasked sky. Dewdrops on my blankets sparkle, my tiny stars.

Alone. No one to hold in my arms. Sleep now, to wake to the crimson dawn.

Slowly rising from the silent sea, Khímaera crouching there, inscrutable, patient. Her highest peaks, her goat's horns, now a burning tip of red. Her breath is set afire.

. . .

I'll go now, my path through the maquis, down to the waking village, to my room.

I hang the blankets, the pillow case, on the railing of my little balcony. I run a bath, I float in billows of steam.

I go down to the office to leave my key. It stinks still of harsh tobacco smoke, sour fish. I take my passport from its pigeonhole, hang my key. An ashtray has overflowed on the desk, the inn's register lies open. The manager had entered my name and date for me. I turn back the pages to the date of Aidan's death.

*Aidan Allard*

*Gióia Venere Toccacielo*

Down through the village—cobbled alleys, blue shadows, blazing whites, violent scarlets, the pungent greens of geraniums, basil in cans. To my usual rusty table.

Morose, a heaviness, resigned. Idly moving bread crumbs into patterns on my plate. Gulls mutter impatiently for the next boatload of fish to dock—the fish heads, the guts to be ripped out. A crowd of them, they pace back and forth by the empty berth—they seem to know. And yes, black diesel smoke behind the breakwater, a caíquia, their mid-morning meal appears. Low in the water, a rare good haul. Moored to the quay, the unloading. Men roll out barrels—of fuel. Gulls, outraged, they swarm off in disgust.

A woman steps out of the caíquia, looks about, uncertain. Beret, dark glasses, shirttails tied in front, sleeves rolled, jeans, sandals, a small knapsack. Not your usual villager, not at all. Nor I, for she sees me, comes straight to my table.

—"Joel? Thank God! I'm Gióia, Gióia Toccacielo. So afraid I'd miss you. You know who I am? Yes, of course. May I join you? Yes, a glass of water too, thank you. My English? Well, I did a nanny tour in Bristol, later au paired in Norfolk for a year, Greeks, I married their son. We lived on Milos for a time, didn't work out, separated, then... poor dear Aidan.

"Tracked you down, I'm so glad. Andréas, yes, your son, Athens. I met him by chance at Aidan's grave, we each had flowers, the day after you left for Khería. No, I couldn't bear the thought of a funeral, but was so relieved to find the grave in all those garish acres...and Andréas...and you. I heard so much about you, Joel, he'd go on and on. Admiration, love, wry stories."

I watch her as she talks on. Dark hair held back under the beret, a sprinkle of white, calm and lovely, hands forever gesturing, joined to her voice. Open, pleasantly informal, easy rapport.

My responses—at first they are stilted, my old reserve, my doubts. Between her stories, I tell her a bit about my quest here, my Silda, my Aidan, their talismans here in my pockets. The visitors of my dreams, my doubts, confused conclusions, Aidan's death.

Her candor softens my reserve.

The violence, the drama of that death. I tell her of yesterday, the crumpled bit of Planters Peanuts foil here on this table. He would take his life? Despair, Greece, me? My dream last night—the woman in white, the black figure on the cliff, the picnic, the seizure, the angry despairing leap, the raised fist, the curse, the uncaring sea.

—"No, no, Joel. A self-fulfilling morbid wish perhaps. It was just not at all like that, just not. Like…look, I'll run through it. Wait, though, I must collect myself, sorry, my coffee cup clatter, I'm trembling I guess. It was weeks ago, but that scene, that loss of my sweet Aidan, it's with me always, right here, my eyes, my ears, my heart."

She pauses, breathes deeply, two three times, looks up at me.

—"Okay. Woman in white, Aphrodite? No, I was dressed much as I am right here. That man in black? No such thing that I ever saw. The peanuts? He had another little bag in his pocket, I saw him munching on them before we set out for our picnic. We did make love, as you call it. Quite the miracle, with the impotency he'd bemoaned when we'd moved into one room at the hotel. Miracle for me too, oh yes. He was truly transported. Said something like: *My beauteous Aphrodite* (we were naked, of course—do I shock you?), *born from the foam of the sea. I your Hephaestos. Our miraculous union, Eros given life.* Well, it did sound better at the time.

"And there was no seizure—those dreadful seizures. After we'd drifted a bit, like on the edge of sleep, he got up, took his floghéra from our basket, and danced, a proud dance, an island tune. I called out, I remember: *Kalós, kalós, mátiamou! Here, I'll join you, take the end of my scarf.* He dropped the floghéra in the basket, grabbed the scarf, we danced, wild we were, as we sang the tune together. *Ai, enough! My feet on this rock, enough! It's chilly, I'll just dress. You're looking out there, out to sea. You're still set on it, your swim to that rock and back. Okay, okay, come right back, it's getting dark and the wind is making up. Wave to me from out there, amore mio, agápemou. Go with your God.*

"There was no fist. A hand raised in farewell to our new-found love, Joel. Of that I am sure."

. . .

"Must you, Gióia, must you leave this very afternoon? Yes, well, I shall stay here for a day or two, alone with my memories."

## 22

I walk down to that finger of rock. No woman, no dress of white to fly in the morning breeze. The headland, no Mister Death in somber suit, no fedora black against the sky. I stand on the ledge where Aidan, exuberant, leaped into the arms of the sea.

I hear the rhythmic thump of oars against tholepins. A small boat appears, a small boy, close in against the rocks. He's rowing idly, peering into the seaweed. I hail him, he looks up startled, smiles. My breakfast friend, I beckon him, *Here*. He slips in expertly, the ledge at gunwale height. He ships his oars, hops out, painter well in hand. I ask him if I may use his boat, an hour or two, these drachmas, while perhaps he'll pull snails and urchins from the rocks. He looks out to sea, —"Eínai ládhi." Like oil. He looks at me carefully, head to toe. He nods.

I step in, push off, oars back in the tholes, I'm on my way. She leaks a bit, water sloshes about my boots. Nothing much, never mind. I turn to make Khímaera my heading, take a bearing dead astern to steer from. It is good to be on the sea, the smells, the ripple of my wake, the gulls flying by to check me out for fish heads. A dolphin blows beside me.

I arrive on the north side of Khímaera, in the shadow,

a touch of chill, no breeze. I pull in close against the cliffs, skirt slowly to the west. I soon come to a deep cleft in the cliff face, a yard or two of shingle where it meets the sea. I continue on around the isle. It takes me almost an hour, and I find no other break, just cliffs and steep rockslides. I return to that one bit of shingle, a bank of pebbles dropping steeply into the sea. I beach the boat, step off the bow, fasten the painter around a rock.

The cleft is narrow, steep, but there is moisture, a bit of earth, some heather, thyme. No Christmas rose, though, no forage for a goat, a lioness, and a serpent. No, no dreams, fantasies, daemons, no mythic madness. Am I heroic Bellerophon, slayer of that mythic monster, those oars the wings of a horse?

A few steps up the cleft, I see a shallow niche in the black wall. I step up on a ledge to look in. It's no bigger than a trailside shrine—no angry Lord, though, no cup of oil, a dried blossom for its wick. Lichened sides, reds and grays, a bit of mossy floor.

I take the ancient coin from my pocket. Its leather frame is rubbed smooth and shiny, the faces on the coin are blurred, green with age. Dear Aidan, it is time to rest.

And here, my dark red stone, warm, glowing. A girl on a pebbly beach, your curly hair shining in the sun. Your time too, dear Silda.

I lay them gently in the moss and go.

*An islet is mirrored in a placid sea—sheer cliffs, twin peaks dark against the bluest sky. A rowboat's wake leaves a faint trail leading up those peaks, the dip of the oars are twin footprints climbing on to a brilliant sky. The rowing pauses, oars raised, dripping lines of bubbles as the boat slides on several lengths, slows, lies still.*

*The rower turns to look shoreward, estimates his position. He ships the battered oars, leans over the gunwale, reaches deep into the sea.*

*Searching, he finds another's hand, lifts him gently to the surface. He steps out, they embrace. They walk back on still waters to the waiting islet. A tiny cove, a bit of shingle, a mossy cliff, fresh water seeping, a patch of heather and thyme. A cleft, a trail cut in the volcanic rock.*

*That is your path, old friend, take it, go on, go up, with love. No monster lurking, no breath of fire, no madness. Some rock work higher up, you'll do it. On, up, there where the peaks just touch the sky.*

*The rower turns, steps out onto the sea, walks back toward his boat, light and firm of step. He pauses, listening, searching. A woman's voice calls joyously. She is standing in the boat, her body sublime in a delicate veiling of palest blue. She waves, steps from the boat. Barefoot, she skips over the water, she flies, flies to his waiting arms.*

*In the still air, a floghéra's song reaches out to them from the distant isle. They dance, dance as they never have before. They laugh, they kiss, they hold each other's heart.*

*He stands before her, arms down, hands open to her. On the tips of her toes, she turns, she twirls, ever faster, spinning, spinning— a whirl of diaphanous blue.*

*Fading, rejoining the sea and the sky.*

*Returned to the boat, he slides out the oars, rows on, the seas still calm, rows on toward welcoming land. His cheeks are shining with his tears.*

*He smiles.*

*Thanks to:*

MY DEAR WIFE, PENNY, FOR HER EVER PRESENT SUPPORT. MANY of my family and friends for their patient encouragement and advice. Kevin Andrews—glimpses of his life and death are imagined here. Manlio Guberti—for his love of an Italy that soured. My son Alexis, Mika Koutsoyannis, Roger Jinkinson, and Ileana Caramanis for their help on the Greek episodes. Donald Pitkin, 1st Lt Ret, and other US Tenth Mountain Division sources. The MacDowell Colony, the National Endowment for the Arts, the Virginia Center for the Creative Arts, and the Ucross Foundation for their generous fellowships, providing intense months of precious time. Mary Bisbee-Beek for her help in launching this book. And special thanks to the remarkable Bruce McPherson for his determined, inspired, and invaluable editorial advice.

*Notes*

THE ISLANDS OF KHERÍA, KHÍMAERA, ARTÉMISOS, AND REKALÍA are fictitious archetypes of islands of the Aegean Sea. Khería means candles. The asphodel, a common flower on those islands, is popularly and mythically called a candle for the dead. Khímaera—*Chimera*—a fire-breathing monster of mixed animal parts, evolved to also become *chimera*, an unobtainable illusion. The likely origin of the monster-slaying Chimera-Bellerophon-Pegasus myth was not an islet in the Aegean Sea, but rather a volcanic area in Lycia, mainland Turkey. Flaming gas vents, goats, and snakes are still to be found there. Lions have left.

*About the Author*

ROBERT CABOT IS A VETERAN OF WORLD WAR II CAMPAIGNS IN
North Africa and Europe. He enlisted in the U S Army shortly
after Pearl Harbor when he turned eighteen. Some of his experi-
ences in his four years as a sergeant are fictionalized in *The Isle
of Khería.*

Cabot received degrees from Harvard College and Yale Law
School, served for some time in several capacities in the Executive
Office of the President in the Truman administration, and then
for ten years in the Marshall Plan and foreign aid programs in
Italy, Thailand, Sri Lanka, and Washington, D.C.

He resigned from government service in protest over U.S.
foreign policy. US economic aid had been offered to struggling
countries as a sincere effort to help develop free and democratic
economies and societies. He found it to have often become a
cynical and arrogant attempt to recreate the world in the American image, and to use US economic aid as an often secret tool
in the Cold War.

Cabot moved to Italy, then to Greece, years later returning to
the U.S. in a solo transatlantic sail with his thirty-foot sloop. He
settled in Canada and later in Washington State. During these
years, he wrote a series of articles decrying the Vietnam
War and American policies in the Cold War. For several
years he was active in citizen diplomacy in the Soviet
Union and Afghanistan.

With his wife Penny and others, Cabot is a joint founder

of several institutions: the Turtle Island Fund promoting several conservation land trusts, including an agricultural/educational commune in British Columbia where they lived for five years; the Threshold Foundation helping social change projects around the world; a Waldorf School near Seattle; the VWC Foundation; and the Seattle Peoples Fund helping struggling ethnic communities in the Puget Sound area.

Writing, however, is his first love. He has written several novels, including: *The Joshua Tree* (Atheneum, 1970, republished several times, most recently by Bloomsbury in 2011); *That Sweetest Wine* (McPherson & Co., 1999), finalist for an Independent Publishers Award; and *The Isle of Khería* (McPherson & Co., 2012). Cabot is a Fellow of the McDowell Colony, the National Endowment for the Arts, the Virginia Center for the Creative Arts, and the Ucross Foundation.

Cabot now lives on Whidbey Island, Washington, with his wife. Between them, they have six children and a bevy of children's children. For three or four months a year he retreats to a mountain town in Sonora, Mexico, where he is finishing a memoir and another novel.